Love
on
Dove Street

A story of war, passion, deception,
and a dog bone

Cherie Hart

Author's note

It was in the aftermath of Russia's invasion of Ukraine in February 2022 that this story came to be. As our journalist friends left for Ukraine to report on the conflict, our Istanbul neighborhood of Cihangir grew eerily silent without their familiar presence on every walk.

One day, during a leisurely stroll down our cobblestone road, I happened upon a well-known local street dog named Çiçek, which means Flower. From her favorite vantage point in a nearby parking lot, she nudged and directed my attention to the surrounding buildings. Our chance encounter inspired me to write a novel set against the incomprehensible backdrop of war.

While the brutal events in Ukraine are a grim reality, the characters in this narrative are entirely fictional. Dove Street, or Kumrulu Sokak in Turkish, is an actual place where we lived for nearly ten years. Çiçek, a real Turkish Kangal dog, was once a frequent presence in our neighborhood until her inexplicable disappearance after the completion of this very tale. We persist in our search for her, scouring all her favored haunts, from dumpsters to cafés.

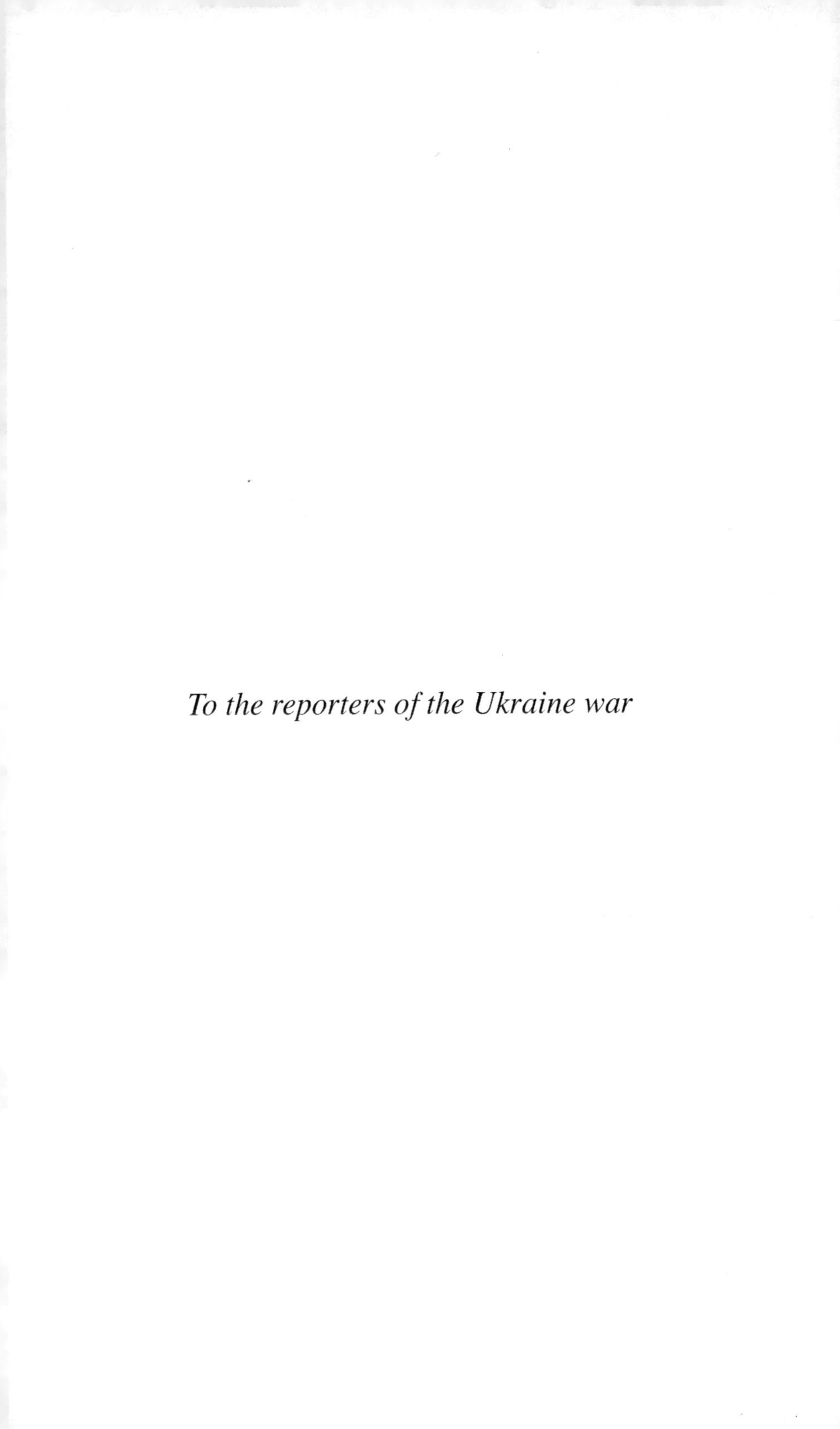

To the reporters of the Ukraine war

ÇIÇEK

I see everything that happens on my street. I mean, everything. And people tell me stuff. I guess they think I don't understand. But I do.

I have a story to tell about love and life and the people on my street. It's not a shaggy dog story—it's all true. Or, at least how I remember it. My story is full of secrets. We all have them. Some are bigger than others. Some we share, and some we don't. You can't always believe what you think. Things aren't always as they seem.

I could write a book about what I've seen.

Most everyone, of course, thinks they have a real good story that would make a great book. They think they can write. I am not a writer, so I don't really care. But I do believe my story is good enough for the movies, and I'd be happy to star in it.

First, let me introduce myself. No one gets my name right. I am Çiçek (Chih-Check). I love steak bones and rolling in the dirt.

My favorite place to hide is in the mud between two old cars in the parking lot where I spend most of my time. I live in Istanbul. Have you ever been there? It's a beautiful place with yummy food and a whole lot of cats and tons of people everywhere.

Someone built a ridiculously small wooden house for me at the back of my parking lot. But it's so tiny if I tried to fit into it, my head would get stuck, and where would that leave my tail?

My story is a long one that began back when I was almost thin enough to fit into that mini house. Even then, I preferred sleeping out in the open. That's how I met Happy Girl. She is the first of many friends in my story.

I heard her before I saw her on a night when the moon was shining full. All the dogs in town were howling, and the cats were screwing like rabbits. That's probably a mixed metaphor, but you get my drift. The bright moon was this gigantic flashlight illuminating the world and igniting animal passions.

I listened to Happy Girl's laughter as she skipped down our cobblestone road, Kumrulu Sokak, which means Dove Street in Turkish. At first, her sounds reminded me of the yelps I made once when a speeding car swiped my back hip. Biting tires is one of my favorite pastimes. Dove Street is way too narrow for my leisure pursuit, but sometimes I get bored and can't help myself. I especially like to chase those speeding motorcycle guys that smell like pizza and Indian food. I can sniff them a mile away. When they zoom past, I'm right on their tail.

Anyway, Happy Girl would never chase a car or a motorcycle. Her two legs would be too slow. Her noises were not sounds of pain but ones of joy.

She spotted me peering around the metal gate in front of the lot. I must have looked funny because she grinned even wider when she noticed me. Instead of running away, she approached me like we were long lost friends, her arms reaching towards me for an embrace. I didn't cower. I could tell she was one of those friendly life forms that would never hit me on the nose or kick me in the rear. Believe me, I know when to hide from those types.

"Here, boy."

I knew it was me she was talking to even though I'm not a boy. Çiçek is the Turkish word for flower. Have you ever heard of a boy named Flower? I didn't think so. I can't blame her for the mistake. Sometimes my fur hides my girl bits.

Happy Girl wrapped her arms around me and buried her soft face into my neck and giggled. Warm and gentle, she rocked me in her skinny arms. She smelled like honey. What a treat, almost as good as a juicy bone. I could have stayed like that forever, especially if she brought me food. I listened as Happy Girl muttered nonsense into my ear, the way humans often do.

HANNAH (Happy Girl)

That huge dog with its clods of dirt and oil-stained fur somehow shared in my joy. At first, I thought she was a boy, but then I realized he was a she. And what a filthy mess she was. She reminded me of an enormous stuffed animal I clung to as a little girl. This street dog's cobalt blue eyes resembled hers and gazed at me with such kindness and intelligence, I knew she understood how ecstatic I was.

"I've met a wonderful man," I whispered to the dog.

There's nothing like the early days of infatuation, when all that matters in the world is you and the person you adore. Not climate change, not COVID, not Putin. Nope. The excitement surging through my body blocked out the world, at least temporarily. I love feeling in love.

I buzzed Sophie's apartment, which was in the building next to mine. We both live across the street from the dog's parking lot. I couldn't wait to tell her about my new man. She was always the first person I wanted to dish to when I had news about my life.

I sprinted up Sophie's tiled stairwell, gave her a quick hug at the door, and plopped myself on the banquette in her front window.

"I've met someone!" I exclaimed, breathless from dashing up four flights.

"What do you mean?" Sophie asked as she tucked a strand of coal black hair behind her ear. Her sapphire eyes met mine, a look of curiosity tinged with skepticism.

Sophie was my neighbor, a foreign correspondent for one of those UK networks that still takes news seriously. She gave up on love years ago when her husband abandoned her for a CNN anchor.

"I think I finally found the perfect guy," I said, hoping that sharing the news with her about my romantic encounter would be more satisfying than confiding in the stray dog that resembled a doormat. But I was wrong.

"No one's perfect," Sophie cautioned. "I thought my husband was perfect, until he ran off with that botoxed news anchor."

"I'm telling you, this guy is genuine," I declared. "He's amazing. He's funny, smart, and he looks like he walked off the pages of GQ. I met him on my flight to Madrid a few weeks ago. He was so easy to talk to. He had smiling eyes."

"Hmmm." Sophie's only comment.

"His name is David. He's half Spanish and half English.

He has a curly mop of dark hair and eyes the color of that green dress you wore to the Emmy Awards."

"OK. What does he do?" she asked pointedly.

"He runs some kind of trading company."

"Tell me more."

I knew Sophie well enough to know she was restraining herself and didn't want her questions to sound like the start of an interrogation.

"I don't know. What can I say? He was dreamy, all cheekbones and gorgeous eyes, and lean-muscled arms of a guy who does more than just sit at a desk. We exchanged WhatsApp numbers when we landed in Madrid. He had to catch a train to see clients in Valencia—but he messaged me even before I left the airport. We've been trading texts ever since."

"That's really romantic," Sophie laughed. "Do you use emojis?"

"No, we do not!" I smiled.

"Ha! I'll bet you do," she said, throwing a pillow at me. She was right, as always.

Sophie knows how to crawl into my head and figure out whatever I'm thinking. That's probably why she's so good at what she does. Her interviews are always empathetic. She understands people and asks the difficult questions without seeming aggressive.

She's nearly six feet tall, slightly built, almost waiflike, and the most fearless woman I know. She was held at gunpoint in Syria, survived a bomb attack in Iraq, and barely missed a Taliban massacre in a Kabul hotel. But when it comes to finding love, I think Sophie has lost her nerve. Burned once, big time, she shows no desire to touch those flames again. I'm the opposite and keep putting myself out there. I want the whole thing: a house, a husband, two children. Not much. Maybe David is the real deal.

Sophie works with a British cameraman, Ted, who lives on the road below Dove Street. Like me, he keeps searching for someone to fill that lonely hole in his life. He doesn't talk much about it, but I see him hanging out at coffee shops with a different woman each time. His long legs don't quite fit under the rickety metal tables. He always looks squished and uncomfortable while chatting up each potential conquest.

I used to think he enjoyed the variety of women in his life, but one day he admitted to Sophie and me, "I'm getting tired of running around. I'm too old for this shit."

"You're not old," Sophie assured him. "You're forty-eight but look much younger, maybe forty-five."

"Thanks, pal," he said.

Sophie and Ted come and go frequently on their overseas assignments. I never know when either or both of them will head to the airport for a story. That's just the nature of their work, especially now when the world seems to be falling apart. We don't bother making plans beyond the next few days. It doesn't seem to concern either of them that they take off for weeks at a time, their personal life interrupted, whenever news breaks.

I usually meet up with Sophie when she returns. She manages to come back whole and wise and calm, as if she never saw babies dying, or families fleeing in desperate caravans, or TV towers toppled by missiles.

I'm always here for Sophie. We catch up over long chats, although not to discuss what she's seen while covering the latest conflict or disaster. Even after the horrors she has witnessed, she still shows interest in the mundane news from home. What's the new pastry the local bakery is selling? What's the hot show on Netflix these days? Is that ice cream kiosk up the street going to stay open through winter?

She never mentions her personal life. I think she lives for the assignments and bides her time in between. We sometimes meet up at a neighborhood café where Peter the Coffee Guy, as we call the owner, hilariously reads the Turkish coffee grounds at the bottom of our cups. He delivers vague prognostications with deadpan seriousness—"What you seek should be apparent. Just open your eyes." Or "Look up. That's all."

I wish that one day Sophie would look up and see more than just her work. Maybe then she'd understand.

ÇIÇEK

Before long, I saw the honey-scented Happy Girl again. She was in the window talking to the dark-haired tall girl. Those two sure liked to natter. Well, that day, mostly Happy Girl talked and waved her arms while Tall Girl listened.

There were three of these humans who had their own pack: Happy Girl and Tall Girl and Tall Guy. They were all from somewhere else, not Turkey. I could tell because of the way they talked. They said "hello" and not "gunayden". They called me "dog" and not "kopek".

Dove Street is a magnet for people like them. Not many Turks live on our cobblestone street, except me of course. Our road seems a little foreign bubble in a very big city.

There are two more people in my story: Sad Girl and Old Guy, who live in the same apartment at the far end of the street. He is from here, but she is not. His skin looks like old tissue paper. She smells like peppermint. Eventually, their story connects with everyone else's. Stay with me. You're in for a real shock.

Back to Tall Girl. She traveled a lot. I'd see her drag her box on wheels down her stairs and then climb into the yellow car with the sign on top. I loved chasing those cars. Anyway, Tall Guy would also climb in after lugging several large boxes of his own. They didn't look like cases of food.

I liked Tall Guy. He brought me a big bone every now and then, even though he didn't live exactly on our street. I'm a sucker for anyone who gives me a bone, especially if it has steak on it. Tall Guy would walk up from the hill below us just to bring me a treat. He always smelled like salt and sea. I know all about that smell because I used to live with a family who took me to the beach. I don't like to talk about them. I don't like to look backwards. It's too sad.

I usually only think about my next meal. Fortunately, people on my street fed me. I had a big rubber dish, and different folks filled it. Sometimes I didn't like what they put in my dish, but rarely did I go hungry. No one ever invited me inside their building, though. I wouldn't have gone even if they did. My open-air parking lot was my home.

The steep grassy hill behind me had a few trees and heaps of old rocks that sometimes rolled down in the rain. I had a perfect view of all the apartments on the other side of the street. The buildings were not very high, with a mix of brick and wood and large windows where cats peered out from behind dark metal bars.

Every morning a head-scarved wrinkled lady roamed the neighborhood, dropping handfuls of cat food everywhere. There were tons, and I mean tons, of cats on our street. There were so many felines in the entire city that some people called it Catstantinople. That's what they call a play on words because Istanbul used to be known as Constantinople.

Oh. Did I tell you about One Eye? I guess not. She was the only cat I ever got along with. She never tried to scratch me. She had only one eye, but I'm sure you worked that out. One night, a big truck came by and sprayed something that smelled sour, and the next morning One Eye was spitting up. I didn't feel too good either. And all the bugs were gone.

A few days later I saw her sleeping at the entrance of my parking lot, but she wouldn't wake up. A nice man took her in his arms, brought her up the hill, and put her in the ground under a tree behind my lot. I like to think that One Eye can still see me from there, out of her one eye.

I miss her. I hate it when you make friends and then they up and die. I guess it's better than never having made a friend.

But I'm getting way off track. Back to my tale. I saw Tall Girl driving off with Tall Guy.

TED (Tall Guy) and SOPHIE (Tall Girl)

Ted rearranged the luggage in the trunk to fit Sophie's case. His Peli case filled with his best camera gear stayed on the back seat between them. He stooped into the taxi and turned to glance at the mutt wagging its tail as their cab disappeared down the street.

"Hey Sophie, do you ever notice that big galoot of a dog that watches us when we head to the airport?" Ted asked. It doesn't matter if we leave in the middle of the night or at sunrise, she's always there, like she's wishing us good luck."

"We could use some luck on this trip," said Sophie. "I have a feeling we'll be covering this war for quite a while."

"It's been ages since I've had to pack a flak jacket," he said. "What do you think Putin's game plan is?"

"No one knows what's going on inside his head, and he certainly isn't going to tell anyone," said Sophie. "He's been building up his military on the Ukrainian border for months. It was just a matter of time before he launched a full-scale invasion."

"I wonder how long we'll be gone. I sure hope that model I met last night remembers me by the time we get back."

"Another woman? Jeez, Ted! What happened to the last girlfriend? You seemed so enthralled with her."

"I had to end it fast. Her brother showed up on our third date and asked what my intentions were. What kind of crazy is that? This dating scene in Istanbul is confusing."

"I wouldn't know," said Sophie. "I can't remember the last time I was on a date."

"Last night was amazing," Ted continued, oblivious to her comment. "I've never spent an evening with anyone who was so captivating. She's a model who moved here a while back. Apparently, Istanbul has become a hub for modeling agencies for Eastern European and Scandinavian women."

"I've seen some of them in our neighborhood," said Sophie. "They travel in herds, like giant giraffes roaming the streets. They're usually clutching designer water bottles and crushed cigarette packs. Hannah told me that they look so gangly and hungry, she always wants to give them a sandwich."

"How is Hannah?" asked Ted.

"Happy as always. She thinks she's found love. Maybe this time, she has. His name is David, and he lives in Spain. She seems to be pinning her dreams on him, like she always does with any man who shows any interest in her. She can't help herself. I blame her neediness on what happened with her father," said Sophie.

Sophie and Ted sat in silence, looking out the backseat windows at the intricate Istanbul highways with their web of loops and tunnels, the malls and housing complexes, and the periodic patches of barren landscape dotted with stray dogs. Spring was less than a month away, but the weather was neither warm nor sunny for their departure to Ukraine.

Sophie's mind raced as she watched the gray clouds hang over them. She could see her smile reflected in the windowpane. It was too soon for her to tell anyone what was happening in her own life. She'd let her friends know when the time was right.

She knew that Ted was absorbed in his own reverie, reliving his evening with the model, and unaware of her beaming face.

Then, suddenly, Ted yelled, "There she is! That's her!" He pointed up at a massive billboard that spanned the highway to Istanbul Airport. "That's the woman I had dinner with last night!"

A pair of enormous sultry gray eyes stared down at them in an ad for a luxury brand of cosmetics.

ÇIÇEK

Do you want to know why dogs sniff each other's butts and stick their noses in private places? Well, a good butt sniff is like a handshake. We smell things a hundred thousand times better than humans do. I'm not saying we're better than people. We just have some superpowers that they don't have.

Our snouts are a true wonder. They can even ignore that poop smell when we take a whiff of a rear end. Plus, we learn so much from a backside inhale, like if a dog is a boy or a girl, if it's old or young, what it eats, how healthy it is, and even what kind of mood it's in.

Butt sniffing can keep us out of trouble, kind of like speed dating. If we don't like what we smell, we just move on. It saves everybody time and heartache. Imagine if humans had such ability. Maybe they wouldn't hook up so often with the wrong people.

I once heard a man tell his wife, "Don't stick your nose in my business." What better place is there to stick a nose than in business?

Another thing. People shouldn't be scared when we get the zoomies. I know we look funny when we run around real fast, up and down a street, or around a yard. It just means we have a lot of pent-up energy, and we need to let it go. It feels so good to shake off that anxiety. If you ever see me with the zoomies, just get out of the way, and let me pass. If you don't step aside, don't blame me if I crash into you.

That's how I met Old Guy. He saw me coming, but he just stood there. What did he expect? I plowed right into him, and he did one of those slow-motion falls and crumpled onto the street. I kept going.

"Hey!" the Girl who was with him called after me. I kept running like a scalded dog. I didn't do anything wrong. The Girl should have moved her father out of the way. I'm not sure why, but I circled back when I finished my sprint down Dove Street.

Old Guy was back on his feet. And wouldn't you know, the two were kissing—on the lips. I know enough to understand that's not what a father and daughter usually do. I wandered up to them and pressed my head against Old Guy's leg. He reached down and stroked my ears. He wasn't mad at all. His hand smelled musty, like the rocks that tumble down the hill when the soil gets moist in the rain.

"Her name must be Çiçek," said Old Guy, as he looked at the tag on the collar that my family had wrapped around my neck long ago, before they lost me.

The Girl knelt to look me in the eye. I thought she was going to scold me, but she wasn't angry either. "Çiçek," she said with a smile. That's when I saw such sadness in her eyes. I don't recommend that people stare at dogs so close like that. Stares can be misunderstood. I met a dog that bit off a girl's lip because she put her face in his. He was a hothead and should not have done that, but he wasn't completely at fault.

I sensed that the Sad Girl in my face was presenting a gentle offering, so I licked her, right where Old Guy had just kissed her. She smelled and tasted like peppermint.

I liked them immediately. Imagine my joy when Old Guy and Sad Girl walked together hand in hand into the apartment building. We were neighbors! They lived on the far end of the street, which is why I had not smelled them before.

NENA (Sad Girl) and HAKAN (Old Guy)

Nena and Hakan were the names on their doorbell. Kismet was written in elaborate typeface on the front door of the couple's building, the lettering was beginning to chip and fade.

"My God, that was a bit scary," panted Hakan as Nena opened their apartment door. "I thought that creature was aiming right for me. I was so frightened I couldn't move my legs to get out of the way."

"That dog wouldn't hurt anyone. She just wanted to play," said Nena.

"It's good to know that someone still wants to play with me," he mused. A wispy rain cloud moved past the mosque in full view of their living room window.

"That's an odd thing to say."

"I'm just feeling so old and in the way these days," Hakan said.

"That's ridiculous, you beautiful old goat."

"Do you ever want to turn back the clock?" he asked. "Go back to that magical time when we first met in Berlin?"

"Stop, Hakan," she insisted. "I don't want to hear any ancient history."

"You realize that you're still younger than I was when I first met you? You're wasting your life with me."

"Don't be absurd."

"You say that, Nena, but I see how men look at you," he said.

"You're talking nonsense." She pulled Hakan into an embrace just as tears filled her eyes. She could see Çiçek through the window, staring up at them from Dove Street. Hakan had blinked hard to hold back tears of his own.

ÇIÇEK

I caught a glimpse of Sad Girl at her window. She looked like she was about to cry, and not the happy kind of cry, or that soft sadness that almost feels good. It was the real sorrowful kind.

I know all about that despair. It's how I felt when my family abandoned me. When the wind shifts over the Bosphorus, the fresh sea air triggers my memories. I try hard not think about them, but some days I just can't help it.

I keep trying to make sense of what happened. I thought my family loved me. Those little boys were my friends. We played ball together and even slept in the same bed. I thought we'd had a fun morning swimming in the sea that day. One minute I was with them, running on the beach, and then they were gone. I watched their car take off down the highway without me. I tried to catch them, but they were too fast and too far away.

I wandered for weeks trying to find them, following their scent but eventually losing it. My nose is good, but not that good. Strangers threw food at me from their cars. I slept by the road. The traffic was noisy, but I didn't mind. I kept hoping one of the passing cars belonged to my family.

I ended up in this neighborhood, where I met a homeless man. He smelled deliciously of dirt and sweat. He spent his days walking through these streets, carrying a muddy burlap sack of sticks and flowers and trash. He offered his bent bouquets of dried wildflowers to anyone who might exchange them for a few coins. A couple of mangy mutts followed right behind him, not far from his heels. They didn't seem to mind when I joined their pack. For a few weeks, they were my foster family.

But I'm a homebody. I didn't like endlessly wandering with them. When we walked past this parking lot, I peeled away from the pack, and I've been here ever since. The homeless man sometimes passes by and waves, while his dogs come over for a good butt sniff.

Anyhow, enough about me. Back to my story. I saw Happy Girl again, this time in her window with a tiny box in her hands. She didn't look anywhere but at its glowing bit. She laughed. Then she covered her mouth in horror. Then she laughed again. Then she looked aghast. Then she giggled. Then she looked alarmed. Then she chuckled. Then her jaw dropped like she'd seen a ghost. You get what I'm saying. She sure skidded through moods.

HANNAH (Happy Girl)

I was feeling like a teenager, indulging in giddy loved-up exhilaration every time a WhatsApp message from David appeared on my phone. At the same time, I was following Sophie's live reporting from a war zone. David's messages from Spain would be interrupted by a disturbing Sophie Tweet from Ukraine. Then came a YouTube link to a love song sent by David, followed by horrific photos from Sophie of a dead Russian soldier covered in snow and a Kyiv apartment building with its top floors obliterated. If my phone screen was a person, it would have been diagnosed with schizophrenia.

David: I can't believe it's only a month since we met. I feel like I've known you forever.

Me: I feel the same way!

Sophie's Tweet: Constant loud explosions and gunfire here in #Kyiv as the city braces for battle. Photo: sandbags and tank traps along a road leading to the city.

David: I miss you more than I ever thought possible.

Sophie's Tweet: Short video of an old woman handing sunflower seeds to a Russian soldier. Sound: "Take these seeds and put them in your pockets so at least sunflowers will grow when you all lie down and die here."

David: Did you get the flowers I sent you?

Me: Yes. They're beautiful. How did you know I love sunflowers?

David: Everyone loves sunflowers.

Me: I have them in my window. They're thriving in the sun.

David: Let's move with the sun! Why don't we go away to the beach together?

Me: Really?! But who will watch my shop on such short notice?

Sophie's Tweet: Reports of #Russian cluster bombs in #Kyiv. Tonight, I am in an underground metro station where an entire hospital unit of ICU babies has been moved.

David: You can find someone to take care of your shop. Maybe one of the artists who buys supplies from you?

Sophie's Tweet: Even grannies are making Molotov cocktails to hurl at Russian tanks as they move into #Kyiv. Civilian defenders take up arms. Accountants wield machine guns. Teachers care for the wounded.

Me: Going with you to a beach sounds very enticing. Let me think about it. It's all so fast.

Sophie's Tweet: Russian forces advance rapidly on the city of #Kyiv. Ukrainians are fleeing by the thousands. These are refugees shaking in fear as they head to #Poland.

David: I have a friend who has a small villa in Menorca. I know he'll let me use it.

Me: I need to think about this. Give me some time.

Sophie's Tweet: Time is running out for the residents of #Kyiv. Is Putin betting the West will fold? Only time will tell in this deadly game.

David: I'll buy your ticket.

Me: Thank you, but no need. I can handle it.

My phone screen was dizzying. The news from Ukraine was horrifying, and I worried about Sophie and Ted being there. They were far braver than I ever could be. They just threw themselves into conflicts where no one was safe.

After the Ukraine story, they'd likely come home for only a few weeks and then move on to the next crisis. Their work depended on messes. No mess, no press.

As selfish as it was, I wanted to run away to Menorca to see David. Yes, there was a war going on and COVID was still on the rampage. But all I could think about was a romantic weekend on a Spanish island. Why not? Time in a villa and a sun-soaked Mediterranean beach sounded perfect to me. David did too.

I had turned down his offer of a free plane ticket because I didn't want the weekend to feel like a *quid pro quo*, that I'd owe him sex if he paid for my flight. I was overthinking everything.

"Just do it," I told myself, as I clicked on the Turkish Airlines app.

TED (Tall Guy)

Sophie and I hunkered down to edit our first feature piece about the terror in which Ukrainians were living. We traveled with a producer, a local fixer, and our security guy.

We stayed in a family-run hotel in Kyiv that looked as if it hadn't been refurbished since the fall of the Soviet Union. The wallpaper was coated in thick cigarette residue, and the wobbly wooden furniture had lost its luster, just as the chairs had long been separated from their padding.

We needed a break and headed to the empty dining room, dimly lit by a dusty chandelier. The place must have been grand back in the day, but hey, weren't we all.

We quickly ordered from the limited menu. I sensed that Sophie was about to interrogate me about my evening with the model, especially after she saw her face on the billboard.

But I was hesitant to reveal anything. Usually, by the time I tell Sophie about my latest girlfriend, the relationship is about to fall apart. I didn't want to jinx this one.

I have passionate but volatile relationships with Turkish women. They're sexy as hell, but explosive. American women usually don't do it for me. My wife was an exception, but even that didn't last. I have to say, this Russian model sure had my attention.

"Okay, spill it," said Sophie. "Who's that gorgeous woman on that big highway sign? And how in the world did she spend an evening with you?"

"I'm insulted," I said, in mock outrage. "Why wouldn't she spend an evening with me?"

"Oh, I don't know. Because you're a messy man-child who likes eating cold beans out of a can?"

"Well. You're wrong. We met at a restaurant in our neighborhood. We were both dining alone, and I asked her to join me. That's the story."

"That's it? You're not telling me anything else?" Sophie asked.

"Nope."

"At least tell me her name."

"Elena."

I didn't tell Sophie anything else. It was all so new, and I was still trying to process that evening. I didn't tell her how Elena was utterly captivating when she walked into the restaurant and tossed her leather coat on a chair. Her silk dress clung to a taught body attached to a pair of legs at the crossroads to heaven. Her auburn hair tumbled down below her shoulders.

I couldn't stop conjuring Elena in my mind. Everything about her portrayed a woman who had lived through years of experiences that had enhanced her exquisiteness rather than diminished it. The faint wrinkles around her eyes reflected an understanding of the vicissitudes of life, as did the slight lines above her brow. She was a timeless beauty. Yet, a kind of mystery.

I calculated she was likely older than most of the women I had dated, though still a bit younger than me, but she looked so much sexier.

I watched as Elena dug into her designer purse and removed a book with a Russian title. She glanced up from its pages and stared right past me, lost in thought, and unconsciously shook her head.

I caught her eye and, somewhat embarrassed, almost turned away. But she was simply too beautiful not to look at. I couldn't believe my luck when she returned my stare, smiled, and her mood seemed to shift. Without hesitation, she accepted my invitation to join me at my table. We closed the restaurant that night.

There were so many questions I had avoided asking her though, worried they would come across as intrusive. I mainly listened.

Switching subjects so I didn't have to tell Sophie any of this, I asked, "What about you, Sophie? Anyone in your life these days?"

"Nope."

"Come on, not all men are terrible. You married a shit, but there are still some good ones out there."

"I know. In fact, I'm certain that I'm going to find a dashing Danish guy, and we'll spend the rest of our years together."

"Are you serious?"

"Absolutely."

"How do you know that?"

"I just do. I've always liked guys from Denmark. They usually have a sense of humor and are open and honest, not like the creep I married."

"You're not generalizing or anything..."

"Maybe. But even when I was a little girl, I had a thing for Danes. I used to watch old Victor Borge black-and-white comedy sketches on TV. Remember him? That Danish musician and comedian? My parents and their friends adored him. He combined playing classical concert piano with a deadpan monologue, always satirical, irreverent, and hilarious."

"I do remember him!" I said. "He'd sometimes take pratfalls off the end of his piano stool, all while continuing to play."

"That's right. Zelensky reminds me of Victor Borge when he was a comedian before he became a politician. I watched some of his routines on YouTube. He'd poke fun at Putin. He was very witty, just like Borge."

Zelensky rose to prominence as the star of a popular TV show, "Servant of the People", in which he portrayed a history teacher who improbably becomes president. In real life, he is the unlikely wartime president.

"I bet Zelensky wishes for those simpler times when he could just tell jokes instead of motivating his nation to fight the Russians," I said.

Both of us sat pensive for a moment.

Sophie smiled. "Anyway, my dashing Dane is out there."

"I hope one day you find him," I told her.

"Oh, I definitely will," she grinned. "And I hope you see Elena again, and not just on a billboard."

HANNAH (Happy Girl)

I did it! I booked my flight to Madrid to meet David there before flying together to Menorca. I had two days to pack, find someone to watch my shop, get a haircut, and buy a few dresses. I hadn't bought any new clothes since before COVID. I had no reason to wear anything fancy to the shop, but I had gotten lazy and wore the same red wool sweater and black jeans for far too many days.

When I texted David that I was coming, he called me immediately.

"I can't wait to see you again. I can't get you out of my mind." I could hear his smile through the phone.

I was smiling too, but I was also a bit scared. I knew he wasn't a psycho killer, but I was nervous about spending an entire weekend with a guy I'd only known for a few hours chatting on a plane. I hadn't really thought as far as waking up with him.

"And don't worry. There are plenty of rooms in the house for each of us. We'll have time to know each other better."

What a relief. He had sensed my uncertainty and saved me from making any awkward explanation. His understanding reassured me. It was all so exciting and romantic.

I wished Sophie were around. I wanted to share my news, but I never disturbed her when she was on assignment. The goings-on of Dove Street were saved for her return. We'd meet in each other's apartment or at Peter the Coffee Guy's café up the street. Until then, the only communications were my occasional WhatsApp comments about her latest news story and her quick return notes, regardless of the stress and constant deadlines she faced.

I wondered what she'd think of me hopping on a plane to spend a weekend with David. I doubted she would have been encouraging.

"I'll take you to my favorite restaurant on a cove that overlooks a rocky beach," David had said to me. "Not too many people know of it. The place has the best wine on the island, and the grilled fish is always from that day's catch."

I pictured beautiful painted tiles adorning such a restaurant, the surf whirling below us, and an open kitchen where we watched the fish blacken. The more David spoke about our weekend, the more thrilled I got.

My anticipation that night kept me aroused. Maybe the bedroom situation in the villa would not be a dilemma.

NENA (Sad Girl)

Hakan used to tell me, "I treasure our late afternoons at Susam Café."

My husband was still alluring. With his shock of thick gray hair, sea-blue eyes, and tanned face, he looked like a classic movie star and frequently attracted doubletakes from older women.

He held my hand across the round metal table where we always sat. The waiters knew to bring us the usual: Negronis, a basket of thin French fries, and an extra dish of olives.

Susam Café was situated at the top of the one hundred stairs that connected Dove Street to Susam Sokak, which means Sesame Street in Turkish. The road has no connection to the American children's show, but someone with a quirky sense of humor had installed rubber replicas of

Big Bird and Ernie on a stone wall across from the café. The TV characters looked so incongruous against the ancient rocks.

Standing at the crossroads of a few cobblestone side streets, Susam Café is a perfect meeting spot for the neighborhood journalists, musicians, painters, and other locals. From the wobbly metal furniture outside, diners easily watch the world go by. Its cozy interior is an eclectic wonderland, with items like a 1950s typewriter and a poster of one of the early European jazz talents, Django Reinhardt. None of the furniture matches, from the sunken sofas to the well-worn leather armchairs. The place has the vibe of an eccentric musician's living room.

Hakan's oldest childhood friends would join us some evenings for cocktails on the patio. They typically would talk about politics and the sinking lira, although recently the war in Ukraine dominated the conversation.

One of Hakan's friends had seen a pack of submarines pass through the Bosphorus. "Dark hulks that looked like a flotilla of Loch Ness monsters," was how he described them.

During our last cocktail gathering, they discussed the Montreux Convention, which allowed movement of warships between the Mediterranean Sea and the Black Sea, and debated Turkey's conflicted position on the war. Turkish officials called the Russian invasion of Ukraine "unacceptable" and a "grave violation of international law" but opposed the Western sanctions imposed on Russia. And yet, one official had announced that Russian oligarchs were "of course" welcome and free to do business in Turkey.

Putin's misinformation campaign that prevented most Russians from knowing about the barbarous assault bewildered Hakan and his friends. Shockingly, most families in Russia refused to believe that their own soldiers could bomb innocent people.

"How can so many people be so deceived?" asked one of them. "Even when their relatives in Ukraine tell them about the destruction, they refuse to believe it happened."

"Sometimes people just want to believe one reality," said another. "If they dare to accept an opposite truth, it obliterates the core of who they are."

After the second round of cocktails, their discussion lightened, and they rehashed familiar stories from their youthful years and roared with laughter as if hearing them for the first time. Then their conversation turned to long-winded monologues about their aches and pains, their tennis injuries, and the medicines they were taking.

"We must be boring to young Nena," one of the old guys sighed.

"Not at all," I responded.

I bristled whenever they made a point of saying young Nena. I was nearly forty, but they couldn't resist making subtle jabs at the thirty-year age difference between Hakan and me. After all these years with Hakan, I resented their comments and their leers, which had become worse of late. Hakan squeezed my hand and beamed at me with pride, oblivious to their attitude, which only made me feel like a trophy.

I had nothing and was nothing twenty years ago when I met Hakan—bad memories my only possession. Hakan took me back to his hotel after we struck up a lively conversation in that Berlin park. He felt familiar from the start, like I had known him forever.

Our unexpected afternoon in bed didn't feel sleazy. Even then, Hakan looked and acted much younger than his years. He was charming, dynamic, and full of life. I wasn't looking for love, but I found it. Before long, he convinced me to come live with him in his Istanbul home.

It wasn't a leap of faith for me. I had nothing to lose.

Hakan recharged my life. He introduced me to artists, photographers, and actors. He opened my eyes to books that I never would have known to read.

He welcomed me into his breathtaking apartment that overlooked the Bosphorus, filled with antiques and colorful art that he had accumulated on his travels to Asia and Africa. From his balcony, we could see the famous Hagia Sophia, the Blue Mosque, and Topkapi Palace. I had only heard about those iconic sites and never dreamed they would become part of my daily landscape.

I grew up these past two decades of living with Hakan. He has been my lover, my friend, and my teacher. I never thought about him as an old man. In fact, I had never thought about him getting old at all until lately, when he seemed so terribly frail.

As we finished off the third round of cocktails, the night air turned chilly. A cold front had moved in fast, and the wind had picked up. Hakan was afraid of closed spaces and contracting COVID, so we didn't move inside. We said our goodbyes and headed home.

I held his arm tightly as we traversed the stairs down to Dove Street. Just when we approached the bottom, that big old dog ambled out of her parking lot and watched as I steered Hakan down the street and into our apartment.

ÇIÇEK

Dove Street was quiet for a long time. Tall Guy and Tall Girl were still away. I knew when they returned because their yellow car stopped near my parking lot. It always took a while for Tall Guy to dig out Tall Girl's box on wheels amid his mound of boxes on wheels. The two of them always looked more tired, with deep rings under their eyes, when they returned. They were usually skinnier too. I wondered why no one fed them when they went on their trips. Maybe they didn't take their big rubber bowls with them.

They were still out of town when Happy Girl left in a yellow car. She seemed more cheerful than ever. And that's saying a lot. She'd come to talk to me the day before. I told you that people tell me stuff. I don't understand the specifics, but I definitely get the gist of what they're saying.

And it's not only "blah, blah, blah, FOOD, blah, blah, blah, FOOD". When Happy Girl spoke to me, she said things like "water" and "beach" and "boy" and "love" and "good".

After Happy Girl left, there was not much action on Dove Street for a while.

Old Guy stepped out with Sad Girl, but only to go up the stairs for a few hours. I hoped my latest fit of zoomies hadn't scared him too much. I sometimes saw Sad Girl leave their apartment alone. She'd come back with bags of chicken and meat patties. I could smell them all the way down the street.

Periodically, Sad Girl took walks on her own. I could see Old Guy in the window, waving to her. Sad Girl didn't always wave back. She'd be gone all day and return before it got dark.

A few times she would come hang out with me. She'd squeeze me too tight, but I didn't mind, especially when she'd cry into my fur. She seemed calm when she left the apartment, but the floodgates opened when she reached my end of the street. She'd sob and sputter into my neck. My fur was too thick to ever get soggy. I'd just sit there and listen. She'd say things like "love" and "old" and "time" and "life" and "sad".

Her peppermint-smelling face was lickable. Once, I stepped on a sticky blob that someone had spit out of their mouth. It smelled like Sad Girl. For the life of me, I couldn't get that mint stuff off my paw. It clung to the fur between my toes. I licked it furiously and even tried to bite it off, but it still stuck to me. Eventually it wore off. Maybe Sad Girl's sadness was like the sticky stuff lodged in my fur. One day, it would be gone for good.

HANNAH (Happy Girl)

I couldn't find David. I scanned the crowd across the Madrid airport arrivals area, my eyes darting in every direction. Mobs at airports around the world have the same expectant vibe—people waiting for their friends, lovers, or family members to emerge from baggage claim. I glanced from left to right at the elderly faces, young faces, anxious faces, men holding flowers, children jumping with excitement, but no David.

I began to panic. The frenzied airport crowd made me flash to a devastating moment when I was eight years old, with my father in a crowded department store in Virginia. He'd told me to wait at the perfume counter.

"Don't move. I'll be back in a few minutes," he promised.

I waited patiently while some people pushed past me, and others stopped to sample the fragrances that were arrayed in elegant bottles on the counter. No one paid any attention to me as my anxiety grew with each minute my father didn't return.

My thoughts snapped back to the airport when I spotted David at an ATM, shoving cash into his pocket while talking on his phone. As he jogged over to the crowd, with a baseball cap covering his unruly curls, I caught his eye. He grinned, waved, and pointed for me to meet him at the end of the arrivals throng. Without looking at it, he tapped his phone screen off, and tucked it inside his jacket.

"You thought I'd stood you up?" he asked, having noticed my momentary alarm. "I'm so sorry. I didn't mean to scare you. I was just running late."

He pulled me into a tight embrace, so there was no awkward decision about whether we should kiss. He clasped my hand, grabbed the pully on my luggage, and we scooted quickly to make our connection to Menorca.

"At last!" he exclaimed as we boarded the domestic flight.

Still reeling from the possibility that he might have been a no-show, my heartbeat had no chance to slow through the scurried airport transfer. When I caught my breath, we looked at each other, face to face from adjacent airplane seats.

"We have to stop meeting like this," David said, cupping his hands around my cheeks and lightly touching his lips to mine. The intimate kiss was over in an instant, but the heat of a hundred fires flushed my face and probably my neck and legs and every other part of my body.

My heart wouldn't slow down. I barely remembered the flight, all my thoughts hung on that spontaneous brush of lips.

After renting a car at Menorca's small airport, we drove along a single-lane road lined with farms and stone walls and fields speckled with meandering cattle. Less than an hour later, we pulled into the driveway of a compact white stucco villa perched on a cliff overlooking a blue-green surf. On the private beach below sat a lone pedalo waiting just for us.

We didn't go to the beach that day. We didn't leave the villa. We barely left the bedroom. All my fears about awkward moments with a stranger disappeared as soon as we walked into the main bedroom. With the sea breeze wafting through open windows across a sumptuous bed, it was an invitation impossible to decline.

David leaned in towards me and put his mouth next to my ear, his hot breath sent goose bumps up and down my frame. His dark eyes scanned my face, and his hands grabbed my hips so lightly they could have been a light wind. The heat in my body spread towards my center, wrapping around my thighs like a vine. I realized I wasn't breathing and forced myself to exhale, the rise and fall of my chest producing a gasp of exhilaration.

"Am I in a dream?" I asked.

David laughed. "It feels that way, doesn't it?"

We spent the weekend jumping in and out of bed, taking short strolls around the villa, dipping in the warm Mediterranean surf, and spinning around the cove in the abandoned pedalo. We ambled on empty beaches, his arm wrapped around my shoulders and the wind pulling at his dark curls as we laughed for no reason but sheer happiness.

We never ate at his favorite restaurant because as we drove up to the front door, David thought the place was too crowded.

"I want you all to myself," he said.

Instead, we drove to an intimate café with only four tables. The couples around us looked like honeymooners. I didn't feel out of place. His knee touched mine, and the heat burned between my legs. His fingers touched my leg and slowly slid up until he found my hand. His thumb drew circles on my palm, and he laced his fingers into mine. We ate off each other's plates and shared an enormous lobster stew.

After dinner, we strolled into galleries with local artists' dramatic paintings of seascapes, crashing tides rolling onto craggy rocks, and ominous thunder clouds hovering over stormy seas.

He asked questions about my life and my shop. There wasn't much to tell. I had an older brother in Virginia, but my parents were both gone. I didn't want to tell him about my father. I didn't want his pity. I did tell him my dream of expanding my art supply shop and how I needed better marketing to attract more international business online.

"You've got so much creativity and love of art. You'll find a way to do it," he said. "I'd like to come and see your life in Istanbul."

"I hope you do," I told him. "I'll introduce you to my friends. Most of us live on one street. It's like a tiny village in the middle of the megacity."

"I want to be part of your village," he declared.

I couldn't believe what I was hearing. I had to stop myself from jumping ahead in my heart and mind. I had just met him. I couldn't dare to dream about where this was heading. It was all so magical.

We snuggled together our last night in the villa. Rain clouds had moved in, and we watched the light downpour from the bedroom window. Our parting at the Menorca airport the next morning was hasty. David had business in Seville, so we took separate flights.

We made promises to see each other soon. I waved at him from the plane before my flight took off. I could still see him in the tiny airport lounge. He stood rigidly, glancing around the room, his arms wrapped tightly across his chest. I was already planning what we would do the next time we got together.

TED (Tall Guy)

Sophie and I finished editing a heartbreaking story about a family of four killed while crossing a Kyiv bridge. The footage was painful to watch. Bright-colored backpacks clung to the tiny lifeless bodies that still clutched stuffed animals. I've seen some horrible things through my camera lens, but nothing compares to the dead eyes of innocent children.

Even after covering numerous wars, I had to remind myself that I wasn't there to mourn. My job was to show others what was happening. Memories of Elena were a welcome diversion. In the midst of all the madness, I thought of her smoky eyes and what she'd look like naked and how she'd move in bed.

"Maybe I'll see you around," was what she had said when she kissed me on both cheeks before we parted outside that Istanbul restaurant. It was noncommittal at best, or maybe she was just not that interested in me. Hell, I was terrible at reading women. That's what my ex-wife used to tell me anyway.

"How do I reach you?" I asked Elena.

"We'll find each other," was all she said.

Why hadn't I pushed to get her number, an email, or any other contact details? I had no idea where she lived or how she happened to wander into that restaurant.

I kept replaying our conversation. She talked with me as if it had been a long time since she had a conversation with anyone. The words poured out of her in a great rush. It took a mountain of restraint for me not to reach across the table and touch those lips.

Elena described her childhood in Russia, which was still part of the Soviet Union then. She had been the product of a love affair between her mother and a Turkish construction industry businessman who sometimes worked in Russia. Her mother had been a receptionist at the Moscow hotel where he stayed, and they got together when he visited every couple of months.

It was the 1980s, a time of blossoming trade between the USSR and Turkey. The Prime Minister of Turkey, Turgut Ozal, sent his country's businessmen to the Soviet Union for trade deals. Four enormous contracts to build housing for members of the Russian military back from duty in East Germany were all awarded to Turkish companies and spurred a big drive to sell Turkish construction goods for export.

Elena remembered her father as a nice man who doted on her mother. When she was about ten, he was able to move her and her mother into a larger, better-appointed Moscow apartment with heat that actually worked.

"He took care of us, but he never married my mother or moved to Russia," Elena told me. "She didn't pressure him. She loved him and waited patiently for his week-long visits."

One day from Elena's bedroom window she watched a man drive up to their apartment and pull a big suitcase out of the trunk of his car. The driver caught her eye for several seconds and shook his head before he buzzed their door. After the man left, she went downstairs and found her mother on the floor, sobbing inconsolably, digging through piles of cash stacked in the suitcase. Her father had died in Turkey of virulent brain cancer and had sent the money so they would be financially secure.

I thought Elena had finished her story. But after a moment's pause, she continued, as if in a trance, talking to no one in particular.

"My mother joined my father in death two years later," she said. "I believe she died from a broken heart. I really think that can happen when you love as much as she did. I was twelve years old. My only survival kit was the suitcase."

I had wanted to reach over and comfort her, to hold her, but I was paralyzed, uncertain what move to make, if any. She had shared a shattering tale of her childhood. I didn't know her that well. Any physical move towards her seemed inappropriate.

Her eyes briefly swept over my face. "I'm sorry I've

unloaded so much on you. I don't even know you," she said, as if reading my mind and standing up to leave.

Our intimate conversation was abruptly over, like a stage curtain coming down at the end of a tragic play. I wanted more. But I was out of luck.

ÇIÇEK

I had visitors today. The homeless man's dogs came by for a sniff. They told me an incredible story about Boji, an old friend of mine. I'd met him during my wanderings on the highway. Boji looked just like me—white fur, dark blotches. At least, that's what we looked like in a store window reflection. His eyes resembled chocolate chips that I had seen once in a roadside trash heap. I don't know what color my eyes are. But someone once pointed to them and said "blueberries". So I assume I have blueberries for eyes.

I didn't realize at the time that Boji was a celebrity. He had gotten popular because he knew how to ride the Istanbul metro. He even hopped on buses. He was a real free spirit. Boji tried to talk me into coming with him on those big moving vehicles, but I was too scared. We lost track of each other after he climbed aboard a tram one day. That's what happens with friends sometimes. They just take a different route in life. But they're still your friends.

Well, my dog friends told me that Boji became so famous that people read about him all over the world. Can you believe it? To think I had smelled the butt and shared a cardboard box with a celebrity!

Boji was so popular that he became the target of a scam.

A bad man brought poop into a tram and placed it on a seat to frame Boji. There are a lot of sick people out there. Boji would never poop in a tram, but folks blamed him anyway.

It was a setup. People took sides. Some of them wanted Boji killed because they thought he was a dirty animal who made messes in their trains. Other people loved Boji and defended him. Well, the truth came out. Cameras in the tram caught the man secretly pulling the poop out of his pocket and putting it on the seat.

But it was too late. Too many people had read about Boji and reached their own conclusion. They didn't want to know the truth. Boji got death threats. People screamed at him and even kicked him, all because of a pile of poop that wasn't even his.

But good thing for Boji, he had important friends. The mayor of Istanbul came to his rescue. He called the richest guy in the city and asked him if he would adopt Boji. And you know what? Boji now lives in a mansion with the wealthy guy. He has his own garden and can do his business whenever and wherever he wants.

I'm glad for Boji. I hope he's as happy as I am in my parking lot.

NENA (Sad Girl)

Hakan told me, "I wouldn't want to live if I ever lost you." I had always felt special to be at the receiving end of his adoration. Lately, though, his expressions of devotion verged on desperation.

We had reversed roles. I was the grown-up and Hakan was the child. But he needed far more care than I ever did.

I had learned to survive on my own when I was very young. I made my way to Berlin after many difficult years.

Hakan's friends had never understood that he and I had fallen in love. What I needed to remind myself was that our love had taken a different form. For some people, love grows stronger and deeper over time. For others, it weakens and fades away. Our love was steady and calm, but I had become more caretaker and mother than lover. I booked his doctor appointments, monitored his heart meds, and consoled him when he could no longer make love like the insatiable bull he once was.

Hakan had asked me if I ever wanted to turn back the clock. I suppose part of me hasn't given up wanting to have that rush of overpowering yearning. I never want to be who I was in those days, but I did want to keep on living instead of doing nothing more than watch Hakan pass from middle age into decrepitude. That was selfish, I know, but I couldn't help it.

I found comfort in the studio and was grateful that work was picking up. I could leave the apartment when jobs came my way with a legitimate excuse to disappear for an afternoon. Each time I walked out of the building and down our street, I felt a release, like a plastic bag had been ripped off my head. I could breathe at last. That gigantic dog, Çiçek, would come bounding up to me. We'd sit by her parking lot before I turned up the one hundred stairs, and she would let me dump my pent-up emotions onto her. I don't know how many tearful sessions I spent crying into that old hound's fur.

I told that dog everything, even thoughts I found too difficult to admit to myself. I knew she wouldn't tell anyone. She was better than a therapist.

HANNAH (Happy Girl)

I repeatedly checked my phone, but there was no message. It had been two days since Menorca and not a single call or text from David. He usually sent a flurry of messages early in the morning, during lunch, and, occasionally, extremely late at night. So basically, he messaged day and night. I stared at my phone, willing it to beep.

Maybe something terrible had happened to him? How would I ever know? There'd be no one who would inform me. My panic returned as I tried my hardest to fight a sick feeling in my stomach.

Of course he was fine, I told myself, as I invented new reasons for his silence. Maybe he just didn't want to see me again? But I rehashed every moment of our weekend on the island and remembered his comment about wanting to be part of my village. Didn't that mean he wanted to be in my life? I knew I hadn't imagined his feelings for me. I sent him a few messages but thought better than to bombard him with texts, demanding to know where he was.

I made pacts with myself: I would allow myself to check my phone after ten customers had walked into my shop, or five cars drove by, or until I just couldn't stand it any longer. I'll just pick up my phone one last time before closing, or maybe two more times.

I convinced myself that he had lost his phone or was stuck somewhere, and that's why he couldn't contact me. I just wanted to hear from him once, to know he was thinking about me. A week passed like this. I wanted to call him, but I had already left too many messages. Any more and he'd know how obsessed I was with him.

Then, hallelujah! My phone made that magnificent beeping sound that changed my worldview. I loved my phone so much at that moment I could have taken a bite out of it.

David: Hi.

I craved to write back with too many exclamation points, too many questions, and too much desperation. His text greeting was like cool water on a burn. A relief. A balm.

Me: Hello.

Proud of my restraint, I waited patiently for the blue tick. He had read it, and I could see he was typing. I smiled at those three pulsing dots on my phone and eagerly anticipated his reply.

David: I've missed you. I've had some crazy stuff at work.

I counted to ten before replying. He may have had a busy schedule, but he could at least have sent a quick message. But I didn't want to nag.

Me: Me too. I've been so busy.

I lied. Business had been slow. I didn't want David to know how lunatic I had become, how I thought of him all the time.

David: I want to see you again. How about I visit you next weekend?

I waited a full ten seconds that felt like a century.

Me: Yes!

The rush of joy made my insides tremble. David told me that he would book a flight. My mind raced with places I'd take him and friends I'd introduce to him.

But Sophie and Ted were still on assignment in Ukraine. They wouldn't likely return soon. The war had escalated. A prominent journalist had just been killed. It seemed no one was off limits in this war. Even reporters had become targets. I was afraid for my friends.

TED (Tall Guy)

Two years from now, will people still think about Ukraine and what happened when Russia stormed in? Will they remember the mayhem? Will they merely think about the bloodshed as something that happened in another part of the world that wasn't on their border? Is this a turning point in history, or is it yet another foreign invasion that will be forgotten among all the others?

I couldn't answer any of those questions.

One thing was certain: I had looked into the face of yet another dead woman today. This one's uncanny resemblance to Elena made me turn my camera off and stare unfiltered into her lifeless eyes and over her skin, which had already turned the eerie pallor of death. That inert Ukrainian woman had once lived and laughed and loved but was now extinguished by a single bullet that found its way to her head. She had been a beauty, her angelic face enveloped by a thick auburn tresses.

She was not Elena. She was not anyone anymore, except a memory in the minds of those who had loved her. A life lived but brutally cut short.

"What do you think about when you're covering a war?" Elena had asked me a month ago at the restaurant in Istanbul.

"How to stay out of danger and avoid snipers and stray bullets," I told her. "How to find the best images that will tell the most compelling story. How to capture life and death."

I also told her about coming home to an empty apartment

with no one waiting for me and nothing in the refrigerator but a dried-up lemon and a half-empty mustard jar. For a few years I'd had a wife, Karen, who I returned to. But I spent years putting my life on hold to hop on a plane to a war, a coup, a tsunami, an earthquake, or a flood. Even after Karen had had enough and my marriage had fallen apart, I still believed that my work was important, that it might possibly make a difference, to somebody, somewhere.

Will the world feel the impact of this war forever? Most likely, yes. That's why the reporters and cameramen like me dropped everything, grabbed camera gear and bulletproof vests, and left our comforts to record the horrors of war and make sure that the tragic stories were told.

I admitted to her that adrenaline plays a part. However important the role of war reporting, it requires an internal ambition, and sometimes insanity, to remain with the gunfire rather than flee it.

My marriage had been a casualty of war. My wife was alone in New York more than I was at home. It wasn't fair to her. I can't blame her for running off with a guy we both knew in college. They reconnected at a reunion that I couldn't attend because I was five thousand miles away. She deserved to be happy. I wasn't ready to give up my globetrotting.

What I hadn't admitted to Elena was that alone at night in my hotel room, I was no different from any other guy in any other circumstance. I thought about sex. Well, not entirely about that. Well, actually, yes, sex was the main topic of my random nightly attentions.

But with Elena on my mind, I didn't feel any urge to hop in the sack with anyone else. And my arousal wasn't from any leftover adrenaline from the day's fear. She was like a wounded bird, but so enchanting that the mere thought of her made me want her, and her alone.

It made no sense, yet this perfectly gorgeous stranger filled a void in my head and my loins during those early depressing days of filming that senseless war. She was a beautiful canvas against which I could project all of my fantasies. What can I say, I'm just a hound dog at heart. I can't help myself.

HANNAH (Happy Girl)

David texted me: "We'll make this work. We can find a way around the miles and countries between us."

He seemed so certain. He gave me hope.

I needed to prepare for his visit and didn't want him to see my shabby apartment in its present form. I gave it a facelift with new sheets, towels, and pillows on the couch. I hung the small painting I bought in Menorca. Its luscious layers of oil paint depicted the same cove that we could see from the villa bedroom. We both remarked what a coincidence it was and how perfectly the artist had captured the scene. The delicate painting was far more evocative of our weekend than any photo could have been.

"Who needs photos when we have such beautiful memories," David had said. "I prefer the pictures in my mind's eye."

I hoped that his visit to Istanbul would be just as perfect as our Menorcan adventure. I debated whether I should meet him at Istanbul Airport because the ride there meant more than an hour in dense traffic. The debate lasted all of a minute. I closed my shop early and went to surprise him.

This time it was me at the airport arrivals gate waiting for him to emerge from luggage claim. I stood amid the crowd, with plenty of time to spare. I didn't want to miss him. The first dozen people who burst through with laughter and loud chatter wore the matching workout clothes of a school sports team. More clusters of travelers meandered through the exit, but no David.

He sure did keep me in suspense. I reminded myself that he had no idea I'd come to meet him. I checked my phone to see if he had left any messages. No text. No WhatsApp. Nothing. I texted to see if he had landed. Silence.

I stood there trying to subdue the growing panic. Again! Had I been stood up, or worse still, had something happened to him? I was just about to leave when David wandered through the door with his phone plastered to his ear. He was yelling, his face contorted with rage. I couldn't hear a word, but as soon as he saw my alarmed look, he abruptly ended his screaming fit and tapped the phone off without any farewell to the person at the other end.

His face immediately softened, and he ran towards me.

"Well, this is a surprise!" he exclaimed, as he planted one of his delicious kisses on my lips. I don't remember much of the ride back to the city or how we ended up in my bed for the next twelve hours.

We lounged the next morning, sipping coffee at the tiny table that fit snugly on my balcony as we watched the ferries sliding across the Bosphorus between Asia and Europe. Istanbul is the only city in the world that spans two continents—I wondered if our relationship could endure the distance.

After more languorous hours in my bedroom, we showered, dressed, and took an hour-long stroll through Cihangir, my neighborhood of cafés brimming with young foreigners and well-off Turks. Famous and not-so-famous artists, writers, and celebrities could be found sipping coffee in the sidewalk restaurants or ambling through the antique shops and boutiques. By evening, the hipsters overcrowding the open-air bars and hoping for hook-ups would spill onto the streets.

We made our way along the uneven sidewalk hugging the busy road that paralleled the Bosphorus, and passed by the famous Kiliç Ali Pasa mosque, a stunning Ottoman specimen decorated with beautiful Islamic tiles and calligraphy.

At the Galata Bridge we watched the ferries, cruise ships, and cargo boats pass below and scanned the outline of the Princes' Islands in the distance, and the Asia side of the city almost close enough to touch. A row of patient fishermen, their rods extended over the metal railing, threw their meager catch into buckets at their feet.

David and I zigged and zagged through the throngs of tourists walking across the bridge. He periodically stopped in the midst of the chaos to kiss me, and we laughed at how our noses got in the way, as did the bill of his baseball hat.

We finally reached Topkapi Palace, home to all the Ottoman sultans. What stories those ancient walls could tell of voracious sultans, ambitious courtiers, beautiful concubines, and attendant eunuchs. We skipped the lavish pavilions, and the Treasury filled with cases of sparkling gems. The lines were too long.

"I want to head to the harem house," David suggested.

"Why am I not surprised?" I laughed.

A guidebook informed us that the harem was a place where the sultan could engage in sex any time he wanted. It was also where the imperial family lived. By Islamic law, the sultan could have four wives but countless lovers. The word "harem" means forbidden or private. The sultans supported as many as three hundred concubines who lived in a labyrinth of lavish bedrooms, tiled courtyards, and waiting rooms with painted ceilings and mother-of-pearl inlay, all surrounded by marbled fountains and baths.

"What a life with all those wives and lovers," David remarked.

"It's a terrible idea," I said.

"What's so awful about it if everyone is on board with the plan?" asked David.

"But what if they're not? What if they want the guy all to themselves and aren't into sharing?"

"Everyone involved would need to be okay with it."

"I don't see how it's sustainable. It would take a lot of energy and a lot of money to keep all the women satisfied."

"I think it's possible," said David. "But probably not practical."

"Seriously?" I retorted. "You don't see anything wrong with the idea of harems?"

"Not really," he deadpanned. But then he broke into laughter at my appalled expression.

We moved to the eunuchs' living quarters. We read the guidebook's explanation that eunuchs were used either as soldiers or as court servants because of their lack of reproductive threat. They would never have sons who could threaten the allegiance of their fathers or put the court at risk. Surprisingly, eunuchs were castrated simply by removing only their testicles and not their penis.

"Ouch," was all David said, as he protectively cupped his hand over his crotch.

ÇIÇEK

I've seen people do it doggy style. You'd think they'd come up with a better name for it. I really think that folks just want to be dogs. They can't be us, so they sometimes act like us.

I realize I've strayed far from the story. But actually, it all ties in. I saw Happy Girl and a new boy doing it "doggy style" in their window. Nobody ever thinks anyone can see into their windows. You can see out of a window, so of course folks can see in.

I saw everything they were doing. Maybe I'm invisible to them. Maybe that's another one of my superpowers. Happy Girl and the new boy were sure going at it. I couldn't hear anything, but I could see their mouths opened and their eyes closed.

I met the new boy with Happy Girl when, after a long time, they stopped humping in the window, put some clothes on, and came down to Dove Street. I watched the way he had his arm around her. She sure liked him. That made me want to like him too. He wore a hat but briefly took it off when he approached me. The sniff test confused me. He carried so many smells, mostly flowers and Happy Girl's honey scent. I couldn't help myself. I took several more sniffs of his crotch.

"Hey Dog, that's enough of that," said Hat Guy. He pushed

me away as they climbed up the stairs. He didn't have to shove so hard.

NENA (Sad Girl)

Another sunset at Susam Café with the old men. A young couple I had never seen before sat near us today. I couldn't take my eyes off the way he caressed her arm and how close they sat to each other. The baseball hat didn't hide his sculpted face and dark green eyes. She had wild brown curls that blew in the breeze. They were a beautiful couple.

They cuddled and touched as if they couldn't bear to ever be separated. Locked in a world of their own, they hardly noticed the arrival of the waiter, or the menus placed in front of them. They oozed that peaceful air of two people who had just finished making love. I was envious of their ardor and wanted the same for myself. One day, maybe that could be me across the table from a young lover. Would I ever dare?

The guy's phone rang and jolted him from their intimate moment. He glanced at the screen, jumped to his feet, and dashed out of the café with the phone pressed to his ear. The woman caught my eye and appeared both surprised and embarrassed to have been abandoned so abruptly.

From my angle, I could see the guy gesticulating angrily as he spoke. He returned a few minutes later and seemed not to have been phased by whatever had transpired. I saw him wave off his girlfriend's concerned look.

What was he up to? Everyone has secrets. I certainly did.

This guy had something eating at him. His mood switched

too fast, and he pretended all was well, when it clearly wasn't. His girlfriend didn't appear to be clued in to whatever was irking him.

None of that was my concern. I had a delicate notion of my own that made me hopeful whenever I dared to think about it. My private thoughts were a refuge, an open door, to daydream about another reality, another life. I confided only in that old street dog, my trustworthy confidante.

A larger issue occupied my mind these days that made me angry and sometimes despondent. I needed to get to the bottom of it. If my gut was correct, then everything I had believed to be true was wrong.

That dog on our street knew my secret, and she let me cry rivers of tears into her fur. I told her what I had seen in a magazine, something I hoped with all my heart was not as it now seemed.

"Nena, you are so deep in thought this evening. Is everything okay?" Hakan asked. His words pulled me out of my head and back into the familiar.

"I'm fine," I smiled.

"I know you're preoccupied with something," said Hakan. "Is there anything I can do to cheer you up?"

"Yes! Let's go on a trip," I exclaimed.

"I don't know how wise that is with all these new COVID variants," he replied.

"Not an international trip. Let's go to that cute fishing village that was featured in *Why Not Spend It?* magazine a few weeks back. Eskifoça, just outside Izmir. We've never been there. It's an easy flight."

He paused for a moment. His eyes went far away and

pensive. "I want to stay home until this pandemic is behind us, but why don't you go? The sea air will do you good."

Part of me selfishly hoped that he wouldn't want to come. I was pleased that it had been his idea for me to go alone. I needed some time alone to figure things out. I desperately wanted my suspicions to be wrong. There was something in that magazine photo that didn't sit right. I had to go to Eskifoça and hunt down the truth.

TED (Tall Guy)

Sophie and I spent another night in a Kyiv metro station huddled in sleeping bags beside a family with two young children. I was in awe of their resilience. One of the little girls sang the alphabet song to calm herself against a steady backdrop of explosions and the roar of planes above. I was left alone to adjust the lights and focus my camera lens through the darkness onto the child's face. Her heartbreaking humming was the sound of innocence.

Sophie had nerves of steel. She never flinched from the blasts that shook the earth around us. She never demanded to be the star of her stories like so many reporters. On camera, you'd catch only a quick glimpse of her long black hair or her hand holding a microphone to whomever she was interviewing. It was her clear and steady non-emotional voice as well as her fair and accurate reporting that had become familiar to so many viewers.

Her composure soothed everyone around her, and her empathy elicited the most remarkable reactions from her interviews. She'd give people space and time to cry or laugh or admit their deepest fears.

Once, when we maneuvered through an empty street that had been obliterated by Russian strikes, I focused the camera on a burly military officer who broke down in tears after only a few calmly delivered questions from Sophie: "Where is your family? How are you coping? Why is this happening?" Those basic queries, never asked in a hasty barrage, drew responses that revealed to the world the truth through those who were suffering it. I continued filming her as we walked down that street of sorrow. She spoke with one hollow-eyed man after another who had lost everything, absorbed the grief around her, empathized, and never cracked.

Although Sophie made it easy for anyone to tell her their inner thoughts, I felt absurd unloading any more about Elena, a woman I'd only met for a few hours but who had become my lifeline to a saner world.

I was well aware she was nothing more than a wet dream. But that buoyed me through the days and weeks on assignment in this incomprehensible war. Putin's battle plan was to demolish cities, terrify the population, and drive them out. It was going to be a war of attrition, and I was happy to have Elena with me, even if only in my fantasies.

ÇIÇEK

I have been busy. You know how it is. You start cleaning the mud off your feet, chase a few cars, and then another sun comes up and goes down.

I need to fill you in on some strange goings on. First of all, Happy Girl's new friend with the hat spent a great deal of time alone in my parking lot yelling into his talking box. I heard him say, "Stop!" I sure understood that word. It usually came with "No!" He also yelled "take it" and "leave it".

The Hat Guy put his talking box away whenever Happy Girl showed up. Maybe if I had a talking box, I'd bark into it when I was angry. I don't know. I wondered why he was so irritated. He had no reason to be upset because he got to spend so much time with Happy Girl.

They'd been taking long walks away from Dove Street. When they returned, they usually looked tired, like they'd been trekking for miles, or maybe they'd been chasing motorbikes. That can be exhausting. Their day always ended with humping activity in the window.

I have news about Sad Girl too. I saw her a while back with her nose in a magazine as she walked past my parking lot. She kept yelling, "No! No! No!" as she frantically turned the pages. There was that "no" word again. I think the magazine must have been very bad.

A few sun ups later, Sad Girl drove off in a yellow car. She waved to me as she clutched that magazine. I wondered where she was going and when she'd return.

As for Tall Girl and Tall Guy, they had been gone a really long time. Wherever they went must be far away.

But the big news was the arrival of so many new people on our street. Young parents pushing babies in strollers and old ladies who couldn't walk very well moved into the empty apartments across from my parking lot. They didn't carry many bags.

I could tell they weren't from here. They said strange words like "Da" and "Nyet" and a really weird sound like "U Crayon" and "Rush uh" when folks on our street came to welcome them. They looked so sad and tired, like I do when someone forgets to feed me. Why were they so unhappy? I wished those DaNyets had come over to see me. I would have licked them and made them feel better.

NENA (Sad Girl)

I didn't waste a second before booking my flight to Izmir and the connecting ride to Eskifoça. I waved to Çiçek as my taxi drove past her parking lot. Hakan was so understanding about my trip. He had no idea what I was planning, but he knew me well enough to let me go without asking any questions. He wanted me to get a change of scenery at the sea.

Settled into my seat, I pulled out the now tattered *Why Not Spend It?* magazine to study the photo making my blood run cold. Every weekend I devoured this glossy addition to Hakan's financial newspaper. The slick magazine typically featured exotic vacation hideaways for the super-rich and over-the-top ads for absurdly conceived items like diamond encrusted bustiers and solid gold cigar boxes.

But never had a travel piece caught my attention like this one with the old photo that made my pulse race.

The article explained that Eskifoça was an ancient Greek settlement named after the rare Mediterranean monk seals who once lived in nearby islands. The area stretched along two bays, the larger one home to a medieval castle. The spectacular beauty of the village's small coves was under strict environmental protection, so even an abundance of tourists couldn't ruin it. New construction was no longer permitted in many sections of the district.

The article included old pictures of what had been a resort

on a hill above the sea, a secret sanctuary for the fabulously wealthy, that had been reduced to nothing more than a dilapidated, abandoned complex, and a cluster of derelict villas.

That's where I spotted him in a photo. Or at least someone who looked like him. Fatih Demirtaş. It had to be him. But the date made no sense. The thought made me sick to my stomach. I needed to find the deserted resort. I needed to find him.

I spent the quick flight to Izmir obsessing about what I might discover. The minibus from the airport dropped me a minute's walk from a family-run boutique hotel overlooking water so clear and blue it blended seamlessly with the sky.

My room in the converted ancient stone house had everything I needed, including a small balcony with a view of the magnificent yachts and colorful fishing boats that dotted the marina. I could see lovers and family vacationers strolling along the waterfront.

The hotel manager showed me a map of how I could walk up the narrow, rocky road along the various inlets to reach the famous "ghost villas".

When I arrived at the rundown entrance, after a two-hour walk that left me parched and exhausted, I climbed through a hole in the rusted gate that had once undoubtedly been a grand doorway with a guard box to keep out riffraff like me.

No longer a paradise for the obscenely rich, with its secluded woods, beach, private villas, Turkish bath, and tennis court, the abandoned resort was an eerie refuge for snakes and who knows what other creepy crawlies.

My eyes focused on the enormous canopy of trees, terrified that something slithering would fall on top of me. A massive swimming pool, filled with fetid water, leaves, and a few turtles, nestled in the middle of the trees.

I found the deserted concierge office and check-in area at the top of a hill in front of a driveway that was barely visible through the decades of overgrowth. A rusty bell was all that remained on the front desk. The whole place was frozen in time, as if abandoned in a hurry.

From there I made my way down to the sea and was treated to an uninhabited white sandy beach with an expanse of blue Aegean waters that stretched uninterrupted to the horizon. This was the location of the photo in the article, except that the sepia picture showed the beach in its heyday, with bikini-clad guests and big-bellied men adorned with gold chains and eating barbequed seafood from beach grills. The hill above the cove still housed the dozens of vacation villas that had become neglected concrete hulks with rotted wood beams.

If indeed that is Fatih Demirtaş in the photo, he must have stood in this very spot, I thought. My heart ached.

HANNAH (Happy Girl)

After another morning frolic in bed with David, we turned on the TV. David's attention shifted quickly to a one-hour news special about the war. Sophie was on air with the lead story. She had interviewed a man whose small village on the outskirts of Kyiv, which was of no strategic importance but was home to a few dozen farm families, had been destroyed.

"I don't know how she can keep covering these tragic stories week after week," I told David. "She never seems to rest."

Sophie's piece was followed by a Russian business story. David turned up the volume as the news anchor read:

> "Several Western countries, including Britain, the United States, Canada, and Australia, have moved to ban imports of Russian oil as a reprisal for Putin's invasion of Ukraine. Nevertheless, the oil trade continues to earn foreign currency for Russia. And traders can quietly sell its oil to refiners who don't worry about sanctions or reputational issues."

The news story ended with a vehement comment from an economic adviser to Ukraine: "Whoever is buying Russian oil is financing war crimes."

David stared blankly at the TV. After a long pause, he said, "There will always be buyers."

"But Zelensky said it's like giving money to a terrorist," I countered.

"Sanctions are complicated," was all that David replied.

The Ukraine news continued with a short segment that hit even closer to home:

> "Many anti-war Russians are flocking to Turkey. While the majority of Ukrainian refugees have fled to neighboring EU countries, a large number are also settling in Istanbul."

As if on cue, David peered out my living room window and exclaimed, "Take a look! There seems to be a rush of new people who have found their way to your street."

Sure enough, a steady stream of young families wandered down the road. We could hear their muffled voices, all speaking what sounded like Russian.

"Those are the fortunate ones who have made it to Dove Street," David said.

"I wouldn't call any of them fortunate." I noticed they had little or no luggage with them. "I'll be right back."

I ran downstairs with a large bag full of clothes I had been meaning to take to the collection box at the mosque up the street. All the families were heading into various apartment buildings. They may have secured housing, but they had precious few belongings. They happily accepted my old coats, boots, pants, and sweaters and hugged me in gratitude.

Çiçek watched it all. Nothing happened on our street without her noticing. I ran over to give her a belly rub that she loved so much.

Back in the apartment, David smiled when I walked through the door and abruptly ended a phone call as I heard him say, "That's the price they're asking." He slid his phone back into his front pocket.

We both turned to the TV again when a breaking news bulletin announced that peace talks were scheduled for later in the week, this time in Istanbul. It seemed that the war was spilling in many ways into my backyard.

"I hope they can break the stalemate in those talks," I said.

"Well, some fights just can't be settled," said David.

"That's dark," I countered. "I hate to believe that."

"You're right. The news is bringing me down. Let's take a walk. I don't want to let the world ruin our last day together."

"I was thinking the same thing. I have one more place I want to take you."

The Basilica cistern was next on our must-see list and would certainly lighten our mood. We strolled back to the heart of the city's tourist district, not far from the harem house we had visited the previous day. We walked down fifty stone steps, feeling the dampness from the fifteen-hundred-year-old cistern that had once provided water to Topkapi Palace and its surrounding buildings. This was the perfect escape from the world above.

All we could hear were whispers from tourists and occasional drips of water. A vendor at an underground souvenir kiosk called us over to entice us to dress up in his Ottoman turbans, like the ones the sultans wore, and have our picture taken.

"No need for photos," David said. "It's a silly tourist gimmick." He was right, but I realized I had no photos of him at all. He didn't even like selfies. "They are absurd and narcissistic," he'd say. I had never met anyone so camera-shy.

Instead, I took pictures of the spectacular view in front of us. We were forty feet underground and standing amid rows of tall, slender, granite columns from the Byzantine era that radiated from a dozen long archways, visible only through faint lights scattered on the walls.

We walked to the back of the cistern to find two columns held up by the heads of Medusa, the famous winged woman in Greek mythology whose hair was living, writhing venomous snakes. Our guidebook explained that Medusa was once a beautiful priestess of Athena, cursed for breaking her vow of celibacy with the sea god Poseidon, which produced two children. Anyone who gazed into Medusa's eyes would turn to stone, so the curse went. One of the Medusa figures in the cistern was upside down, and the other lay on its side. No one is sure of the reason, but a favored theory is that the skewed positioning of the heads meant anyone who dared to look into her eyes would escape being turned into stone.

"Wow. Medusa paid a tough price for love," said David.

"You're such a romantic," I smiled, as I leafed through the guidebook to find more fun facts about the cistern.

I read aloud: "The 1963 film *From Russia with Love* shows James Bond sailing through the Basilica cistern columns to reach a secret door, no doubt on his way to catch some devious people."

"Let's hurry back to your apartment where I can do some devious things to you," David said. I was okay with that.

NENA (Sad Girl)

I asked at the front desk of my Eskifoça hotel, "Have you ever seen this man?" The manager squinted to scrutinize the magazine photo more closely.

"His name is Fatih Demirtaş," I added.

"I don't recognize him or the name," the manager told me. "I'm new here. My girlfriend's family has been running this place for a long time, but I live in Istanbul and just came down to help for a few months."

He was familiar with the magazine story, though, which he said had attracted a flood of tourists.

"It's the best advertisement we could have asked for."

"Do you know anyone who might know him?" I persisted.

"It's a small town. Your best bet is to walk up and down the beach and hang out at the restaurants on the marina."

"Is there a bar or café where locals hang out and would be more promising than the tourist haunts," I asked.

"Not really. There isn't a huge choice of places to eat and drink. The whole village is a mix of families who have been here for generations, along with tourists like you who come with that magazine," he said. "But before you do anything else, I recommend a swim in the cove out front. You'll have a refreshing afternoon. It's still cold this time of year, but it's rejuvenating."

That sounded like a perfect plan. I put on my favorite plum-colored swimsuit, slightly revealing through the metal loops across the front but not enough to make me uncomfortable at the public beach. I slipped on my white linen tunic, walked through the tiny lobby, crossed the path at the foot of the entrance, and stuck my toes into the refreshing in front of Aegean Sea. Colored buoys bobbing on a red rope marked off a large area to separate swimmers from the nearby boats.

I dropped my things onto the sand and dove in. As soon as my body adjusted to the chilly water, I relaxed. The salted surf and fresh sea air were a perfect way to clear my head. The longer I swam, the more I thought how absurd my suspicion probably was. Why would Fatih have lied for so many years? What purpose would that have served? I'm sure he would not have wanted to hurt me.

Pushing my obsession to find him to one side, I decided to simply enjoy myself for a few days at the beach. The photo was probably just someone who looked like him and worked at that resort.

The sunlight sparkled on the water in front of me as I swam through the gentle swells. Only an occasional cloud cast a shadow over the beach. Seagulls squawked as they dove into the schools of fish that freely cruised just below the surface, oblivious to the hungry prey above them.

An afternoon nap that followed my swim turned into a deep sleep and the first dream I'd had in a long while, a dream so vivid that it produced tastes and smells of fish that sizzled on an open grill. An old man wearing a large chef's hat offered me platters of freshly cooked sardines and sea bass, but when I tried to serve myself, the fish turned to dust.

I was no closer to solving my mystery. Perhaps there was no mystery at all. I had never been able to turn up any information online about the Fatih Demirtaş that I knew. Maybe he was gone for good. Out of guilt for being away, I called Hakan. His excitement at hearing my voice made me feel worse about my selfish adventure without him.

"Stay as long as you need," he encouraged. "I am doing fine. I'm even getting along better with that dog down the road. She doesn't jump on me anymore. I've been bringing her leftover bones and meat scraps."

His updates from home included a description of Russians who had fled Putin and had moved into our neighborhood.

"I've heard they've filled all the vacant apartments in town," he said. "And landlords are increasing rents. It's amazing how people are happy to profit from this war."

Hakan also shared his cynical views on the peace talks in Istanbul. “I don’t believe any breakthroughs will happen there,” he said. “The Russian negotiator believes there is a long way to go for a peace agreement. The Ukrainian side thinks conditions are sufficient for the leaders to meet. It doesn’t sound very promising.”

“And where exactly is Turkey in all of this?” I asked.

“Turkey is pro-Ukrainian but not outright anti-Russian. Turkey doesn’t want to antagonize Russia because its wheat, gas, and oil are important. Russian oligarch money is looking for a new home, and Turkey is a welcome haven for it. Plus, Russia is Turkey’s biggest source of tourists.”

That was certainly the case in Eskifoça. Despite the war, Russian tourists continued to check into the seaside hotels. I wondered if many of the yachts in the cove were owned by wealthy Russians.

Hakan encouraged me to stay a few more days at the beach. I had no recent calls from the studio for work, so my schedule was wide open.

“Then I’ll see you at the end of the week,” I told him, grateful that he asked no questions.

“I love you,” he whispered.

“I love you too, Hakan,” I said before hanging up.

My growling stomach required attention. I ambled over to the liveliest restaurant on the pier that was chockablock with noisy diners, a mix of locals in colorful cotton beach clothes and tourists sporting not much more than their sunburns.

Scanning the front room of the restaurant and deciding it was much too crowded, I strode instead to a smaller café off the main pier.

FATIH DEMIRTAŞ

Good God in heaven! That could not have been her in the restaurant. I must be losing my mind. But where did she go so fast?

TED (Tall Guy)

Sophie and I wrapped up a story on a military night patrol. The magic of the evening skies ceased to exist with the drones that roamed above us. I remembered childhood evenings on Cornwall beaches, where I'd lay on my back on the cool sand and try to find Orion's Belt or the North Star by following the handle of the Big Dipper. Beauty is anything that makes us aware of the wonder of life. Stars included. I would stare upwards, open-mouthed at the countless pinpoints of light traveling through space, and time, and try to differentiate stars from planets and satellites. It was impossible to take the magnificence for granted.

Now, with skilled Ukrainian soldiers wielding laser beams, we could identify the drones moving among the twinkling stars, surveilling our whereabouts. Glimmering constellations would never look the same to me.

I believe that most wars are fought over real estate. That's certainly the case with this barbaric invasion. Putin was never able to get over the collapse of the Soviet Union. Judging by the destruction we could see around us, his apparent aim was to obliterate all signs of Ukrainian identity and condemn the country to suffer dictatorship inside a newly imagined Russian Empire.

We woke up to the news of a temporary ceasefire in the battered southern Ukrainian port city of Mariupol that would allow civilians out and humanitarian aid in. Russian troops had also left the defunct Chernobyl nuclear plant and returned control to the Ukrainians.

Each day during the past week, Ukraine took more land than it lost. We all wanted those victories to carry on, but each small advantage was negated by too many deaths. The soldiers we met insisted that Ukraine would prevail. Their hope seemed unflagging, but I couldn't relate to their fortitude, especially after the Ukrainian government reported a massacre northwest of Kyiv. Their horrific narrative sent shockwaves around the world. Even the most hardened news watchers were repulsed by the gruesome photos of corpses, some with their hands bound behind their backs, some with their heads cut off. Too many recent assignments had left me questioning what has happened to our humanity.

While I wouldn't have wanted to be covering any other story, my mind still wandered to Elena each night in my hotel room. The distant sounds of shelling did nothing to erase her from my thoughts.

As the days passed, I had such a strange longing to contact her. After a bit of online searching, I emailed the cosmetics company behind the highway billboard ad that featured her face and tried not to sound too stalkerish:

> *"I am a photographer and recently met one of your models. I subsequently saw her on your billboard on the way to Istanbul Airport. I am interested in contacting her for future work. I would be most grateful if you could send me her contact details."*

A few days later I got the not-unexpected response:

> *"We are unable to send you contact information for our models, but we will forward your message to her agent."*

A polite brush-off. A dead end. The agent would never help. They must get dozens of requests from people who want to contact one of their stunning models. My email would be just one of many from creeps who fall hard for a beautiful face.

Another idea popped into my head. It was a long shot, but I had nothing to lose. I sent off a note to a photographer friend who had gone commercial after too many close calls in war zones. He had gotten married, had a few kids, and no longer wanted to put himself in the line of fire. He now made a lucrative living in the commercial arts world in Eastern Europe. Maybe he'd know a photographer who would have contact information for Elena.

In my evenings of doubt, I thought that maybe I had in fact become a weird stalker. Being away so long made me desperate. On the other hand, trying to find Elena online was a harmless distraction, especially during evening curfews.

But as the weeks passed, I wondered if I had made any impression on her at all. Did she ever think about me? Was I reading too much into our brief but intense time together? I knew she'd likely remember me, but were my fantasies completely delusional? I couldn't let myself believe that I meant nothing to her. I needed to hold on to her. This bloody conflict made no sense. In my head, my lust for the elusive Elena made sense.

And then there was something else that made no sense at all: Will Smith's slap. You'd think we'd have no time for Hollywood news, but many of us covering the war were obsessed with the TV footage of the Oscars when Will Smith slapped comedian Chris Rock for making a joke about his wife Jada Pinkett Smith.

Surprisingly, even Ukrainians, with the intense fighting going on in their country, watched the replays of the Academy Awards shocker. Audio was remixed into TikTok dance songs by musicians searching for fame. We found groups of young Ukrainians hovered around their phones viewing memes of Will Smith on Twitter, on Instagram feeds, in mashups and remixes.

I suppose we all needed a distraction.

ÇIÇEK

Big news on Dove Street today. A loud car barreled down the street and almost ran me over. At first, I thought it was a bunch of screeching seagulls. It sounded like the hullabaloo those birds make when the old head-scarved lady roams the neighborhood with open buckets of cat food.

After I jumped out of the way and the noise passed, I saw it was a big truck with blinking lights on top. It came to a sudden stop in front of Sad Girl and Old Guy's building. Two men jumped out and ran inside while their noisy truck blocked the whole street. Motorcycles that smelled like pizza whizzed by but got stuck behind the truck. So did lots of cars.

After a very long time, the men came out of the building. But they weren't alone. They carried Old Guy, who was tied down on a narrow bed. I wouldn't want to be strapped down like that. I sure would bark if they tried to do that to me. I might even bite too.

Old Guy had a plastic cup on his face. That was a strange way to drink water. Maybe it wasn't water. Maybe he was eating. But that cup was much smaller than my rubber dish. The men opened two big doors at the back of the truck and slid the Old Guy inside, slammed the doors, and drove off in a big hurry, making screeching seagull noises again.

People watched from their windows, and several even came downstairs to see the uproar. Some of the new people who talked funny came to watch too. I call them the "DaNyets." They're now living in several buildings on our street.

Sad Girl was still gone, so she missed the excitement. Where did they take Old Guy? How would Sad Girl know where to find him? It would be terrible if she came home and he wasn't there.

I hoped he'd come back soon. We were getting along so well. He had started to bring me big bones to eat and gave me the best belly rubs, even better than Happy Girl's rubs. I could tell it wasn't easy for him to bend down to my belly level, but he made himself do it. I don't like it when friends go away for too long. They smell different when they come back.

Happy Girl was still around with the guy who always wore a hat. He came to my parking lot again but didn't bother to talk to me. He had a long chat with someone in the box in his hand, but he didn't yell this time. I heard him say "Good boy" and "Go for a ride." I assumed he was talking to a dog. Maybe he lived with a dog.

HANNAH (Happy Girl)

David's work seemed to have gotten more frenetic during his last day in Turkey. He constantly checked his phone, apologized for being so distracted, and was clearly anxious to get back to Spain.

"I hate to leave you," he told me. "I just need to take care of a few things. Business is like a pressure cooker these days. I promise, I'll see you soon."

I knew he had to leave, but it was painful to put him in a taxi to the airport. I tried not to cry as he held me tight and gave me one last lingering kiss.

"I honestly didn't know you were going to be this important to me," he said. "We'll be together soon, as quickly as I can iron out a few difficult deals I'm working on. I can't be without you."

"I'll miss you. I've loved these few days with you here in Istanbul. Maybe next time I can come visit you in Madrid," I suggested. I knew I sounded pathetic.

"Or maybe we'll meet somewhere else for another romantic getaway," said David.

We made no definitive plans, but I felt that our goodbye was not forever. Ever the vigilant street dog, Çiçek loped over to me, stood by my side, and together we watched the taxi disappear down the hill at the end of the street.

I had a funny random thought as we gazed at the now-empty street. Dogs can only see blue and yellow. That would mean that Çiçek would see everything and everybody in the colors of the Ukrainian flag. At that moment, though, I couldn't see much of anything through my tears.

The dog licked my hand and wagged her tail. That was my cue to give her a belly rub. I noticed with envy a young couple who were embracing on the stairs, and I wondered when and where David would be back in my arms.

A flock of doves flew off in unison, perhaps spooked by a silent predator, as clouds floated in front of the sun, casting a long cool shadow over Dove Street. The sudden traces of darkness fit my mood.

I headed to my favorite neighborhood coffee shop and wished Sophie could be with me. Peter the Coffee Guy always made us laugh. His jolly demeaner was as big as his burly build and beaming smile. I ordered a Turkish coffee. Per his usual antics, he studied my coffee grounds with mock solemnity and pretended to read their prediction with keen wisdom: "Your soul will be brimming soon. But you will always need more coffee."

TED (Tall Guy)

After two months of covering this unimaginable war, I needed a break. I had seen too much slaughter and filmed too many devastated parents who had lost their children to the violence. It was becoming unbearable.

We witnessed ghastly butcheries on a regular basis. More cruelties were coming to light each day. Yesterday we filmed a family home that was hit by a missile, burying a two-year-old boy under the rubble, his hand clutching a fuzzy brown teddy bear. Too many rotting bodies, so many eyewitnesses to atrocities. How could this continue? How could there be any debate about whether war crimes were being committed?

At last, the foreign desk told us to rotate out and take a break. New teams were coming in to replace us. We would definitely be returning to Ukraine because this conflict was not ending anytime soon. For the immediate future, we could pack up and go. As I was preparing to leave, I got an email from my photographer buddy.

> *Hey Bro,*
>
> *You must be one horny dude if you're trying to track down a model who you only met for a few hours. I hope you're staying safe in that bloody war. What a shitshow.*
>
> *I have to say, I kind of miss the action when I see your stories. Half of me wants to grab my gear, jump on a plane, and meet you in Kyiv. The other half tells me to stay put and read bedtime stories to my kids.*
>
> *Anyway, about your lusty question. You're in luck. A guy I know had a contact at her modeling agency. Your gorgeous lady friend is Elena Petrovitch. That's her professional modeling name. Here's her gmail address. Good luck. From the looks of her, you'll need it.*

Elena Petrovitch. I had a full name to bring into my dreams. The timing was perfect. I could email her and hope there'd be a response by the time I got back to Istanbul. My optimism made me chuckle. Who was I kidding? My note would probably be nothing but spam to her. But like the New York lottery ad used to say, "You gotta be in it to win it." If I didn't try, I'd have no chance of reaching her.

There was no time to be Hemingway. Sophie and our producer were waiting for me in the lobby. Christ! I wanted to strike just the right tone: friendly but not friendly like a friend; romantic but not too slobbery because we didn't know each other.

I needed Sophie's wordsmithing talent on this one, but I was too embarrassed to ask her.

Dear Elena,

I don't know if you remember me. We met at that Greek restaurant in our neighborhood a couple of months ago. A photographer friend of mine gave me your email address. I keep thinking about our evening together. My assignment in Ukraine is wrapping up for now.

I'd love to see you again when I get back. Coffee or lunch somewhere close by?

Looking forward to hearing from you,

Ted

I had zero seconds to edit it: jack it up, tone it down, or delete it? I hit send. I threw my gear into my bags and dashed downstairs to catch our long ride to Chisinau, the capital of Moldova and then on to Istanbul. Ours was one of the rare foreign desks that wanted us to stay a couple of days in Chisinau to decompress. We were all eager to get home to Istanbul, but we had to abide by their desire to take care of our mental health. Maybe I'd hear from Elena by the time we reached Moldova. That would certainly do wonders for my sanity.

My mind jumped back and forth, from my feelings about Elena to my reflections on the Ukrainians we were leaving behind. I felt guilty. We had the luxury of returning to the safety and comfort of our homes in a country that was not under attack. Those brave Ukrainians were fighting for their very existence. Their lives irrevocably broken, they refused to cave in.

"I'm so sorry, Ukraine, for what has happened to you," I said out loud to no one in particular as we drove away.

Once we reached Moldova, our London-based bosses told us to eat and drink as much as we wanted by way of a big thank you. We checked into a luxury boutique hotel, one of those places with beds the size of a city block and enough pillows for an entire harem. What a waste that I was alone in a room that screamed of sex. Worse still, I had no reply from Elena. I knew that it was way too soon to expect any response, but a guy can hope, especially in a hotel room like this.

Sophie went to sleep down the hall in her room. She was physically spent from the two months of war reporting, the best work she'd ever done in her two decades as a journalist. I was proud of what we did together. She never looked away. She walked into the fray, no matter how harrowing or heartbreaking.

I was too jazzed to sleep so I strolled through the streets of Chisinau. At first glance, it wasn't the most interesting city I had ever visited. Maybe a bit of dull was what I needed to unwind. I walked past an enormous WWII memorial that celebrated the long-ago defeat of the Nazis. Opposite the parliament building sat a smaller version of Paris' Arc de Triomphe. After a saunter through the chaos of the central market, I was ready for some of the tasty Moldovan wine I had heard so much about.

I bought a bottle and plopped myself in one of the city's

leafy parks and watched the world go by. It was a sunny day, the birds were chirping, and tulips were just starting to break through. It was mind-boggling to think that only a short distance away, life as Sophie and I had seen it seemed to be on the brink of exterminating itself.

But even this safe haven in Chisinau could be under threat. In no more than an hour's drive from here, a Kremlin-backed regime, not recognized by any country, had controlled a 400-kilometer strip of land called Transnistria since 1990, separated from the rest of Moldova by a river. The war loomed ominously close to Moldova. No one knew where the madman Putin was going to take this conflict.

NENA (Sad Girl)

The hotel kitchen staff packed a grilled fish lunch for my late morning walk around the Eskifoça marina. I watched children playing tag in a small park and found myself staring at an old couple silently holding hands as they sat shoulder to shoulder on a wooden bench overlooking the sea. They had no need to talk. I imagined they shared a lifetime of memories to constantly relive. What a luxury to grow old together.

My mind turned to Hakan, and my stomach clenched. I had no right to be mad at him for getting old or for resigning himself to being old. His mind was sharp, but his body was getting feeble. I was angry at myself for wanting him to walk faster, stand up straighter, keep moving. It wasn't his fault that his body could no longer keep up with his mind or move at my pace. I was the problem, not him.

I yearned for new love that could be stoked. But as

tempting as it was, I couldn't betray Hakan. You can't simply discard someone because they're frail. Some mornings, I'd wake up and wish for the vibrant Hakan I once knew. But that was not fair to him. Other days, I'd think about how incomplete my world would be without him. He sharpened my brain, made me see beyond our village to worldviews I never would have known.

I set up my picnic lunch on a large, blue-striped Turkish towel that matched the color of the sea. Just a few feet from the water's edge, I breathed in the briny air and made a silent pact with myself to be more patient and generous in my heart with Hakan.

Suddenly, a gust of cold wind disturbed my meditations. The sunny sky disappeared behind ominous dark clouds that materialized from nowhere. I gulped my sandwich, rolled up my towel, and sprinted back to the hotel before the downpour. As I arrived at the lobby, the cobblestones echoed with the tapping sound of bouncing rain. I was amazed at how fast the weather had shifted without warning.

I had left my phone in my room all morning and was happy to have had the break from it. But my heart stopped when I saw dozens of missed calls and text messages from a neighbor: "Please call as soon as you can."

My hands shook as I returned his call. "Nena! Finally! I'm sorry to tell you, but Hakan has had a heart attack. He's in ICU at Taksim Hospital."

A shiver went through me, as did self-blame. I should have had my phone with me. I shouldn't have come to Eskifoça without him. I should have stayed at home with him.

"How bad is he?" I asked.

"Well, his ticker is tired. He needs you."

"What does that mean? Will he be okay?"

"He's stable for now. But he may be in the hospital for a while."

"I'll leave immediately. Thank you so much for letting me know. Call me if there are any changes, good or bad. I'll have my phone on before I board."

I could barely focus on checking out of the hotel and booking the next flight home. This was all my fault. I was being punished for my selfishness. This was the universe telling me I had been neglecting Hakan and following my own fancy. How ridiculous I was to come down here, chasing an idea that made no sense, all because of a photo in a magazine.

The hotel manager phoned for a taxi and loaded my suitcase into the car when it arrived. I could just about make the next flight to Istanbul if we hurried. As the car pulled out of the dirt driveway and picked up speed on the approach to the highway, I looked back for a final farewell to Eskifoça.

My heart skipped a beat, and I gasped at what I saw. Unless my eyes were tricking me, there was Fatih Demirtaş, walking towards a market with two young men.

I screamed at the taxi driver to turn around. I knew we'd have to go all the way to the first highway exit to backtrack, and it was a frustrating lost cause. We had missed our chance for a quick U-turn. The driver was not pleased and, of course, when we got back to where I had spotted the three men, they were gone. There was no more time to waste if I wanted to make my flight. I'd just have to come back.

I know he's here. I was certain that was him.

SOPHIE (Tall Girl)

Ted and I arrived home in mid-April after nearly two months in Ukraine. After a few days of COVID precaution, we met up with Hannah at Peter the Coffee Guy's place. Exhausted and sad, neither of us was in the mood to talk about what we had witnessed. We certainly had no positive predictions about where the conflict was heading.

A dose of Hannah's sunny disposition was badly needed. She came bounding into the café, ecstatic that we were back and effusive with praise for our stories. Our response was half-hearted.

"I get it. The last thing you want to do is talk about it," she said. "Anyway, there's plenty of news to fill you in on."

"Yes, there is," I interjected. "Ted told me about a gorgeous Russian he met before we left on assignment. I'm dying to hear if he found her since we got back."

"You don't know how to keep a secret, do you?" said Ted in mock anger. "And the answer is no, I haven't found Elena or heard from her."

"I'm sure she'll show up sooner or later," I assured him.

"I hope so," he said. "In the meantime, I got a call from a news agency where I used to work. They asked if I could help a Russian filmmaker, Mila, settle in. She had to flee Moscow because of her political documentaries."

Ted had suggested that Mila look for a place to live on Dove Street, which she had already done. She was fortunate to have found a place so soon. She had moved in, Ted said, and as part of her own therapy to adjust to her new home, she was making short videos. She had been forced to leave her camera equipment in Russia, so she was using Ted's older cameras while he introduced her to the neighborhood and to Istanbul.

"Her new apartment is also directly across the street from Çiçek's large parking lot, so she's had a few days to see the dog in action," he said. "I think she's fallen in love with that mutt," he laughed. "Mila considers Çiçek a symbol of all that is good and hospitable in the world because the dog welcomes so many strangers, including refugees who are flocking here. Mila wants Çiçek to be the focus of her videos. We've had a great time filming these last few mornings."

"That's a fabulous project," reflected Hannah. "I hope we can meet her soon and see what's she produced with our favorite mutt."

"You mean me?" Ted joked.

"Of course not! I mean Çiçek. You're not a hound dog."

"Ha!" I exclaimed. "Yes, he is."

I asked Hannah what she had been up to. I had a feeling she had news to share.

She exhaled forcefully and smiled. "Where do I begin? I've met up with David for a few romantic days in Menorca, and he came here to visit."

"Wow. We missed a lot," I admitted. "Tell us more."

"Well, so far, my time with David casts a magical spell on my life. Every moment gets bigger and brighter and better than the last," Hannah enthused.

Neither Ted nor I knew how to react. She sounded like a teenager in lust.

"When I'm with him, I can see a life together. He loves adventure," she continued. She talked fast, as if her enthusiasm would convince us of David's merits.

"He is exactly the love story I always imagined for myself. He's up for any getaway, has curiosity about the world. I feel alive when I'm with him," she gushed.

More silence from Ted and me.

"That sure sounds hopeful." I couldn't hide my utter lack of enthusiasm.

"I had a feeling you'd be skeptical. Don't worry. He's the real deal. I want you to meet him in person and see for yourself," Hannah responded.

"Have you looked him up online?" I asked.

"Of course not!"

Hannah must be the only person on the planet who doesn't online research someone she has just met.

"I'll do it right now," I told her. "What's his last name?"

"Morales. David Morales," she huffed.

I typed his name on my phone and immediately found a short bio that sounded like him. There were no Facebook or Instagram posts. I read to Hannah what had popped up: "David Morales, born in 1980 in Madrid, Spain, an international commodities trader, hedge fund manager, financier, and businessman."

"I don't see that he's married," I added.

"Of course he's not married!" she exclaimed.

Now I had gotten her upset.

"There's no photo anywhere. Do you have one of him?"

"Actually, he hates having his picture taken," Hannah explained.

"International man of mystery. I look forward to meeting

him the next time he comes to Istanbul."

Hannah bristled at my negativity. Instead of fighting with me, she made a subtle but slightly snarky response. "It sounds like you need some rest, Sophie."

"You got that right," I told her. "I'm so exhausted. I'm going to head home to London for a visit. I need some 'normal' with my nieces. I'm craving their hugs. I'll travel in Europe for a bit after that."

"Good idea," Ted and Hannah said in unison.

Before we paid our bill, Peter the Coffee Guy came by to read our coffee grounds. He carefully scrutinized my mug and beamed at the message at the bottom of my cup. He said out loud, as if reading actual words: "It's time to take the big step!"

"Don't worry," I grinned at him. "I already have."

ÇIÇEK

Joy of joys, my old buddies were all back home again. The only one missing was Old Guy. But I had a feeling he'd come back soon because I saw Sad Girl return in the same yellow car she had left in. This time, the car stood outside her building. She sprinted inside and then quickly reappeared and jumped back into the yellow car. I had never seen that trick before. Maybe she was going to pick up Old Guy somewhere. I hoped so. He had brought me yummy bones before he disappeared. I was getting sick of the mushy food that people were putting in my rubber dish.

Also, I made a new friend with one of the DaNyets. I didn't understand her words, except Da and Nyet, but I knew she liked me. We played tag all the time. I wanted to jump on her, but I didn't. If I was too rough, I might have scared her away.

But guess what? The DaNyet showed up in the parking lot with Tall Guy. I couldn't believe they knew each other. He just returned home, and she had only recently appeared on Dove Street. How did they have time to meet?

Tall Guy carried a dark metal box with him and showed it to the girl. They looked through a window in the box and played with some buttons. Then, they pointed it right at my face. How annoying was that! It made me very uncomfortable. I turned away and yawned, hoping they'd get the hint that I didn't like their game with that thing aimed at me.

But then Tall Guy gave me a scrumptious biscuit every time I looked at their box thing. He said I was a "good girl". Maybe the box wasn't so bad after all. I liked it better each time they gave me a treat.

They came back a few times with some food, a ball, and a chew toy. The DaNyet held the box to her face while I jumped and ran and barked and ate the food. I was having as much fun as I used to have when I lived with my family.

I guess Dove Street was officially my family now.

NENA (Sad Girl)

God, how I hated the sounds and sights of hospitals: Sick people pulled along in gurneys down long sterile corridors. Muffled voices behind half-closed doors of bedridden patients. The constant hissing and beeping of monitors. And the wretched food in the cafeterias, made worse by the mass-produced shrink-wrapped snacks on offer due to the COVID restrictions.

I could only observe Hakan from the hospital hallway. A tear rolled down my cheek and fell to the tile floor.

“I’m so sorry, Hakan,” I said out loud.

We were separated by a window where I could see that he was still asleep. I couldn’t help but think this was all my fault. I hadn’t been paying enough attention to the signs that his health was failing. I knew he was getting feebler, but I did nothing to help him address his frailties.

The doctor told me that Hakan was doing a bit better but still floating in and out of consciousness. There were beds to spare in ICU, so he could remain there for now. His heart doctor advised that I keep my distance because new COVID variants made it unwise for me to get too close.

Thin and pale, Hakan’s transparent skin looked like tissue paper draped over his bones. The lines around his eyes showed the traces of a lifetime of laughter, smiles, and affection.

“He’s a strong man,” the doctor told me. “I can see that he plays sports.”

I’d told the doctor about the Negronis that Hakan enjoyed at Susam Café and explained what an avid tennis player he was.

“Well, he’ll be in the hospital for a while, and tennis may not be part of his near future. And juice may have to replace those Negronis,” explained the doctor. “His muscles will lose strength in bed, so you’ll need to walk him regularly around the neighborhood. You could even take him down to Galataport by the Bosphorus, where he can take in some fresh sea air while he strolls.”

I could do that for him. I could be his nursemaid and bring

him back to health. I owed him that. I wanted that. In a few days he probably would be strong enough so that I could talk to him at his bedside. It was too painful to stand here helplessly gazing at the tubes and monitors attached to his once virile body.

I'd tell Hakan about Fatih Demirtaş. I knew for certain that's who I had seen in Eskifoça. The man I'd glimpsed had to be him. Hakan would be as shocked as I was. Maybe one day I could take him with me to Eskifoça to discover the truth together.

TED (Tall Guy)

I hadn't heard back from Elena and couldn't find her anywhere. I tried to convince myself that she wasn't ghosting me. Maybe she hadn't seen my note, even though I had sent it a week ago. Maybe she rarely checked her emails and was more of a WhatsApp person. I didn't have any phone details for her.

Fortunately, filming in the parking lot with the dog was an entertaining distraction. I helped shoot action videos of Çiçek in the mornings with Mila. She told me she'd edit the dog's antics and overlay music and graphics to tell stories.

She had stumbled on an old YouTube video of musicians around the world singing "Peace Train", a song, she learned, Cat Stevens wrote in 1971 about unity and understanding. Funny how lyrics change but the themes never do. When the video ended with a gray-haired, blue-spectacled Yusuf Islam giving a peace sign as he sat at a white piano in a leafy yard somewhere in Istanbul, Mila hit on the idea of PeaceDog calling for peace.

At least it was something to distract her in what I could only imagine was a hard loneliness, having been forced to leave behind everything and everyone she had ever known and loved.

I was so determined to find Elena, I would leave Mila in the late afternoon and head every evening to the same neighborhood restaurant where Elena and I had met. I brought a book each night and used it as a prop so I could stare at the entrance without looking too obvious.

After almost two weeks of eating at the same place, I had become so friendly with the restaurant owners that they plied me with extra desserts and raki after each meal. I knew the menu by heart and had become all too familiar with the tangy olives and the tzatziki that was produced with the thicker Greek yogurt instead of the thinner Turkish kind.

All I wanted to taste was every part of Elena.

I was treated like one of the family and given the best seat in the restaurant, which also happened to be the most convenient vantage point for my clandestine lookout. One night, just as I was paying my bill and the evening dinner rush had disappeared, I heard the familiar swish of the front door being pushed open by another customer. I looked up, and there she was. I couldn't believe it.

I had trouble breathing. I had no control over my heartbeat. She looked more drawn, but even more desirable than I remembered. Oh my God, how I wanted to bring her home with me and never let her out of my bed.

"Elena!" I blurted.

No reaction.

"Elena!" I called out again.

She lifted her head and searched the room, seemingly confused. Our eyes locked, just for a second. A smile flickered across her face, tremulous at first, and then radiant like the sun on a hot August day. A rush of adrenaline in a dopamine bomb blasted through my brain. I wanted to skip from "nice to see you" to seeing her naked.

"Ted, how wonderful to see you," she said.

I moved towards her, at once wanting to kiss those inviting lips but knowing that was just a fantasy I had lived a hundred times in my head.

"May I join you?" I asked. May I join you in bed for the rest of my life? Can you climb on top of me?—that's what I really wanted to plead.

"Of course! I'm just having a late-night drink. I want to hear all about your assignment."

I had no interest in reliving the hell that was Ukraine when I was staring at heaven in front of me. I wanted to tell her how thoughts of her helped me survive the scenes of death and despair that I filmed. How dreaming of making love with her carried me through my nights alone in blacked-out hotel rooms that rattled from explosions.

"The devastation I saw was as cruel as all the news stories you've seen," I told her. "But I had a great farewell when I left Istanbul for Kyiv. I saw your face on that enormous billboard on the way to the airport."

She blushed and shook her head in embarrassment. "There aren't many modeling opportunities for women my age these days. I take what I can get, even cosmetic ads for older women. I think that ad was a one-hit wonder. I haven't had much else since. It's a silly business. It takes no courage, not like what you're doing. You're making a difference."

"I think you've been courageous finding your way in this world after being orphaned so young in Moscow," I told her.

"That was just survival, not heroism," she said. "There was nothing brave about cleaning rooms, mending other people's clothes, serving slop at cheap restaurants, and getting my ass pinched as a waitress in scummy bars."

"I disagree. You are brave."

"Not really. I just learned fast how fortunes can change. I had no choice. One minute, I had a comfortable home with a loving mother and a kind father, even if he wasn't always there," she said. Sadness swept across her face and then disappeared like a cloud passing quickly in front of the sun.

"The next minute, I was alone with nothing but my teenage wits. But I think 'brave' describes the Ukrainians fighting for their lives and anti-war Russians fleeing a despot. And you. You bring the war to people's living rooms so they can't look away."

I reached for her hands that rested in clenched fists on the table. She didn't pull back, but she also didn't open her hands to return my grasp. When her phone rang, she pulled away to frantically dig through her purse and retrieve the goddamn device. Our moment ruined, her silky hands now grasped the phone instead of me. She missed the call, but a shadow of alarm crept across her face.

"I've got to go, Ted. I'm so sorry," she said. I saw anguish in her eyes. But then, astonishingly, she pulled me towards her across the table and put her velvety mouth on mine. For those few seconds, with her lips melding with mine, nothing else mattered in the world.

"I'm so sorry. I have to leave," she repeated. And dashed out of the restaurant.

"What the fuck?" I muttered. I ran out to follow her, but she turned and shook her head at me. Tears ran down her face. She had the look of a cornered animal.

"Elena! I don't have your number! I wrote you, and you never replied!" I called out to her as she sprinted off. If I chased her, I'd be nothing more than a creepy predator. I had to hope I would find her again.

HANNAH (Happy Girl)

Me: I miss you. Where do we meet next?

David: In a bedroom.

Me: That's an igloo.

David: I couldn't find a bedroom emoji. Ah, here it is.

Me: Hahahaha. I can come to Madrid for a long weekend.

David: I want to go back to the beach. I just read about Eskifoça in *Why Not Spend It?* Let's meet there. I've found connecting flights that will get me from Madrid to Izmir.

Me: You've planned it already?

David: Of course! I desperately want to see you.

Me: How soon can you come?

David: Next weekend? Early May is a perfect time. Not too many tourists yet.

Me: I love your plan. I'll book a Friday flight.

My first impulse was to call Sophie to tell her that I was heading to the beach to see David again. But I stopped myself. She definitely disapproved of him, even though they had never met. His presence in my life, even if remote, had started to put a wedge between Sophie and me. I knew she was just trying to protect me, but I was disappointed that she didn't understand how happy he made me feel.

My face actually hurt from smiling. My business also had picked up dramatically and unexpectedly. My favorite customer, an art teacher who now took care of my shop when I traveled, had suggested that his students buy their supplies from me. One of them was so impressed with the range of art materials that he mentioned it on Twitter. Sales skyrocketed. Everything was going my way.

Late Friday afternoon, David and I found each other at Izmir airport. He looked more relaxed. No phone was glued to his ear this time.

We jumped into a limo, nestled into the soft leather seats, and cuddled during the drive along the spectacular coastline dotted with small islands, tiny fishing boats, and some enormous yachts. The driver's eyes staring back at us from the rearview mirror made us too uncomfortable to go beyond cuddling—much as we both wanted to.

Instead, and to distract us from the anticipation of love-making in a sumptuous hotel room, we read some of the *Why Not Spend It?* article that explained that two of the islands here were known as Siren Rocks, mentioned in Homer's Odyssey. According to the Greek myth, the sweet sounds of the Sirens, creatures who were half bird and half woman, lured sailors to their deaths, crashing their ships into the rocks.

"I can't sing at all, but let me lure you to our bedroom," I purred to David.

He laughed and nuzzled my neck. We checked into an opulent boutique hotel—a former Ottoman mansion constructed from giant beige stones that held floor-to-ceiling windows overlooking the sea.

Our bedroom reminded me of the luxurious Topkapi Palace harem house, with a bed large enough for an orgy, silk pillows piled high, and intricately tiled geometric-patterned floors the colors of lapis and onyx. I had barely scanned the gigantic room when David pulled me into his arms, and his mouth broke into a smile even as it sank hot and light against my lips. He tasted sweet, the flavor of the pomegranate juice we drank at the check-in desk. Lust oozed through me, reaching all the recesses between our bodies.

As we tumbled onto the bed, I pulled at his shirt, feeling the warmth of his skin through the linen. With ease, he unbuttoned, unzipped, unsnapped, and removed my layers of clothes. I tugged at his pants, and with a quick assist from him, he too was naked on the crisp cotton sheets. I wanted him closer to savor how it felt to be pressed against him, to be swathed around him. One of his hands moved up the length of my neck, his fingers webbed under my hair. I sighed as he kissed me again, softer, slower. His finger nudged my mouth up to him for more, and I hugged his ribs to move closer.

His breathing came fast and steady. I raked my hands through his hair, arched into him, and a low groan rumbled through his throat. A pulse swept through me as we both cried out in ecstasy. This felt more intimate, more lovely than any of our previous sex romps in Menorca or Istanbul. I couldn't remember ever feeling so turned on. My body would never feel the same after such bliss.

ÇIÇEK

Tall Guy and the DaNyet came to see me every morning. The three of us played jumping and running games for hours. I was so used to their metal box that it didn't bother me anymore, no matter how close they put it to my face. I even licked the tiny front window of it, which made them laugh and got me more excited. I leapt, chased, barked, pooped, peed, and once farted, while they aimed that thing at me. They seemed to have as much fun as I did.

The DaNyet didn't need to stand on her toes to talk to Tall Guy. She met him eye to eye when they looked through the box together and laughed at what they saw.

I liked her hair. It swung behind her head like a long tail. When she wasn't holding the box, she fiddled with her mane, twisted it around her fingers, and knotted it into a ball that always fell apart.

Tall Guy watched her every move and smiled when she looked his way. He touched her arm, the small of her back, and made a light squeeze of her hand when they shifted the box in my direction. When his back was turned, the DaNyet stole glances at him. She looked him over from head to toe.

I'll bet that if they could sniff each other's butts, they would. That's our advantage. We can just go and do that, take a bold sniff wherever and whenever we want. People have to pretend like they don't want to do it, then whammo, they go and do it. Think about all the time they waste.

I watched them watch each other as they pretended to watch me. It would be dog years before they'd finally see each other and notice what was right in front of them.

Suddenly, a plastic bag caught my attention when a gust

of wind blew across the lot. I sprang off my hind feet as the bag gained height, and I caught it in my mouth. It tasted like meat juice. This was my lucky day.

With the bag in my mouth, I trotted outside the parking lot and up the street. The DaNyet and Tall Guy didn't even notice I had left them. They were too busy looking into their box with their heads nearly touching each other. Come on, you two! Why don't you just turn your faces and lick each other.

Just as I reached the far end of Dove Street, that yellow car with a sign on top pulled up and honked at me. I never understood why they do that. I hear them. I know they're there. I know they know that I know they're there. But they still beep that deafening horn.

Sad Girl climbed out, rushed around the back of the car, and opened the other door. She crouched and tugged and pulled, and slowly one foot then another emerged from the back seat. Old Guy needed some serious help getting out of that car, but he was home.

Someone definitely forgot to feed him while he was away. His clothes hung limp and loose on his bones. I brought my tasty bag over to him and dropped it at his feet. He coughed and laughed while he scratched my head with one hand and grasped Sad Girl with the other.

He smelled different. Not so much like the musty rocks on my hill anymore. I wondered if I smelled different to him, like the poop I had rolled in earlier in the week, even though I thought I had rubbed it off in the grass.

I pressed my head against Old Guy as he and Sad Girl shuffled to the front door. He felt brittle like a chicken bone.

I promised myself that I'd never do a zoomie into him again because I don't think he'd be able to get back up. Sad Girl had no time for me. She focused all her attention onto Old Guy, gripping him tightly and moving him carefully inside.

Just as the two of them disappeared into their building, I heard a shout behind me. Tall Guy and the DaNyet called me back to the parking lot. I sprinted down the street towards them, picked up my pace, and advanced to a full-throttle zoomie in their direction. I didn't mean to do it, but my speed and momentum toppled both of them as they laughed uproariously and tumbled onto each other. Well, maybe I did mean to do it.

NENA (Sad Girl)

I was shocked when the doctor called to say I could bring Hakan home. At first glance, seeing the hospital number on my phone, a nauseating wave of terror swept through my stomach. I thought the worst, that Hakan would not be coming home, ever. But relief replaced fear. Hakan's recovery had been faster than anticipated, the physician told me, and he'd be safer from COVID at our apartment. I rushed to pick him up but had little time to prepare for his homecoming.

We hardly spoke in the taxi. I had too many checklists for his homecare spinning in my head. We'd figure out an exercise routine with his walker—first down the hall in the apartment, then down Dove Street, and eventually along the new Galataport boardwalk on the Bosphorus. One small step at a time.

Hakan seemed delighted to be greeted by Çiçek. He and that adorable smelly dog clearly had bonded while I was at the beach. It was as if she knew how frail Hakan had become and leaned into him to provide extra support when we entered the apartment building. She was such an empathetic creature, a great listener, and the perfect keeper of my secret thoughts.

My goal now was to restore some of Hakan's vigor and then talk to him about what I'd seen in Eskifoça. Without any doubt, I had recognized Fatih Demirtaş, despite the decades since he had been gone from my life. He looked remarkably the same, just grayer, but still lean and strong. I recognized that wry smile and the twinkling eyes, that same warmth from so many years ago, which was why any betrayal on his part was incomprehensible.

Hakan and I curled up together and binge-watched the latest season of Bridgerton. He fell asleep beside me while I couldn't stop watching. All those youthful bodies, virile men with testosterone pulsing through them, and women in ornate taffeta dresses, desperate to be noticed and ravaged. In my own life, I was definitely noticed and even by the man I lived with, but that was not enough. I longed for something more. How I hated that Netflix and its soft-porn corniness that awakened a hunger in me.

I wondered about Fatih. He must have been frustrated or unfulfilled to have turned his back on love, to have denied what was right in front of him, and then to have walked away in such an unceremonious manner. I believed in him. He shattered all that I thought to be true and lovely.

I tried to recall the last time I had seen him, the last words we exchanged, the last gifts he delivered. I couldn't remember any specifics. All that came to mind was a bright glow that filled my heart with anticipation and happiness.

The mind is magical sometimes. It blocks out the worst and shines light on the best. I suppose if all we remembered was immense grief, we'd never get out of bed, or bother to face a new day. Hope would never exist.

TED (Tall Guy)

That dirty dog knocked Mila and me down to the ground and wagged her tail in excitement at the havoc she had caused. She let out a shrill bark as if laughing at the chaos. I wasn't in a hurry to pick myself up, and Mila didn't spring up either. We lingered on the street, lying next to each other as our laughter died down and our eyes met. She smiled as I offered her my hand, and we slowly stood up and dusted off the dirt.

Mila lowered her gaze and turned away while she retrieved my camera that had fallen out of her hands. As if to avoid any awkward eye contact, she spent an inordinate amount of time inspecting the equipment. All was in order with the camera, but my heartbeat was out of whack, and my palms were as wet as a damp beach towel.

I hadn't seen any of this coming. I had spent so much time lusting after the elusive Elena that I hadn't fully twigged on to the beauty in front of me. Mila had the energy of a young colt, while Elena floated through space like an ethereal mist. Both women were sexy as hell, but one was real, while the other was fantastical. Mila's long blonde hair and round violet eyes contrasted with Elena's red-brown wavy tresses and hooded gray eyes. While Elena had curves where they counted, Mila had muscles where they were attractive.

"Want to call it a day on the filming and go have a drink?" I asked.

"I was just about to ask you the same thing," Mila grinned.

Hallelujah. No games. No guile. No mystery. I tried not to jump ahead and picture her naked in my apartment, but I couldn't help myself. Through all those hours of filming Çiçek in the parking lot, I had never fully noticed the soft round swells of her breasts under her baggy flannel shirts or the trim waist hidden beneath her oversized jeans. Until now. Maybe it was my subconscious keeping me in line, not wanting to take advantage of her rootless situation.

As we climbed the stairs to Susam Café, her hand brushed against mine. Or was I imagining it? The wind ruffled her hair, and I realized how much I missed stroking the soft locks of a woman. I noticed the downy hairs along her swan-like neck as she took powerful strides up the steps, two at time. Athletic but graceful.

I ordered a beer, and she surprised me by ordering a double shot of vodka.

"To peace!" she exclaimed.

We clinked glasses and locked eyes. Again she smiled, which gave me hope that the fluttering in my stomach might be mutual. Her gaze gave me the courage to place my hand on hers, and when she didn't pull away, I knew I wasn't imagining some kind of shared desire.

If I had had my way, I'd have paid the bill and taken her home with me as fast as we could run down those one hundred stairs and around the corner to my place. But I knew better. I didn't want to appear as desperate for sex as I actually was.

I also wanted to learn more about her. I was sure there

had to be depth to her hidden beauty. I had only focused on her filming project and had not felt comfortable enough to ask about her personal upheavals.

As I listened to her remarkable tale, my longing for her only intensified. She had to flee Moscow when she received a message from a friend at the European news agency where she had done some work. He had written, "enjoy your vacation in Turkey". It was a signal to get out fast.

Immediately, she erased all the apps on her phone, deleted all her email contacts, and quickly packed a small suitcase of beach clothes and a few other basic outfits, in case anyone rifled through her luggage. She wanted to appear just like any other vacationer, not like an activist filmmaker who was fleeing persecution.

Miraculously, she made it onto a commercial flight direct to Istanbul, after only minimal questioning at the airport border control. And fortunately, she had substantial earnings from her European-financed documentaries. The funds were stashed away in foreign banks.

"I was making anti-Putin movies with generous foreign funding. That was a dangerous combination," she said. "If I'd stayed, I could easily have been arrested and jailed like some of my friends."

"Did you have to leave family behind?" I asked.

"My parents had me late in life, so both are gone. They died a few years ago, soon after I turned thirty. I'm glad they're not around to see what Putin has done to Russia and how this conflict might escalate into a wider war."

"Did you have a boyfriend or partner back home?"

Nosy. But I was dying to know.

"I have no one now but you and Çiçek," she said, squeezing my hand. "I feel safe on Dove Street. Çiçek was the first to greet me, and you were the first to help me be creative again."

What a buzzkill. I didn't want her gratitude. I didn't want her to feel indebted to me. And I certainly didn't want to take advantage of her vulnerable situation. As if reading my disappointment, she leaned across the table, gently pulled my head towards her gorgeous face, and kissed me, soft and moist and hot and breathy in one timeless, passionate moment. As she pulled away, I opened my eyes to see hers shining bright and the heat rising in her cheeks.

"You were taking too long," she laughed. "Let's get out of here."

Good God in heaven. Thank you! I yanked cash out of my pocket, threw it on the table, and we sprinted down the stairs. Çiçek was peeing near the dumpster and watched us turn the corner to my street. I don't know which one of us was panting the hardest.

I pushed open my apartment door and couldn't rip off Mila's clothes fast enough. What a body she had hidden under those oversized clothes. She felt hotter as her taut waist moved up and down mine, and her wet fingertips and full lips moved across my chest. I couldn't breathe. I didn't want her to stop. I wanted more of her, to devour her. She gave and gave until I was dizzy, until I found that sweet spot, until we both screamed in ecstasy, and fell damp onto my unmade bed.

While we both gasped for air, trying to catch our breath and think of any words that could possibly follow our lovemaking, my phone rang. I glanced at it on the nightstand.

"Shit! I have to take this." I rolled away from her with my phone in hand.

"Such romantic words," she laughed.

"Not fair!" I countered.

The realities of the world came crashing in as soon as I answered that call from my editor. I was to return to Ukraine. Sophie would follow later with another cameraman. Russian forces were concentrating on Ukraine's eastern Donbas region while air strikes had hit residential buildings in Kyiv during a visit from the UN Secretary-General. The onslaught was becoming more intense.

"I'll be heading back to Ukraine," I told Mila when I finished the call.

She took it in stride. She knew the business.

"I'll be here when you return," she smiled.

"Well then, I'll have something to look forward to. That's a rare occurrence for me."

"Just keep your head down and get home safely."

It had been a long time since someone would be waiting for me at the end of an assignment. I had forgotten what a reassuring feeling that was. I wasn't exactly firmly rooted with Mila, but knowing she'd be here when I returned gave me an inner calm.

She had borrowed my old back-up camera. "I'm done filming for now, but your equipment will be useful in the future. I've got a bit more editing to do. The Çiçek series is almost ready for launch. Want to see it?"

"Of course. But let me show you something else first. Meet me under the covers," I grinned.

HANNAH (Happy Girl)

Sex always makes me hungry. David and I showered and dressed for dinner after getting reacquainted with each other in bed. We strolled along the stone walkway that hugged the small marina in Eskifoça. David draped his arm around my shoulders, and our hips moved in sync. I loved the way we fit together.

A small gift shop stuffed with handmade crafts and wooden toys caught his eye. We stood holding hands, peering through the shop window.

"I have a couple of nephews," he said. "My sister's kids. Let's go inside and see what they might like."

Until then, he had never revealed much about his family.

"I didn't even know you had a sister. How old are her children?" I asked.

"Four and five. They're full of energy. They get excited about anything on wheels."

"Do you ever want children of your own?" I asked.

I knew it was a bold question, but I had wanted to ask him ever since our trip to Menorca. He stopped and turned towards me, with a questioning look.

"Of course. What's life without children?"

His answer moved me. I was relieved to know we were on the same page. We entered the store, and he gravitated towards two hand-painted wooden cars, one red and the other blue.

"These are perfect." He held them up to inspect the handiwork.

Wandering over to another section, he picked up a mother-of-pearl inlaid jewelry box, opened it, and rubbed the soft red velvet cushion.

"I'll get this too. For my sister."

"I can't remember the last time I bought anything for my brother in Virginia, except when we get together for Christmas every few years," I said.

It had been a while since I thought about my brother. It was just the two of us now, our mother had been gone about ten years and our father so long ago, so abruptly. My thoughts drifted back to that department store, the last time I ever saw him.

"We're a close family in Madrid." David's comment interrupted my thoughts and brought me back to Eskifoça.

"I hope I get to meet them," I told him.

"Soon, I'll introduce you."

His dark eyes looked straight into mine. The seriousness of his assurance bolstered my belief in us. Slowly, he was opening up his life to me. I looked forward to learning more.

I wished that Sophie could see how family-oriented and thoughtful he was. David was much more than his brief online profile. Sophie didn't understand. She saw the world as a reporter and was too clinical in her assessment. I knew with time she'd come around.

David and I grabbed his purchases and continued our stroll down the seaside walkway. The entire port was filled with the aroma of grilled, fried, and baked seafood wafting from dozens of open-air dining rooms. We stopped at the largest and liveliest one, where we were seated at an intimate table away from the center of the fray and nearest to the water.

Around us we listened to the mix of Russian, German,

English, and Turkish languages. A gray-haired gentleman, fit and tanned, rambled through the restaurant, chatting with diners at each table. We figured he must be the owner. He had a lengthy conversation in Russian with the group next to us. We listened intently, understanding nothing but appreciating his facility with the language, which was not his own.

When he reached our table, he introduced himself as Fat Demi and welcomed us to his restaurant. "My name is Fatih Demirtaş, but Fat Demi works better with the tourists, and it's a name they can remember. That's how you can find me and my restaurant online."

"Your place is beautiful," I told him. "You've attracted tourists from so many countries. We even heard you speaking Russian."

"I pick up languages easily," replied Fatih. "I've learned basics from the tourists here."

"Well, you have certainly built a popular place."

"I couldn't have done it alone," he said. "My British wife gave me the courage, and the capital, to open this restaurant here in my hometown. Our two grown boys are part of the business too. You could say this restaurant is our third child. Anyway, enjoy your meal!"

We watched Fatih work the room, chatting with each table of customers. His sons and wife periodically came out of the kitchen with hot plates that they proudly presented to the hungry customers.

His wife looked like a classic English rose, delicate and fair-skinned, with berry-stained full lips and flush cheeks. She was likely closing in on sixty but could easily have passed for ten years younger. Even her brown hair, tucked up in a loose bun, had the shine that you find on much younger women.

Fatih's sons looked like mini versions of him: tall and lean, as if born with a tennis racket in their hand. But they clearly worked fast and hard in their father's kitchen.

"I don't think I could do what he does," said David.

"What do you mean? You couldn't open your own business?"

"No. I mean he works every day and night to keep this place afloat. He should be retired, but he and his wife and sons, are all laboring frantically to keep this restaurant alive."

"Maybe he likes the work. He looks like he's enjoying himself."

"Nah. I'll bet he's always on, always here, always working," said David.

"What's the alternative?"

"I like making a killing, fast. A quick high-risk deal can be stressful, but then you can sit back and enjoy the cash once the transaction is done."

"What kind of transaction? You never really told me much about what you do. Are you a drug dealer?" I laughed.

"Yes! I am! How did you know?"

After a few seconds, he said, "Seriously, I trade commodities. It has its excitement, and anxiety, and huge payoffs. Most of the time it's dull. But let's take care of this evening's business by ordering dinner. I'm starved!" He stroked my hand across the table and concentrated on the elaborate menu.

I was famished. In any case, commodities trading didn't

sound like the most scintillating topic for discussion.

We ordered a feast. We dined on oven-baked sea bass after watching the waiter expertly remove the skin, pull off the crisp silvery scales, and lift the delicate spine, leaving not a bone behind. The mouthwatering mezzes included artichoke hearts, hummus, thin slices of pastrami, hot spicy yogurt, and roasted eggplant with garlic. We easily finished a bottle of crisp white wine from the Arcadia vineyard and topped it off with a bottle of local raki.

"I feel alive when I'm with you," David told me as we embraced on our walk back to the hotel.

"Funny. I feel the same about you."

Both of us, a bit wobbly from too much booze and an abundance of rich food, propped each other up as we tottered through the narrow alleys between ancient stone houses and lush backyard gardens, never far from the rhythms of the full moon tide.

TED (Tall Guy)

Sophie called me from her London holiday while I was throwing clothes and gear into suitcases for my return trip to Ukraine. I was sorry she wouldn't be the correspondent on this assignment, but glad she was taking some time off. She deserved it.

"Hey! You and that Russian filmmaker have certainly been busy."

I was confused. I hadn't told her anything about the exciting change in my relationship with Mila.

"What are you talking about?" I asked.

"My niece showed me some online videos of PeaceDog. That's Çiçek's TikTok name. All the kids are watching her, and she's becoming somewhat of a sensation."

"Right! PeaceDog. Isn't it amazing what Mila has done in only a few days?"

"She's a real talent," Sophie concurred.

"She sure is," I smiled. "How's your holiday?"

"I'm having a great time. I have to say, I'm liking this café life. But I know myself. I'll be bored in another week. Anyway, have a safe journey, my friend. We'll run into each other in Ukraine, I'm sure."

I noticed a rare cheerfulness in Sophie's voice. Time off was what she needed. "You sound awfully chirpy."

"I am indeed."

As soon as we hung up, I clicked on TikTok and took a long look at PeaceDog. There was Çiçek, jumping and flipping in slow motion while lip-syncing to "Give Peace a Chance". Another video showed Çiçek's movements digitally manipulated to show her waving a Ukrainian flag and singing Jimi Hendrix's "Power of Love". Colorful peace signs floated around her head. And in another video, sunglasses superimposed on her nose reflected more peace symbols. PeaceDog's online profile simply read: "Peace. It beats the alternative."

I called Mila to tell her that PeaceDog was picking up interest. Even Sophie had seen her online while away.

"PeaceDog is definitely getting noticed," said Mila. "I saw a few people in front of her parking lot this afternoon. They must be from the neighborhood and recognized her. They actually took selfies with her."

"I hope stardom doesn't go to her head," I laughed.

"So far, she seems fine."

"How are you doing? I'm going to miss you."

"I'm going to miss you too. Don't be reckless and get too close to the action."

"Don't worry. I don't plan on dying for this story."

"No one ever does. Give me a minute. I'll come down and see you off in the taxi."

Mila was so fresh and breezy. It was hard to believe she had transplanted herself from Moscow into a whole new world in Istanbul in a matter of weeks. She had turned my universe upside down, and it seemed she was about to do the same for Çiçek.

She jogged down to my place, just as I tossed my cases into the trunk of the taxi. Mila looked sexy as hell with her slightly disheveled blond ponytail whipping back and forth behind her head, her baggy sweatpants showing the outline of her lean legs, and her T-shirt hugging the right curves. As I leaned against the car, she threw her arms around my neck, pressed her lithe body against mine, and set her mouth just so for one last magnificent, lingering kiss.

"I'll take that with me," I smiled.

"I wish you could take all of me with you," she said.

The cabbie was in no hurry as his meter ticked, and he focused full attention on his iPhone. Mila and I turned in unison as we heard music coming out of his open window.

"He's watching PeaceDog," I laughed.

"Editing more of Çiçek's videos will keep me busy while you're away," Mila said. "Let me know when you meet up with the rest of your crew and you're settled in."

I jumped in the cab and waved to her from the back window until she was out of sight. I hummed one of the Peace Dog tunes, as did the cabby. I closed my eyes and drummed my fingers to the beat, fully immersed in the happy rhythm.

What a difference between my departure for this Ukraine assignment and the previous one. Last time I lusted after a fantasy. With the unexpected involvement of Mila in my life, I had a genuine and unaffected person to bring with me into my dreams. Her smile, her zest for life, her courage, and commitment to a greater good were intoxicating. Not to mention her remarkable agility in bed. It was easy to conjure her with my eyes closed and my eyes wide open.

She was true. Elena was not.

But then, the woman who had taken up so much space in my daydreams, who had filled my head with lust during those lonely nights in Ukraine, unexpectedly appeared at the crosswalk at the foot of the hill. My cab had stopped at the long traffic light, and there too was Elena, waiting for it to turn green. The reddish highlights in her hair sparkled in the sun, her smoky eyes trained straight ahead at the road, as always lost in thought, seemingly worlds away.

Surprisingly, no surge of adrenaline rushed through me. I was baffled by my own lack of physical reaction on seeing the woman who had been my obsession for so many weeks. How quickly my attentions had shifted from the longing for one woman to the desire for another. Sophie would have made fun of my fickleness. But it seemed there was only room in my heart for one woman, and that woman was no longer Elena.

Nevertheless, I pressed the window button and stuck out my head. "Hey, Elena!" She didn't seem to hear her name.

"Elena!" I repeated.

An expression of recognition moved across her face when she turned her head towards the cab and spotted me hanging out the window. She smiled and waved vigorously.

"Ted!" she exclaimed, sincerely happy to realize it was me who was calling her name.

"I'm heading off to Ukraine," I called out. The cab slowly moved through the intersection as the light changed to green.

"I'll write you," she yelled.

What was she talking about? She had never replied to my email and hadn't even acknowledged it when we spoke. I rolled up the window and wondered why she'd even consider corresponding with me. She had left me in the lurch outside the restaurant after planting that kiss on me.

What a strange, conflicted, stunning woman she was. I didn't expect I'd ever understand why she was always lost in internal conversations and hid such a mystery behind those alluring eyes.

My taxi eventually passed by the cosmetics billboard that still displayed her breathtaking face. "Goodbye, Elena," I whispered. Sophie would have laughed and rolled her eyes at me.

ÇIÇEK

Something very strange was going on in my parking lot. People I had never seen before came to visit me. They acted like they knew me, but I didn't recognize any of their smells. They crouched beside me. They put their tiny boxes in my face. One of them came over and hugged me while

I pooped, with her box held at eye level in front of us. That was just wrong.

I kept my cool and didn't growl or bite or jump on them, but I sure wanted to. What had I done to deserve this rush of newcomers into my space? I didn't ask for any of this.

Who were these oddballs? Some of them carried rubber dishes, just like mine. Had they come for food? I didn't want to share mine with them. Another wore a collar exactly like the one that my family had given me long ago. Did they want to be me? They were weirdos.

Some of them arrived with flags on sticks. And music, so much music, played in the background from the boxes in their hands. They swayed and jumped and danced to the rhythms. I barked and howled with them. I could tell they really liked that because they came closer with their boxes.

They didn't call me by my name. I kept hearing PeaceDog. At first, I thought they said, "hot dog", but no one came with food. What a bummer. I would have appreciated a hot dog.

"PeaceDog, look over here," they said. "Up here, Peace Dog. Come this way, PeaceDog."

It took me a while to realize they were talking to me. I could live with that. I guess I didn't have much choice. They didn't appear to want to leave anytime soon.

Finally, a familiar face poked through the crowd. The DaNyet pushed her way towards me and wrapped her arms around my neck. She was checking on me. I could tell. I licked her face in appreciation, and her mouth smelled like Tall Guy, all salty and fresh like sea air.

She stood up and talked to the visitors. I couldn't understand what she said to them, but I think she was happy to see them. That made me feel better. She talked to them about "U Crayon" and "peace" and "dog" and "poo tin". I knew all about "poo". I wasn't sure about the other stuff.

HANNAH (Happy Girl)

Wrapped in each other's arms, both of us tingling from a slight sunburn and still smelling of saltwater and sea air, we snoozed on the way to Izmir airport from Eskifoça. We rolled the window down to catch the fresh scents before we hit the highway. A giant crow hovering above the beach road released a harsh "caw! caw!" and woke us from the kind of sleep that only a smooth car ride could induce.

David snapped out of his nap and reflected on our weekend.

"I was just thinking about what Fatih told us. I think his life story was too pat."

"Well, considering he had a packed restaurant of customers, I think he talked with us as long as he could, don't you?"

"It didn't make sense. You can't learn Russian that well simply by talking to customers who eat in your restaurant."

"Maybe he studied Russian so he could communicate better with the tourists."

"Maybe."

David rested his head against the back window and stared out at the passing traffic and the soulless strip malls as we approached the airport.

"You have a suspicious mind," I laughed. "He's just a guy running a restaurant. Why do you even care?"

"You're right. I'm always intrigued when I see that someone is hiding something. I guess it's just part of my nature."

"All I care about is when we'll see each other again. Maybe I can come visit you in Madrid?"

"Of course," he smiled. "I need to clear some things at work. This latest trade is a tough one. I'm dealing with some very difficult people."

I knew his work was important to him. I could wait. I was relieved that he was ready for me to visit him at his home.

But I dreaded our goodbyes. It was hard to hold back the tears. I knew I'd be with him again, but each separation became more trying for me. I did not look forward to that final hug as we headed towards different airport security lines.

His embrace was filled with extra love. I felt his eyes on me as we parted, daring myself not to look back in his direction.

I couldn't help it. I turned, and there he was, staring at me with his enormous smile. I waved, and he put his hand to his heart. I watched as he approached his security checkpoint and pulled out his phone for a quick call. He ended the conversation fast, tossed his phone into the security bin, and disappeared through the line.

Alone at the airport I watched the tearful partings of other lovers, or the lucky ones, who checked in side by side, simultaneously handing their passports to the airline agents while on their way to new adventures. I wondered when that would be me and David never having to board different flights, perhaps even boarding together with young children in tow. A girl can dream. It didn't seem so far-fetched with each weekend we spent together. I knew he was someone I wanted to be with for a long time. I could tell he felt the same way. Perhaps my trip to Madrid would seal our commitment.

My flight was delayed, so I gave Sophie a call. I never phoned her while she was on assignment, but I had no concern about interrupting her vacation. When she picked up, I could hear outdoor café chatter in the background.

"Hey! Hannah! How are you? I've been wondering what you're up to," Sophie chirped.

"I can hear you're enjoying yourself as a 'lady who lunches'. But I can't work out the language in the background. Where are you?" I asked.

"I'm loving the cafés of Europe. All of them."

"That's a busy schedule, and vague. Where exactly are you?"

"On lots of trains and planes, short hops. I'm having a great time. What's up with you?"

I told her about my latest Eskifoça trip with David, his promise of days together in Madrid, and his thoughtful gift-buying for his sister and nephews.

"I'm glad you're getting to know him a bit more," she said, although I could still sense her skepticism. "Just take it slow."

"Thank you for your warning. But he makes me ecstatic."

"Then I'm glad for you."

An uncomfortable silence hung between us that Sophie broke by asking, "By the way, have you watched Çiçek on TikTok?"

"Um. No. I don't have the app on my phone," I laughed.

"Have a look. Our favorite street dog is gaining some notoriety. She's PeaceDog now. That Russian filmmaker Ted told us about has turned her into a peacenik celebrity."

NENA (Sad Girl)

The fresh spring weather was too spectacular to ignore. I had taken a few short rambles by myself in the neighborhood but was reluctant to leave Hakan alone too long. The budding flowers, the cooing doves, and the chirping songbirds eventually conspired to lure him away from the living room.

I readied him for his first foray outdoors. He put on his flat cap and his light tweed jacket, both ill-fitting from dramatic weight loss after the heart attack. An outfit that had once looked dapper now transformed him into a wizened old man.

One deliberate step at a time, Hakan gripped me and the wooden railing, as he made painstaking descent down the tiled stairwell to Dove Street. He had to catch his breath at the front door. So did I, but for different reasons. I had so much on my mind. My heart was cluttered with too many conflicting emotions and my brain with too many questions.

As soon as Hakan and I stepped onto the street, we couldn't help but notice the commotion of a small crowd at the parking lot. Music played loudly, a mix of drumbeats and mechanized syncopation, and above the din, we could hear John Lennon's "Give Peace a Chance". The crowd pulsed and rocked, swaying and singing together as they used their phones to film each other.

"I hope Çiçek is not frightened by all that, whatever it is," Hakan said.

The two of us made our way down the street to make sure that Çiçek was not in danger. She seemed to relish the mob, which was now standing in a line, waiting in turn to take selfies with her.

"What's happening?" I asked one of the many tattooed bystanders who was waving a Ukrainian flag. Why had they come to our street and surrounded Çiçek?

"We've come to see PeaceDog," the woman told me.

"PeaceDog?"

"That's her." She pointed to Çiçek. "We're following her on Instagram and TikTok. We live nearby and instantly recognized her as the dog that lives in this parking lot."

I had no idea what she was talking about. Relieved that Çiçek was in no danger, we walked on to the small garden next to the mosque at the far end of our street. We sat on a bench, side by side, our shoulders touching, looking out on the Bosphorus where a few towering cruise ships had recently moored at Galataport, the new high-end open-air shopping mall along the water. From our vantage point, the passengers looked like small ants scurrying on the vast decks that extended longer than several city blocks.

"Isn't it funny how tiny and insignificant those people look on that enormous ship," I said to Hakan. "But each one of them has their own unique story of struggles, triumphs, loves, and disappointments."

"And what about your own story, Nena?" Hakan asked. "Something is troubling you."

"I saw Fatih Demirtaş in Eskifoça," I blurted.

After a long pause, a lone tear rolled down his face, his eyes staring straight ahead.

"Are you sure?" he asked.

"I'm not certain. But I think I recognized him. Why are you so sad?"

"I'm just disappointed that you didn't tell me that was why

you went down there. And if it is him you saw, I'm so afraid he will only bring you unhappiness."

"Hakan, you chose not to come to the beach with me. In any case, I wasn't sure what I was chasing. At first, I thought I recognized him in an old photo in that magazine *Why Not Spend It?* The picture made no sense because it was dated ten years after he was gone. Then I saw him walking with a couple of young men."

Hakan listened in silence.

"I couldn't find the right time to tell you. Then you had a heart attack, and I rushed back. I felt like it was karma, my punishment for going away without you."

"That's nonsense, Nena."

He reached for my hand and squeezed it gently.

"If you believe you saw him, you should go back. Find him. Confront him. You deserve the truth."

"You kind man. You're as upset as I am."

"I love you, Nena. I have only wanted to make you happy."

"You've always watched out for me, Hakan. I owe my whole world to you."

"You found your own path, Nena."

We held each other tight and listened to the music that Çiçek's followers were playing—a recording of Bono's "Stand by Me".

TED (Tall Guy)

We heard reports that some of the people trapped in the Azovstal steel plant in Mariupol had been safely evacuated. The situation in the city in May had been described by the Red Cross as "apocalyptic", with nearly 22,000 civilians killed and almost all of its infrastructure destroyed. The one hundred or so people who first emerged from the factory had lived like rats in dark underground tunnels, hiding from the Russian bombardments for two months. They had found it hard to adjust to the daylight.

Putin had doubled down on his spurious reasons for the invasion, claiming in a speech that he was forced to attack Ukraine because of NATO military action in territories adjacent to Russia.

He continued with the outrageous claim that Kyiv was threatening to acquire nuclear weapons. In reality, NATO had no plans to invade Russia, and the idea of a nuclear arsenal in Kyiv was an absurdity.

Yet, some people believe what they want to believe. Sometimes, people don't want to hear the truth because they don't want their illusions destroyed.

Fortunately, in my own life, Mila showed up and pulled me out of my personal delusion that was Elena. Although Mila had no idea about Elena or how that woman had briefly and inexplicably possessed my heart, Mila's openness and her unfettered delight just to be with me destroyed the Elena mirage.

Alone in my room in Mariupol and scrolling through my emails, the chimera emerged again. There it was: Elena Petrovich's name on my screen. She had sent a message, just as she said she would. However, her name evoked nothing more than curiosity. No lustful anticipation. No expectation of any kind. It was such a change from a few weeks earlier.

Dear Ted,

I have so much to say to you, so much to explain. Fate brought you to me, but life keeps me from you. I am mired in a mess right now. Our fleeting hours of close conversation were a salve. Without knowing it, you gave me an escape from my dark thoughts. You allowed me to picture new possibilities, to be who I actually want to be, instead of who I must be. That kiss in the restaurant was real. You are real. But timing is everything. I hope one day you'll understand.

Your friend,

Elena

"What the hell, Elena?" I screamed out loud to no one. "What kind of nonsense is that?" Her note provoked more questions than answers, her words a waste of space in my computer. I had no idea why she even bothered to write.

As if she knew I was stewing in my room, a WhatsApp message from Mila appeared on my phone: "How are you? I miss you." Never had such simple words meant so much to me.

"I'm fine. I'm so glad to hear from you," I texted back.

"I just wanted to tell you to stay safe. Keep your head down, both of them."

I was loving her humor. "HaHaHa. You don't have to worry about me. I'm all yours."

"I'm all yours too. Your only competition for my heart is Çiçek."

It was tough competition, I agreed and had to text: "She's awfully loveable."

"Sleep well, Ted."

Mila's perfectly timed messages calmed me after a long, emotional day of interviews capped by the frustratingly vague note from Elena. Never could two women have been more different. How fortunate I was that Mila's sensibilities replaced the emotional roller-coaster that was Elena. Plus, there was the added advantage that Mila was spectacular in bed.

HANNAH (Happy Girl)

Me: Why are you texting me emojis of croissants and cheese?

David: Because I couldn't find the Eiffel Tower emoji.

Me: What do you mean?

David: I'm taking you to Paris!

Me: I thought I was going to meet you in Madrid.

David: I just closed a big business deal. I want to celebrate. With you. In Paris.

Me: We can't celebrate in Madrid? I'd really like to meet your friends and your sister and nephews.

David: Paris is more romantic. I need a getaway. And I want to see you.

Me: Well. It's hard to argue about a few days in Paris in May.

David: My treat this time. I'll book the tickets. How does next Friday sound?

Me: Wonderful!

David: I'm counting the days.

A long weekend in Paris! It was so easy to fly there

from Istanbul, but I never really wanted to do so on my own. At long last, I had someone to join me on a romantic weekend in the City of Lights. David was so full of surprises. Always thinking of me and what we'd do next. I'd meet his sister and nephews another time. This time, I was completely comfortable letting him treat me to the plane ticket. Everything felt right.

Bursting with excitement, daydreaming of a Bateaux Mouches cruise on the Seine and an afternoon stroll to the Musée d'Orsay, I was jolted out of my reverie when my phone rang. An unknown number. I almost let it go, but the call persisted. As soon as I answered, the caller hung up.

I decided to call Sophie to get an update on her extended time off. She answered almost immediately. "Hey, Hannah! How are you? I was just going to call you."

"You never call me. I always call you."

"Well. I was about to buzz you because I had an idea. I'm now in London to check in with the new foreign editor. It looks like they're taking me off the Ukraine rotation for a while."

"I'm sorry. I know how much you care about being there to cover the war."

"It's okay. I'll be doing more business stories from Turkey but still related to Ukraine. But that's not why I wanted to call you. I'm going to use my last weekend in Europe to head to Paris. Why don't you join me?"

"You're kidding? That's crazy. I just firmed up plans to meet David in Paris next weekend."

Sophie was silent.

"Are you there?" I asked.

"Yes. I'm here. I don't want to horn in on your romantic weekend with him."

"Nonsense. You can finally meet David."

"Hmm. He may not like my intrusion, even if it's just for coffee. Let's see how it goes," said Sophie.

"Of course he'll want to meet you! I'll let him know. It'll be fun to meet up. I'll call you when we get there. And one other thing, listen to this...." I put my phone to the window for Sophie to hear the music outside on Dove Street. "Hear it?"

The music blared: "Imagine all the people, livin' life in peace..."

"Is that John Lennon's "Imagine?" Sophie asked.

"It is! It's PeaceDog's followers in the parking lot. You were right—Çiçek has become quite the celebrity."

"She's not just a local star," said Sophie. "I was at a grocery store on Fulham Road here in London yesterday and saw a bunch of kids watching her online."

"Ted and Mila are star-makers. But it's only a matter of time before there are too many people gathering on Dove Street. So far, only locals have identified Çiçek as PeaceDog. I recognize many of them."

"I hope it stays that way."

"Anyway, I'll talk to you next weekend. I can't believe we'll see each other in Paris!" I signed off and texted David that Sophie would be meeting us.

I watched the young group in the parking lot as each person jockeyed to film Çiçek or take a selfie with her. I noticed a blond ponytail in the middle of the mob, towering above everyone and periodically ducking down to talk to Çiçek. That must be Mila, the Russian filmmaker who Ted described to Sophie and me. She was so attentive to the dog. I decided to go downstairs and meet this remarkable woman who had escaped Russia and quickly created an unlikely global peace activist.

On my way there, I walked past the beautiful woman I had seen a while back in Susam Café drinking with a group of older men. It was the time I had been eating with David, and she had caught my eye when he walked off to take a phone call.

I remembered she was so solicitous of the older man she was with, whom I had assumed was her father. Here she was again with the old guy, who looked frailer than before and now used a cane. She smiled in recognition as I passed her.

HAKAN (Old Guy)

It's time that Nena learned the truth, even if she'll hate me for it. The years of deception are closing in on me. I knew this day would come. I thought I could forget the past after all this time, but misdeeds are difficult to conceal, no matter how long you try to hide them.

I know the stress contributed to my heart attack. I saw Nena reading that magazine. I thumbed through it and found the photo that got her attention.

There was Fatih, ageless, timeless. Of course she recognized him.

I was complicit in his dirty work. He was a selfish bastard, and I was a coward to do his evil bidding. I sold my soul to him.

How could I ever rationalize to Nena why I deluded her. Even now I can't bring myself to confess. Fatih will have the shock of his life when she shows up and confronts him. I want him to have a reckoning, even if it means Nena will have nothing to do with me ever again. No one, no matter how big their heart, could forgive what I did.

FATIH DEMIRTAŞ

I can't get her out of my mind. It made no sense that I saw her at my restaurant. I need to find Hakan.

ÇIÇEK

Too many strange people and smells began to visit my parking lot. My friend Boji had gotten into trouble when he became famous. This must be how he felt. I was scared. I didn't know why all this commotion was happening. I didn't do anything special. At least Boji knew how to ride subways and buses and trams and ferries. I had no extraordinary talent like that.

My only skills were chasing motorbikes and sleeping in the mud. I didn't know why all these people were here. At first it was fun. They brought me food. I even got new squeak toys, enormous chewies, and an endless supply of juicy bones.

Loud music blared. When it rose too high, I howled and barked. Thank goodness the DaNyet kept checking on me. She'd talk to the people, and they would turn down their noise, and sometimes they'd leave.

She knew when I needed rest. The DaNyet was fast becoming my new best friend. Tall Guy was gone again, and

Tall Girl had been gone for a long time. Happy Girl was still around, but she didn't visit me as much. Thank goodness her rude Hat Guy hadn't reappeared.

I was so pleased when Happy Girl came down to see me again and talked with the DaNyet. Those two wonderful people had finally met, right in front of me in my parking lot.

And you know what? Along came Sad Girl and Old Guy too. They also met the DaNyet. So many of my favorite people were getting to know each other.

I watched them watch their boxes together. I could hear the same music that the crowd had been playing. Old Guy pointed to the box and then pointed to me. They all smiled at whatever it was they were viewing. They clapped hands every time the music changed.

The DaNyet talked with them about "Poo tin", just as she had with the crowd. I could poo too, but I decided to wait. Instead, I let out a big greasy fart. That caused the four of them to roar with laughter. I joined along and howled, which made them laugh even more.

As long as my friends kept me safe, I would be fine with all the new people making their way into my lot. Boji had no one to watch out for him, until the mayor of Istanbul saved him from the bad people who wanted to hurt him. But I didn't want to end up in a palace garden like the one where Boji now lived. I trusted the DaNyet and all my buddies on Dove Street. They wouldn't let anything terrible happen to me.

More cars than usual drove along our street. They'd slow down, roll down their windows, and scream PeaceDog! I'm not sure what I was supposed to do. They'd honk and wave blue and yellow flags at me. There were so many of them that I no longer chased their cars. There was no point. They moved too slowly.

TED (Tall Guy)

I was amazed at how #PeaceDog was catching on in Ukraine. Not just with young kids but even among Ukrainian soldiers. I saw them scrolling through their Instagram accounts where the dog not only captured their hearts but also provided an amusing break from the fighting. I'd heard snippets of "Give Peace a Chance" in my hotel hallways—even the foreign correspondents were following her online and laughing over her short YouTube videos.

I planned to send a message to Mila and tell her about PeaceDog's growing popularity in Ukraine, but I didn't need to. I turned on the news, and there was Çiçek in front of a TV correspondent.

> "Forget about Russia vs. Ukraine for a second and check out #PeaceDog. This ginormous street dog is a rising social media star who has generated a tsunami of interest and a whopping 35 million views on TikTok. Her simple message: 'Peace. It beats the alternative.' You can also find PeaceDog on Instagram, YouTube and as memes while she dances, sings, and does backflips to some of the world's most iconic peace songs.
>
> The video magic is courtesy of an anti-Putin Russian filmmaker activist who prefers

> to give the limelight to PeaceDog. We were asked to keep her and the dog's home under wraps, so PeaceDog doesn't get stormed by too many fans. In the meantime, #PeaceDog swag, including T-shirts and coffee mugs, have cropped up online with proceeds going to various Ukrainian and Russian refugee-support groups. PeaceDog is more than a viral meme. She's fast becoming a global phenomenon."

I was speechless. My God. Mila sure worked fast. "Congratulations on the remarkable news coverage," I wrote to her. "You and PeaceDog are gaining some serious momentum together. Should I be jealous?"

"Yes, Çiçek and I make beautiful music together," she texted back.

"But I thought you and I did that?"

"Of course we do."

"I hope you and Çiçek stay safe. There are plenty of crazies out there to worry about now that PeaceDog is becoming known."

"You're the one who needs to stay safe. You're in the middle of a war zone."

"Don't worry about me."

"Take care."

I found it odd that the TV network had run PeaceDog as the lead Ukraine story. Perhaps they decided that too much nonstop reporting of carnage would cause people to tune out. The sad truth is that before long, the Ukraine war would be nothing but a news-in-brief piece because anything longer wouldn't hold viewers' attention. At least today's Ukraine broadcast headlines seemed brighter, but maybe a bit too optimistic at this three-month mark in the war.

> "Russia has lost one-third of the ground forces it deployed when the invasion began on February 24, and its offensive in the Donbas has lost momentum and fallen significantly behind schedule, according to officials in Ukraine. After driving Russian troops back from Kharkiv, Ukraine's second-largest city, Ukrainian forces launched another counter-offensive. Russian forces, meanwhile, made some advances in the Donbas but continue to suffer from low morale and reduced combat effectiveness. Stay tuned for our business news stories: The Kremlin's crude oil friendships. And McDonald's pulls its golden arches out of Russia."

I had seen enough and clicked off the TV. It was time to reward myself, crawl into bed and dream about Mila. In my head, I pushed away the images of the survivors I had filmed that day, along with the smells of the rotting bodies just a few miles from the Russian border.

NENA (Sad Girl)

Hakan and I stopped by the parking lot where we introduced ourselves to Hannah and Mila. I had seen Hannah with her boyfriend at Susam Café a while back, but we had never met.

Chatting now with the two women made me realize how much I needed girlfriends. I was devoting so much time to Hakan's care, and spinning wheels inside my head, I had forgotten how good it felt to befriend women.

"This street and this dog have been an inspiration for me," Mila told us. "I fled Russia with nothing, and now I have a new home and a new purpose."

She told us of her escape from Moscow that had forced her to leave everything behind, including her cameras. She was borrowing equipment from a local cameraman.

"We're fortunate you ended up on our street as our neighbor," Hannah responded. "If there's anything you need, please call."

The three of us exchanged phone numbers. Hakan looked on as he scratched Çiçek behind her ears and under her collar. The dog licked him in appreciation.

I was in awe of how quickly Mila had created a new life in a new country with nothing but commitment and drive. Somehow, I never mustered such fortitude. Hakan brought me into his world, and it was an enlightened and happy one, but along the way I never really made a life of my own.

"Let's meet up for coffee tomorrow," I suggested. My enthusiastic invitation surprised even myself. I never reached out to anyone like that. Hakan smiled and squeezed my hand, encouraging my effort at making new friends.

"I'm sorry I can't make it," Hannah said. "I'm going to Paris, but I look forward to spending time with both of you when I'm back."

Mila was free, and we made plans to meet.

As Hakan and I walked back to our apartment, I began to regret my impulsive offer. I had spent so much of my adult life hiding from my past that I kept it locked tight in a pandora's box of miserable recollections. Only recently had I permitted myself to pry it open. Now Mila's arrival in Dove Street and my improbable sighting of Fatih Demirtaş in Eskifoça conspired to reignite memories I had long suppressed.

"How come you didn't tell Mila where you were born?" Hakan asked "You didn't even tell her that you know how to speak Russian."

"I get too sad when I think about those years. I prefer to think about my life after we met in Berlin," I told him. "That's when my life truly began."

"You know that's not true," he countered. "You had a life before me."

His eyes filled with tears—a habit that seemed to have become more frequent. I had heard that heart attacks sometimes affect men's emotions and make them more prone to depression. I needed to ask the doctor about that possibility.

"You should take time for yourself, Nena. Get to know those women. They could be good friends for you. They live on our street, and you weren't even aware of them. You're spending way too much time as my nursemaid."

He spoke the truth, but I didn't see how I could leave him alone for any length of time. I couldn't live with my guilt if he had another emergency while I was gone. I never even wanted to take walks too far from home. But I could at least meet Mila at a coffee shop.

MILA (The DaNyet)

Two wonderful women, Nena and Hannah, along with a man named Hakan, introduced themselves to me in the parking lot. I was happy to meet people in the neighborhood. I needed some human contact, especially with Ted in Ukraine for the foreseeable future. I loved hanging out with Çiçek, my first friend in Istanbul, but conversation was a bit limited.

The next day, I met up with Nena. We rambled up Siriselvilar Street through the heart of our neighborhood, past the Pilates studios, pharmacies, bakeries, and local hospital, until we reached Taksim Square.

We pushed our way through the bottleneck of narrow sidewalks packed with tourists, fast-food restaurants, and cheap backpacker hotels, and thankfully reached a break in the throng. Another few minutes of strolling through the tiny green hill in Gezi Park brought us to a coffee shop on the leafy edges of Istanbul Technical University. We sipped cappuccinos as we sat among the students, each with a computer in front of their nose.

I was surprised to learn that Nena was from Russia. She never mentioned it when we introduced ourselves in the parking lot. She had no trace of an accent. She wasn't interested in talking about her upbringing in Moscow or speaking in Russian.

"My memories from Russia only make me sad when I dig them up," Nena told me.

She stared into her coffee and stirred her spoon, distractedly. A cloud passed across the sun, briefly casting a long shadow through the windows across the coffee shop.

"I had some struggles," was all she would say.

I didn't push. She was a new friend, and I had no need to probe if she wasn't ready to share her private life. Instead, she indulged me and let me talk about myself.

I told her about the movie I made that got me in so much trouble with Putin and escaping from Moscow with only one suitcase in a race against time as international flights became more difficult to board.

I had filmed a documentary, *City of Dreamers*, to illustrate why so many Russians supported Putin and his war. I wanted to get to the heart of what was happening now. The movie focused on an unremarkable remote town where the military, as far back as a year earlier, had been preparing for an assault on Ukraine.

My original plan was to make a kind of surreal time-travel movie to portray a place locked into a Soviet past, unable to move forward. But when I started the project, I realized people were falling victim to the government's brainwashing. Like too many others throughout Russia, they were obsessed with past military encounters that the Putin regime misrepresented to keep them paranoid about alleged enemies like NATO.

Putin's party constantly warned against "terrorists" and "Nazis" who had to be defeated. They used doublespeak when they talked about peace but actually meant war. I filmed residents of the town who likened patriotism to their devotion to Putin. My movie showed young children pledging allegiance to the military and singing military songs in classrooms decorated with posters of soldiers and rocket launchers.

"I don't see a way for me to ever return to Russia," I told Nena. "I'm marked as a foreign agent because of the outside funders for my movie."

"Why would you ever want to go back, anyway?" Nena asked. "Life here is so much easier."

"But don't you ever miss home?" I asked.

"My home is here with Hakan."

Hurt briefly took hold of her face.

"Tell me more about Hakan," I asked. I hoped my curiosity wouldn't shut her down. Surprisingly, she wanted to talk about her present life; only her past was off limits.

"Hakan saved me from a life that was always a breath away from homelessness."

"How did he save you?"

"We met by chance in a park in Germany. We fell in love instantly. I know it sounds crazy, considering our big age difference, but it just happened."

I could relate to that. She was fortunate Hakan appeared in her life when he did.

"I feel the same way about a man who lives near our street. I started working with him just a few weeks ago, and I've fallen hard for him."

"I'm glad for you," she said. "You've been through so much. It's nice to have someone watching out for you. I have Hakan, but I feel guilty when I daydream about being with a younger man. I love Hakan, and I owe him my life, but I find myself longing for someone closer in age."

"That makes sense. Nothing wrong with lusting," I told her.

We both laughed. There was only one man in my heart, and I certainly lusted after him day and night. I couldn't get Ted off my mind.

I felt sorry for Nena for ending our chat to return home. "I don't like to leave Hakan alone for too long," she explained.

DAVID (Hat Guy)

Why did Hannah have to invite her reporter friend to meet us in Paris? The last thing I need is a journalist snooping around my business.

HANNAH (Happy Girl)

I'm so excited that David is going to meet Sophie while we're in Paris. I'm sure he'll win her over with his charm and generosity.

SOPHIE (Tall Girl)

I hope I like David. He seems to bring her joy, but she isn't always discerning. I'll know in a heartbeat if he's someone who's going to hurt her. And maybe there'll be time to tell Hannah my own news.

FATIH DEMIRTAŞ

I'm still reeling from what I saw. It's been so many years, but I know it was her. She left so quickly, I don't think she saw me. If she had spotted me, she would not have disappeared without a confrontation.

What would I ever say to her? Nothing could ever bring

back those years. She'd never understand why I did what I did. I didn't even know what had become of her.

After I thought I caught a glimpse of her, I searched the beaches for several days to see if she was still around. I'm not sure what I would have done if I had found her. Thankfully, she never returned to the restaurant. Maybe she just flew here for a quick vacation, and now she's gone for good.

But today, I felt like I was losing my mind. She could destroy everything. I even had a nightmare last night that she showed up at the restaurant as I was serving a platter of shrimp to a group of Russian tourists. Nena came tearing out of the kitchen and screamed, "Why? Why did you do it?" and then plunged a knife through me. It doesn't take Sigmund Freud to analyze that dream.

My God. What a fiasco. I should have known better. It's not so crazy that she'd find her way here. The world has gotten smaller. Hideaways become overrun when word gets out, and people arrive on flights from every point of the compass.

I always thought I could hide from the past, sweep it away, and move on. I've got to find Hakan and see if he knows anything. He must be somewhere in Istanbul, but it's been decades, and our last encounter was so fractious.

He told me back then that I had betrayed him by walking away from our business. What nonsense. Business was business. The resort was barely breaking even in a good month. The only answer for me was to buy him out and let him figure it out. New opportunities came my way. My plans no longer included him. Or her.

Hakan didn't understand. Back then he warned me, "If you lie to yourself about what you're doing and ignore the evil that you're perpetrating, you're building a future on an unstable foundation. The past doesn't just go away. You can't hide from it. It will take too much mental and emotional energy to run from it."

How wrong he was. I was able to rope off the past. I have a beautiful family and a thriving business and no regrets.

Still, I needed to ask him if he knew anything. He always had a soft spot for her.

SOPHIE (Tall Girl)

I met up with Hannah and David at a corner café near the République metro stop. The sidewalks were crowded with street vendors hawking cheap luggage and discount clothes, and every block boasted pastry shops with windows full of pastel-colored macarons.

Hannah had been ecstatic that Paris was the city where David and I would get acquainted. Unfortunately, our much-anticipated meeting came at an inopportune time. Hannah's stomach was acting up.

"I shouldn't have eaten those pastries so fast this morning," Hannah told us, rubbing her tummy. "They were really rich, and I really don't feel well all of a sudden."

"Queasy?" David asked.

"Yep," Hannah replied. She actually burped. "Very queasy."

The waiter arrived at precisely the wrong moment, proffering an array of fresh fruit and gooey cheeses nestled on a large silver tray. Under normal circumstances, the opportunity to enthuse about such a selection of delicacies would have been the perfect icebreaker.

Poor Hannah. As soon as she inhaled the aroma of the cheeses, she groaned, "I have to get out of here" and made a run for the public toilet across the street—a sanisette. It is one of the city's high-tech, self-cleaning toilets that resembles a spaceship from an old sci-fi movie. Before either of us could make a move to help her, she disappeared inside its automatic sliding doors.

David and I stared awkwardly at the doors that had enveloped our friend.

"I hope she's okay," I said. "I'll check on her if she's not out in a few minutes."

He didn't respond. We sat in silence, our eyes peeled on the bathroom entrance. Ignoring my presence, he scrolled through his emails. He expressed no concern for Hannah's situation.

A few young kids raced in front of us on electric scooters. One of them nearly mowed down an elderly couple walking arm in arm, forcing them to break away from each other and stumble to catch their footing. A girl on one scooter was oblivious to the accident she almost caused, too busy watching her phone. It was blasting PeaceDog's version of "Imagine".

"Did you see that?" I asked David in amazement. "PeaceDog almost caused an accident. It's the dog that lives on our street in Istanbul."

No reaction. No acknowledgment that I'd said anything. There was no way I'd sit there and let him be so boorish. Maybe a conversation about him would be of more interest to him?

"So, Hannah told me you're here celebrating a big business deal," I said. "Congratulations."

"Thanks." He didn't even look up from his phone.

"She told me you're a commodities trader."

"Yep."

"I don't know much about the business, but I've heard that some commodities traders can actually do very well in times of war," I said.

A deliberately provocative statement I hoped would stir a response.

"I guess that depends," was all he offered.

I changed tactics.

"Anyway, Hannah told me you have a couple of nephews in Spain."

He merely nodded in agreement. Oh man, this guy was a piece of work. He was tight like a kettle drum. And rude. I'd had enough of his cold-fish demeanor. I left the table, crossed the street, and knocked on the bathroom door to check on Hannah. Whatever was happening to her tummy would only have gotten worse had she witnessed the non-conversation between David and me.

"How are you doing in there?" I yelled through the electronic door.

"I'm okay. I feel much better now. I'm good." Hannah emerged upright and smiling. "I'm feeling completely normal."

At least one of us was. When we reached the table, David grabbed Hannah's jacket from the back of her chair.

"I'm thinking I should take her back to the hotel," he announced.

"I really do feel as if I could stay," Hannah protested.

David paid no attention. Our farewell on the street corner was over before it began. David accelerated the departure. I got a perfunctory hug from him. Hannah moved towards me for an embrace, but even that was truncated when David called out to her. He had already begun heading down the street without her. There was no talk about when and where we might meet again in the city. Before I knew it, they had nearly disappeared into the Paris crowd. Hannah gave me a quick wave as David pulled her along and threw his arm around her shoulder.

How could Hannah be so blind? David Morales was an asshole.

TED (Tall Guy)

Last Friday marked one hundred days since Russia began its invasion of Ukraine. President Zelensky said Russia now controlled twenty percent of his country following recent gains in the eastern Donbas region where I was filming. Photographers and videographers were always vulnerable because we needed to get up close for pictures. Fortunately, Mila understood my job. I know she worried about me, but when we spoke, she didn't overdo the concern.

"I'm watching your stories closely," Mila said over the phone. "I preferred it when you traveled with Sophie. She seemed to have more sense about safety than the correspondent you're with now. He likes being in the middle of crossfire, doesn't he?"

"Don't worry. He knows what he's doing. We're being careful," I assured her.

I missed her like crazy, and just talking to her online

brought a grin to my face and a lift to my nether regions. I had to put my lascivious thoughts aside for now. I had a few more hours of editing to do. Discussion of PeaceDog was a more neutral topic. We talked about the animal as if she were our child. In a way, I guess she was. We were certainly acting like proud parents.

I told Mila that the only reason PeaceDog's music wasn't reaching into Russia was that the company that owned TikTok had blocked Russian users from seeing any content produced outside of the country. The company claimed that the measure would protect its users and employees from Russia's draconian "fake news" laws, some of which threatened prison sentences of up to fifteen years for spreading so-called false information about the Russian government or military operations. Whether a political or business decision, the app could still operate in Russia but without externally produced content like PeaceDog.

Nevertheless, PeaceDog was becoming a presence in the resistance outside of Russia. Her music clips and the lively escapades in her parking lot provided joy to anyone in Ukraine who tapped into her on TikTok, Instagram, or YouTube.

PeaceDog was becoming a national antidote to the grim reality of war. The reporters I knew tuned into her antics. I was amazed at her popularity in the city and even in the parts of the countryside that still had internet service.

Ukrainians young and old, in and out of uniform, gathered around their phones and devoured her uplifting messages of peace.

Mila's latest editing masterpiece was not as lighthearted as the earlier PeaceDog productions but had still caught on.

It was a mashup of President Zelensky's anti-war message delivered via video at the Grammy Awards, along with PeaceDog singing John Legend's song, "Free".

"She's great at covers, but I think PeaceDog needs to start writing her own stuff," I told Mila.

"That's not my area of expertise. Maybe I'll contact a famous songwriter to work with us."

"I'm sure you will," I laughed.

She stayed quiet for moment. I knew she was thinking about something.

"I have to take Çiçek out of town," she said. "The crowd is getting too big in her parking lot. Dove Street can't handle the noise and traffic. I'm worried for her safety."

"I was afraid of that. Where will you go?"

"I was hoping you could suggest a place, maybe a beach town that's not overrun with tourists."

"My friend Hannah recently went with her boyfriend to a village near Izmir. It's called Eskifoça. She loved it."

"Oh, I just met Hannah! She came to the parking lot to introduce herself. I also met Nena. Do you know her?"

"I've never met Nena, but I'm glad you've made a new friend in Hannah. She's great, always happy. Çiçek is a pal, but it's good for you to have some two-legged company. Anyway, check out Eskifoça. Whenever this assignment is over, I could meet you. Stay a while down there. Take my extra camera to film Çiçek at the beach."

Mila thought it was a great idea.

"Oh, I'd love that. It's getting hot in Istanbul. I can work from a beach house and swim in the sea with Çiçek every day. I'm going to book a place now and work out how to get down there by car. I have some new ideas for PeaceDog. A new venue may be a great inspiration."

"I want you to stay safe, Mila."

"I can deal with PeaceDog's followers. You need to keep your wits about you and stay clear of those damn Russians. Except this Russian, of course."

"No chance I'll ever stay clear of you. But I'm afraid I have to get back to work. Take care, Mila. Sleep well."

SOPHIE (Tall Girl)

I decided to pay a surprise visit to Hannah at her hotel off the Champs-Élysées. Her sudden illness yesterday worried me. She told me they were staying at the George V. Of course, a historic renowned, luxury hotel like that is exactly where he'd book a room if he was trying to impress someone. He had just closed some kind of enormous deal, and he was splurging, big time.

I just wanted to make sure Hannah was feeling better. If I called ahead, David no doubt would find an excuse to keep me away.

Fortunately, the morning was one of those rare spring days in Paris when the sky was brilliantly blue, not the usual gray with drizzle on the side. I strolled for an hour to their hotel along the Seine through the bookstalls, sidewalk art displays and touristy kiosks brimming with French aprons, berets, kitchen towels, and all manner of keyrings bearing the French flag.

As I turned onto the Champs-Élysées, the small shops selling chic shoes and handbags gave way to giant windows displaying the luxury brands of Louis Vuitton, Hugo Boss, Hermès, Gucci, Chanel, and Swarovski.

Window shopping on that famous Parisian boulevard was no different from a walk down Worth Avenue in Palm Beach or Rodeo Drive in Beverly Hills. The world had become so homogenized. I never understood why people who could afford these stores always shopped in them. To me, it reflected a lack of imagination.

I arrived at the gilded art deco doors of the landmark Hotel George V and paused to think about how I'd get to their room without David intercepting me. I wasn't concerned about interrupting their privacy, I just wanted to be certain that Hannah was on the mend. I had no confidence in his ability to take care of her. He seemed to show no interest in her welfare when she fell sick at the café.

I approached the front doors of the George V just as David exited the lobby and strode onto the sidewalk, so wrapped up in his own thoughts that he didn't even notice me. I debated whether I should take the opportunity to catch Hannah alone in her room or do something mischievous. Not a difficult choice.

As David turned the corner, I tailed him. If he noticed me, it would be easy enough to tell him I was shopping. After all, that's exactly what he was up to. And what a major speed shopper he proved to be. I watched him enter and leave the Disney Store with several enormous bags in a matter of minutes. He darted into Hermès but exited with none of their bright orange shopping bags.

He spent about twenty minutes in Tiffany's and emerged clutching one of their distinctive robin's egg-colored bags. Hmm. The smaller the bag, the bigger the item from that store. What kind of precious bauble had he picked up? I prayed it wasn't an engagement ring.

He ducked into the Galeries Lafayette department store and came out with a red Cartier shopping bag tucked under his arm. Perhaps he picked up one of their insanely expensive watches? After browsing through another half dozen stores and making no further purchases, he completed his expedition and walked back to their hotel. I gazed through the glass entrance as he consolidated his bags so that everything fit into the Disney Store package before he disappeared into the elevator.

Rather than check on Hannah in their room I headed back to my place. Nearly an hour into my stroll as I approached my hotel, my phone buzzed with a message from her: "I'm sorry we didn't really get together this weekend."

"No problem. I hope you're feeling better now."

"I'm fine, just tired," she wrote.

I gave a rendezvous one last try. "Are you around tomorrow?"

"Unfortunately, David has to head back to Madrid, and I'm returning to Istanbul."

"Let's meet as soon as we're both back home. I'll be there in a few days." Hannah paused a second before writing. The three dots on my phone screen moved again.

"I can't wait to show you something that David got me."

"Oh?"

"You'll have to wait to see. It's a surprise," she said.

I wrote a few responses to Hannah but kept deleting them. I couldn't think of anything appropriate to say.

I settled on, "I look forward to it!"

Oh my God, I despaired that they might be engaged. I hoped a Cartier watch would beat out a Tiffany engagement ring. Maybe I had become hardened and cynical about relationships, but my antipathy towards David Morales Commodities Trader went beyond that. My gut told me that he was a creep. However, my negative opinion alone wouldn't be enough to change Hannah's love-sick mind.

Part of being a good friend is working up the courage to say you think your friend is doing something that will make them unhappy. I felt like disaster was imminent for Hannah. She was putting her heart in peril.

But it would be too easy for her to blow off any worries I expressed if I only cited "a feeling I had". I wasn't ready to flat out tell Hannah that she was making a bad life decision. I had no evidence to back up such a bold declaration.

One real problem for me was that Hannah couldn't describe anything noteworthy about their relationship aside from her romantic attraction to him. Her gushing praise sounded like a hormonal teenager. She seemed fixated on how he made her feel, without any sort of objectivity. Telltale signs of trouble were obvious to me, but I wasn't the one caught up in the breathlessness of romance.

David and I definitely did not get along. I could only hope that his behavior wasn't a sign of how he might treat Hannah down the line. My best option was to wait. I'd let her talk. I'd listen to her recap their Paris weekend. I'd ask her exactly what she sees in him and try my best not to put her on the defensive. Maybe I'd just have to smile and be happy for Hannah.

Who was I kidding? I had to find a way for Hannah to realize that David Morales was a shit. She had to discover it on her own. But she'd get a little help from her friend.

ÇIÇEK

Joy. Joy. Joy. I felt like the luckiest dog in the universe as I perched on the soft car seat next to the DaNyet. She had placed a beach towel on it so I could push it onto the floor. What a treat to sit inside looking out at the world, instead of being outside chasing the car, hoping to bite its tires. I loved the view and the smells and the speed. I hadn't been a passenger in a car since my family left me at the beach. I knew that the DaNyet would never leave me.

You know why dogs love sticking their heads out of car windows? Because they can! I let my gums flap in the wind. My nostrils quivered. A long string of saliva trailed behind my head and slapped itself along the back window.

I was dizzy with happiness. Faster. Faster. I barked at the man who sat in a small booth on the highway as he took money from the DaNyet. I growled at the dog who dared to stick his head out from another car.

"You're such a good girl," the DaNyet laughed. "I hope no one recognizes you where we're going. I'm taking you to the beach!"

She scratched my neck just below my collar, and it felt so good. All I had to do was think it and she'd scratch behind my ears. She was sympatico with me. I licked her hand and then her face.

"Easy there!" she laughed. "I'm driving. Go look out your window."

I loved the rush of the open road. Oh, that wind smelled sweet and made me dizzy. There were infinite amounts of smells to delight in: gas, poop, sweat, banana peels, apple cores, wet dogs, French fries, and dirt, so much dirt.

Also, did you know that dogs can actually exhale and continue smelling things at the same time? That's something that people can't do. You can rub your own belly while you pat your own head. We can't do that. But who would want to do that when you can get someone else to do it for you?

But I digress. The DaNyet whisked me away to a beach at the perfect time. I was ready for a cool swim, and I'd had enough of the parking lot for a while. It had become overrun with too many strangers.

I forgot to tell you that another lady had shown up with one of those big metal boxes. She arrived in a big square car that had enormous dishes on top. I had never seen anything like it. How could anyone climb up so high and eat from dishes so large?

The DaNyet had greeted the lady and directed her towards me. I knew she would be friendly because the DaNyet had shaken her hand. I licked her big metal box and she laughed at that. Everyone seemed to enjoy that trick, no matter how many times I did it.

She placed her metal box in front of me. I did the usual. I caught a frisbee, chased a ball, barked at a car, and howled at the call to prayer from the mosque down the street. She clapped at that last exploit. The lady spoke some more to the DaNyet, and then we watched her drive off in her big square car that had the gigantic dishes on the roof. The DaNyet and I left for the beach soon after.

HAKAN (Old Guy)

Go fuck yourself, Fatih! My God it felt good to scream those words to him through the phone. I don't know how he found my phone number or what he thought I could do for him. He sounded so pathetic.

"I think I saw Nena. She looked exactly like her mother. Remember them?" Fatih moaned.

What an idiot. He and I hadn't spoken for nearly twenty-five years—and that was his opening remark?

"Of course I remember. You are a selfish, ruthless bastard and always have been."

I realized immediately that he wasn't really interested in the past and what he had done. He was just worried that his precious life might be upended. He didn't even bother to ask about my life these past decades. He should have been begging me for forgiveness for shutting down our business prematurely.

"You walked out on everything. Why exactly are you calling me now?" I asked him.

"I thought you might know something about her whereabouts," said Fatih.

"Because you're so worried about her? I don't think so. The time for concern came and went a lifetime ago, you prick."

I hung up on him. I was still shaking from fury when Nena walked through the door. I came so close to telling her everything at that moment, anything to calm her down from her concern that I was on the verge of another heart attack.

"What's happened? Are you okay?" she cried out.

My guilt was killing me. "I'm fine!"

"You're not fine. You're shaking. What happened?"

"Nothing. You worry too much about me. I'm stronger every day, thanks to you. But you must care for your own well-being and that means spending time with others. You don't need to stay cooped up with me."

I loved her so much but was too much of a coward to reveal the horrible reality of Fatih and my complicity in his lies. I sensed everything would soon change. Truth was bubbling below the surface like layers of molten magma in a volcano about to blow.

MILA (The DaNyet)

Çiçek and I checked into our two-bedroom rented bungalow in the gentle hills above the Eskifoça pier. The online photos hadn't done justice to the place; it was far more spectacular in real life.

Our jaw-dropping sea view blurred the lines between indoors and out—the living room seemed to extend directly into the turquoise water. Olive trees and a landscaped garden cascaded down the hill to a secluded sundeck.

I couldn't help but giggle at the fabulous property I had found. We had lucked out. This one was hard to beat.

"I think we can be comfortable here. What do you think, Çiçek?"

I turned on the enormous flatscreen TV to catch the news at the top of the hour. The reporter who had filmed Çiçek just before our drive to the beach had told me the likely time slot for her PeaceDog story and I didn't want to miss it. It was particularly important because it would announce a new direction for PeaceDog's videos.

Her peace messages would stay constant, but we were going to switch things up to attract new audiences.

Çiçek and I sat on the floor, staring at the TV, waiting anxiously for the commercial break to end. When a photo of PeaceDog with her peace-sign sunglasses superimposed on her nose popped onto the screen, I clapped in excitement. Çiçek barked because she too sensed something big was about to happen. The lengthy feature story that followed was perfect for our purposes.

> "The gigantic street mutt known as PeaceDog has rapidly become a symbol of the anti-war movement in Ukraine as she gains online followers around the world. She leaps, chases cars, and catches frisbees all while appearing to lip-sync to iconic peace tunes.
>
> Her clever Instagram account includes photoshopped mashups of the canine hanging out with Ukraine President Volodymyr Zelensky and even US President Joe Biden's German Shepherd, Major.
>
> The brainchild behind this rising TikTok star is an anti-Putin Russian filmmaker who has asked to remain anonymous for safety reasons. She explained that even PeaceDog has had to be whisked away from the parking lot where she lives because local residents began to recognize her and mob the street.

> With 2.4 million followers so far, PeaceDog will be reaching out to an older and influential audience. The hope is that her messages of peace can gather even more attention as the war in Ukraine grinds on with no end in sight.
>
> PeaceDog is tucked away at an unknown beach hideaway and will be teaming up with a glamorous grandma, or "glamma". Together, they plan to increase the number of followers aged sixty and older. New research has shown a remarkable uptake in technology by older people and that includes TikTok.
>
> The message of peace is not bound by age. So, stay tuned for more PeaceDog productions with a still-to-be-discovered older co-star."

"Wow! That reporter gave us an amazing boost, Çiçek. Now we have to find the perfect glamma to make it all happen. Let's go to the beach. It's your job to locate a photogenic older woman to join our cause."

We race down the hill on the winding slate stairs and reached the stone walkway that hugged the narrow beach. Çiçek took off ahead of me, her tail wagging and her nose fully engaged in the mixed beach smells of suntan lotion and ozone.

She zigged. She zagged. She sniffed. She nuzzled. Everyone she smelled seemed to take joy in her arrival at their beach blanket. No one yelled at her. No one demanded that she leave them alone. Çiçek was charismatic. Even without her online graphics and sound embellishments, she was a charmer.

She didn't hover around any particular sunbather, though. She would take a quick whiff and trot off in new directions. She used her nose, almost like a metal detector.

After nearly an hour of combing the sands and making herself known to the several dozen beachgoers on the main strip, Çiçek zeroed in on a woman walking alone, carrying a pair of gold sandals. Her blue linen shirt seemed to catch Çiçek's attention. She galloped towards the lady, who threw her arms around Çiçek's neck and let her lick her face. You would have thought they had known each other for a long time.

"What a beautiful dog you are!" the woman exclaimed. Even though she might have been the far side of middle age, she looked like a classic English rose.

Çiçek had found our glamma.

HANNAH (Happy Girl)

I was so excited with how our May weekend in Paris ended. Now that I was back in Istanbul, my time with David in France seemed like a dream. The candlelight dinner in our hotel room. The champagne. David's loving words. I couldn't wait to tell Sophie everything. I had so much to think about. How soon would I move to Spain? Or would David come to Istanbul and bring his job with him?

My life was about to change but I felt too sick to my stomach to enjoy the moment. I took several home COVID tests, but they came out negative. I was so tired I could barely get out of bed and decided if I didn't feel better soon, I'd go see my doctor.

I had managed to fall into a deep sleep when my phone rang. A call at two a.m. is rarely good news. I fumbled for my mobile. My fingers trembled as I thought about the horrible scenarios that might have warranted a call at this hour. But it was just another annoying hang-up. I had received several lately, all of them from an "unknown caller" who said nothing despite my repeated demands to know who they were. I turned off my ringer and slept solidly until mid-afternoon.

When I woke up, I only had enough energy to turn on the TV. I caught the news at just the right moment. They were running a feature story about the remarkable rise of PeaceDog's popularity. I realized I hadn't seen Çiçek in her parking lot when I returned from the airport or even noticed that her crowd of fans was gone too.

I texted that Russian filmmaker to congratulate her. "Hello, Mila. Great PeaceDog story! Hope you find the right co-star."

"So great to hear from you, Hannah! Thank you. We're excited about the news story," she wrote back instantly.

"Where are you and Çiçek? I promise not to tell anyone. I know you want to hide from PeaceDog's followers."

"Ted told me that you and your boyfriend enjoyed Eski-foça. Çiçek and I just arrived here on that recommendation!" Mila replied.

"Excellent! Check out Fat Demi's restaurant. The food is spectacular."

"Okay. I'll try it. Thanks for reaching out to us."

"Take care," I signed off.

I must have picked up the flu in Paris. But I couldn't even gather myself to trundle up the one hundred stairs at the end of Dove Street and wend my way through the neighborhood to the doctor's office. Instead of feeling elated in the aftermath of my glorious weekend with David, I felt like I was wading through quicksand on my way to the bathroom.

TED (Tall Guy)

I was devastated that Ukraine seemed to be fighting a losing battle in an eastern part of the country. I filmed the panicked departure of civilians as Russia pounded the city of Lysychansk. They struggled to outrun the moving front lines of the war and would likely never be able to return home. Our story reported that Moscow's superior firepower left nothing but scorched earth behind. The Russian tactic was to bomb, shell, and burn—and target civilians. Meanwhile, roughly 10,000 Ukrainian soldiers had died since the invasion began four months ago. No one seemed to be making any moves to bring an end to the hostilities.

The correspondent, producer, and I decided to take a mental break for a day. I texted Mila to get my mind off the annihilation around us.

"I was just thinking about you!" she responded. "Come home now. You are missed."

She excitedly described the breathtaking bungalow she had found in Eskifoça and sent me a link to the cheerful news story about PeaceDog seeking an older co-star. Mila had a way of immediately lifting my spirits. Her creativity was boundless, and her optimism infectious.

"Çiçek has a nose for this," Mila continued. "I think she's

found her perfect co-star. The woman that Çiçek sniffed on the beach was beautiful, age-appropriate, and had immediate chemistry with her. I've invited her for a coffee tomorrow, without mentioning the online project. She agreed to meet us because she wants to see Çiçek again."

"I don't see why she wouldn't jump at the chance to appear in your productions."

"I wish you could jump on me right now," Mila teased.

"If only I could. I'll be back before you know it."

"I hope so. I miss you, especially in this big empty bed."

"You're killing me."

"Ha! Stay out of trouble. If you get bored, check out the latest PeaceDog video. I think you'll like it."

"I'm sure I will. Good luck with the co-star tomorrow. I hope she's what you're looking for."

I spent the remainder of Sunday clearing out my long-neglected emails. They included the usual online credit card bills, headline news updates, some bitcoin ads that evaded the spam filter, and then, an unexpected message.

> *Dear Ted,*
> *I don't know where you are in Ukraine right now, but the dire news stories made me think of you. I hope you stay safe and get back to Istanbul soon. I meant it when I wrote that our brief conversations were a comfort at a difficult time for me. But I wasn't completely honest with you. I know you have no reason to meet with me, but I hope you'll give me a chance to explain myself when you return.*
>
> *Kind regards,*
>
> *Elena*

"What weren't you honest about, Elena?" I muttered to myself. "That kiss you planted on me? Your story about being orphaned as a teenager? You are one confused woman, Elena."

I deleted her note. She was an erratic beauty, one of those gorgeous poisonous flowers best to look at but not to touch, a walking example of how nature says "beware".

Her message made my pulse race, and not in a good way. I decided to calm down by mindlessly scrolling through nonsense on the Internet. There was plenty to choose from: cat videos, babies doing adorable things, dads doing reprehensible things, moms losing weight. The options for unearthing inane crap online were endless. Social media was a virtual gallery of a life I wasn't living. I could find fun I wasn't having, holidays I wasn't on, parties I wasn't attending. It was too easy to get hypnotized by the stupidity.

I wasted too much time going down the rabbit hole of YouTube and other videos about Johnny Depp's court battle with his wife Amber Heard. What a fiasco their marriage had been.

I thanked the universe that my first wife and I were still on good terms, even though we rarely communicated. I was happy she remarried, and I completely understood why she had left me. That seemed like a lifetime ago.

I hoped I had found my balance with Mila—a hot lover with a sharp mind and an easy laugh.

Her latest PeaceDog TikTok production was spectacular, the most moving one she had created so far, a magical montage of PeaceDog dancing with the Lviv Ballet. The merging of the dog's parking lot acrobatics with video from the ballerinas' bomb shelter performance of Giselle caught the resilience of life and culture during a time of war.

A news bulletin popped up on my screen showing that all bridges to the neighboring city of Severodonetsk were now destroyed. Those poor people. When would this end? How would this end? Humans have the power to save each other. They can pull together in crises. But this was something else. This was not human.

MILA (The DaNyet)

The woman who Çiçek had picked up on the beach said, "I'd love to be part of your project."

Her name was Sandra Demirtaş and coincidentally, she and her husband owned the popular Fat Demi's restaurant that Hannah had recommended. Sandra knew little about TikTok and nothing about PeaceDog, so we spent the morning scrolling through PeaceDog's greatest hits and other popular videos.

"What you're making with PeaceDog is so important," she said. "I'd be honored to be in a video with her."

Çiçek had picked the perfect glamma. Sandra was even more attractive than I had remembered when Çiçek first spotted her. She was ageless, as if trapped in amber on her fiftieth birthday. I suspected she was at least ten years older. Her copper-green eyes were still bright and her brown hair still glossy. Her clear skin showed few wrinkles except a smattering of lines around her eyes, the consequence of a long life spent laughing.

"I want to keep this a surprise for my husband," she told me. "We've built a successful restaurant together, but I've never really done anything on my own. I want to present him with something I've helped to create that is worthwhile. Something that is my doing and not just his."

Her motivation didn't really matter. If she was excited about what we were doing, she was our choice for a co-star. We agreed to meet at the beach the next morning, ahead of the crowd and before the sun would get blistering hot. Çiçek gave Sandra a slobbery lick across her face that sealed the deal better than any handshake.

We headed back to our bungalow. I popped open a beer and flopped onto the couch with Çiçek. I caught the news just in time to see Ted's face flash across the screen, along with several of his colleagues. I nearly choked on my drink. What had happened? Why were they featuring him?

A cold prickly wave of fear crept through my body, and with shaking hands I turned up the sound. Overwhelmed with relief, I laughed and cried manically when I heard the news report.

> "Russia has banned dozens of members of international media from entering the country, according to its foreign ministry. Moscow says the action was a response to Western sanctions and the spreading of 'false information about Russia'.
>
> The journalists in the list are involved in the 'deliberate dissemination of false and one-sided information about Russia and events in Ukraine and Donbas,' said the Russian government statement.

> A spokesperson for the International Association for a Free Media commented that this is a disappointing day for freedom of the press. Accurate reporting is needed now more than ever. 'Despite this unfortunate decision,' he said, 'we will stay the course and continue reporting on Russia and its invasion of Ukraine."

The journalists' headshots reappeared on the screen. "There's Ted again," I shouted, laughing giddily, which only confused Çiçek, who tried to comfort me by piling her enormous body onto my lap.

"It's alright, girl. Ted has been banned from entering Russia, just like you and your videos, and me too. We're all in good company. And none of us can ever go to Russia for vacation."

HANNAH (Happy Girl)

The nausea I felt the second I woke up soon went away, and I was ready for breakfast. Or so I thought. The smell of bacon made me retch. I vomited repeatedly, and then felt fine. So much so that I devoured in three bites a buttery croissant I'd brought back from Paris. Then I scarfed down another one in two bites.

It reminded me of the times in college when I drank too much, which wasn't often, I'd throw up everything and then eat a disgusting amount of pizza. It was as if once my stomach cleansed itself of everything bad, it craved to be filled again with more delicious but crappy food. But I hadn't been drinking. I just felt shitty.

I poured a glass of orange juice thinking it would do me good. It didn't. It smelled rancid, and holding my stomach, I ran into the bathroom. My pale sweaty face twisted into another bout of retching. There was nothing left to throw up.

My throat tightened and the taste inside turned sour. I couldn't stop the rhythmic heaving, first in the sink and then into the toilet. The cool tile floor felt soothing but not comforting enough to ease my distress.

I vomited last night too. Had I picked up the dreaded norovirus or gotten sick from bad oysters during the Paris trip? Why else would I be puking so often? I examined myself in the mirror again, and then it dawned on me. I knew I didn't have the flu, food poisoning, or a virus.

I was pregnant.

I crawled into jeans and a T-shirt and took a slow, unsteady walk to the nearest pharmacy. It was a painful journey, like the last mile of a marathon, every step a challenge as I inched closer to the pharmacy's blinking neon sign.

Inside, I snapped up three different kinds of pregnancy tests, put them on the counter, and asked to use the staff bathroom in the back. The pharmacist took pity on me, or perhaps he also was curious about the results of my tests.

No surprise when I pulled down my pants, ripped open the test kits and peed on the strips. All three displayed the telltale double pink lines.

Yep. I was pregnant.

I laughed. I cried. I threw up some more.

Dazed, I remained on the floor of the bathroom that was not much bigger than a broom closet and doubled as a storage room for extra COVID test kits, cold medicines, toilet paper, and other pharmacy supplies. This was not the most elegant locale to have begun a momentous new phase of my life, but it didn't matter. I was going to be someone's mother.

My mind raced. I remembered the full moon night in Eskifoça with David. I took my pill later than usual and then forgot to take one the next day as well. I had made a mistake, and we had made a baby.

I needed to pick myself up, get out of there, and tell someone, tell David, tell Sophie, tell the world! In that instant of jubilation, my phone rang. I rifled through the mess in my purse but dug it out too late. The "unknown number" at the other end had hung up. The call was followed by a buzz that indicated someone had sent an attachment. I clicked on it, and a photo opened.

I struggled to understand. My body shivered uncontrollably. "No, no! This is not possible," I whimpered. But it was too late to un-see it.

How could this be? The picture showed a much younger David dressed in a blue hospital gown, tears in his eyes of a happy man who had just witnessed a miracle. His face was pressed close to a sweaty-headed woman lying in a hospital bed, a newborn baby cradled in her arms.

Who was that woman? Who was that child? I couldn't think straight. I needed help to understand what I was seeing. For a nanosecond I thought about how fragile we are, how in an instant our lives can change forever. Are we just an unexpected phone call away from a completely different life with a future we never anticipated? Was that what was happening now? Get a grip, I thought. You don't know what that photo really is, what it means.

"Please call me," I texted David.

No response. Nothing. After ten minutes, still nothing. I called him, but it went immediately to voicemail.

"Please call me," I sobbed into the phone. Tears rolled down my cheeks.

"Please call me," I repeated in a whisper.

The pharmacist tapped on the restroom door. "Are you okay in there? Do you need help?" His concern made me weep harder.

"I'm fine," I lied. "I'm coming out now."

I gave myself a series of simple directives. Get up. Wash your face. Move your body. Put your phone in your purse. Walk home. Feel the sunlight. Breathe deeply, slowly, and consciously. Let fear float through you.

I'd give David a chance to explain. Maybe things weren't as they appeared. That photo made no sense. After all, he told me he loved me. He gave me that gorgeous diamond Cartier watch. I was going to move to Madrid. Or he was going to live with me in Istanbul. We were going to have a family together.

Now we have an actual family on the way.

SOPHIE (Tall Girl)

I couldn't fight my urge to take a much deeper internet dive to find out more about David Morales. The initial cursory probe I had made in Hannah's presence had turned up little. At that time, I didn't feel compelled to burrow further. Hannah was happy. It wasn't really my business. Their relationship was new and fresh and full of possibilities.

The time for passivity was over. It was my obligation as Hannah's friend to find out exactly who he was before she went too far with the relationship.

I had to find evidence to support my gut reaction. Now that I knew what he looked like, it was easy to locate his photo online with an older man identified as Anthony Morales. Probably his father. The man's arm was casually draped over David's shoulder. They had the same green eyes and curly mop of hair, only the older man's hair was a bit thinner and grayer, and he sported a pot belly. They each held a tennis racket and looked like they had just come off a court.

When I Googled Anthony Morales, I found a gold mine of photos. There was Anthony posing as a proud father with presumably his daughter, who was a beaming bride in a sleek satin gown, likely David's sister that Hannah had mentioned.

In another photo, Anthony was standing with two young boys in a playground. One of the kids was on a slide, the other waiting his turn at the top. They must have been Anthony's grandkids, probably David's nephews who Hannah had also talked about.

I scrolled through more public photos of Anthony Morales, skipping through those I knew had no connection to the man I was searching for. Eventually, I found the right Anthony Morales in another photo where he looked a bit older, starting to go bald, and his belly even more rotund than in the wedding picture. Granddad was on a beach with the same two boys from the playground photo, building an intricate sandcastle. Seashells formed the bridge over a small moat they had dug. Tiny twigs ringed the top of the creation.

Something in the corner of the photo caught my attention. I almost missed it. A scene in the background, along the water's edge. Two people, slightly out of focus. I looked closer. A lean muscled man, wearing dark blue bathing trunks stood next to a bikini clad raven-haired beauty. Their backs were to the camera as they stared off into the ocean. There was no mistaking David's build and curly head of hair. The woman's trim waist and gorgeous thick tresses were those of the bride from the previous online photo.

The pair's closeness to each other on the beach could mean they were brother and sister watching the sunset, or husband and wife. I suspected the latter but couldn't be certain. There had been no mention of a wife and family when I had read David's short online biography to Hannah a while back. Maybe I had been too quick to conclude that he wasn't married.

David had been fairly good at hiding his online presence, but not good enough. His proud father, who was also a doting grandfather, may have ruined the subterfuge by posting so many personal pictures. I wondered what else I'd unearth about David Morales. If he were lying about his personal affairs, there were probably shady reasons why he had been so vague about his work life too.

I hoped I was wrong. Poor Hannah. Her dream guy might be a nightmare. Or maybe I was looking for something that just wasn't there. Maybe I was projecting my own fears about love and longing. I planned to keep snooping. I knew in my heart that David was hiding something, and maybe many things.

ÇIÇEK

Oh boy, a crazy thing happened to me after the DaNyet and I ran up the hill from the beach. She was all excited about the day. I could tell she was happy because she laughed and danced and clapped when we reached the house. I was glad for her, but all the activity made me tired.

I climbed onto the couch and closed my eyes. I badly needed a nap. I think that naps might be the main point of life. I listened to the clock ticking and the birds singing and before long, I set off on an adventure inside my head. It started with a huge crowd of people cheering and waving blue and yellow flags. They chanted "U Crayon! U Crayon!" As they shouted, I joined their group and made my way to the front.

We marched along the beach and then onto a long highway, where we ran into my friend Boji, the former street dog. He directed us onto an enormous bus. Tall Guy, Tall Girl and Happy Girl boarded with us. I was happy to see them because they had been gone for so long. Boji took his place in the driver's seat. I knew he could ride buses and subways, but I had no idea he could drive.

He steered the bus up to a large parking lot, much bigger than mine. Everyone piled out, singing, and waving their flags. I ran around in circles and barked at the crowd to corral them into the lot.

Soft round flower petals dropped from the sky, and the sun shone so brightly we all had to wear sunglasses. White doves appeared out of nowhere and fluttered above our heads. Our faces turned upwards to follow their flight as they disappeared behind some clouds.

I don't know what took place next because the DaNyet shook me.

"Çiçek! Çiçek!" she yelled. "You're having a dream. You're barking and scratching at the couch! Wake up!"

For a minute, I didn't know where we were. I yawned. I blinked. I sniffed. This was not my beautiful Dove Street, and this was not my beautiful parking lot. I wasn't on a bus. What was this pillow under me?

The DaNyet wiped the drool off my face and scratched behind my ears in my favorite spot. Everything around me came into focus and appeared familiar again. When she dumped food into my rubber dish, all was good in my world.

Maybe those white doves would return. That would make everything better.

NENA (Sad Girl)

I needed to get out of the house. Hakan was on the mend and slowly getting his strength back, but he moped and sighed and looked perpetually anguished. I thought that perhaps his heart attack had caused some kind of depression, but something else was bothering him. I couldn't help him snap out of it.

For my own sanity, I had to take a break. His gloom was bringing me down.

"Are you up for a cup of coffee?" I texted Mila.

"I'd love to, but I'm in Eskifoça," she responded. "I'm so sorry I didn't tell you. I had to leave in a hurry. The crowds around Çiçek were getting worrisome."

Eskifoça? Of all the places to choose to hide with that

dog, how in the world did she come up with that town? As if reading my mind, she continued: "I heard that Hannah came here with her boyfriend and loved it."

What? Had the whole neighborhood been there? That article in *Why Not Spend It?* must have been the draw.

"I've found an incredible rental with two bedrooms," Mila texted. "If you ever decide you can get away, come down and visit!"

"I may take you up on the offer one of these days," I wrote. "How long will you be there?"

"At least through August. Çiçek and I are starting a new series of videos with an older woman who runs a restaurant down here. We begin tomorrow."

"Good luck! I'll be on the lookout for your new productions. Maybe I'll see you soon."

"I'd like that," Mila wrote.

I didn't want to pull her into my personal drama, but I was tempted. How easy it would have been to solicit her help in tracking down Fatih Demirtaş, but I just couldn't impose on a new friend. She had her own work to do.

I mentioned to Hakan that Mila was in Eskifoça with Çiçek, filming with a restauranteur. His reaction surprised me.

"What?" he exclaimed. "What restaurant? Who was the owner?"

I told him that I had no idea. It wasn't really relevant to my conversation with Mila about her videos. My response left him agitated.

"You should go down there and find Fatih," Hakan told me. "Confront him. He has a lot to answer for."

"I'm aware of that, but I won't take a trip away from you just yet. Your health isn't stable. Ideally, I'd like to go down there with you."

"That's just not going to happen," Hakan said emphatically.

"Why not? I could use your support."

"This is a demon you must confront on your own. I'll be here for you."

What a strange reaction. Ever since I met him, Hakan was always there to make my life better. This was a bizarre new twist.

But maybe going to the beach without him would offer both of us a mini break. Maybe I would go down there after all. Perhaps Mila would have some extra time to help me locate Fatih.

HANNAH (Happy Girl)

When I returned from the pharmacy, I took a quick shower and examined my body. Was I thicker around the waist already? Could anyone else tell if I was pregnant? That was highly unlikely. I had been vomiting so often, I looked emaciated instead of a rosy and plump pregnant lady.

I sat down on my bed and dialed David again. It rang. And rang. And then it went to voicemail.

"Hi, David. It's me. Call me back urgently. We have some things to talk about. Okay, bye."

I flopped backwards onto my pillows. My heart thumping, I started thinking what I'd do if he never returned my call. I wasn't sure which conversation to have with him. The one about him possibly being married? Or the one about me being pregnant?

At last, David texted: "I have so many calls and mysterious messages from you. What's up?"

"Please call me."

"I'm kind of busy at work right now."

"I need to talk to you," I insisted.

"Can it wait until tomorrow?" he asked.

I shook with fury as I forwarded the photo of him holding the newborn baby in the hospital. That got his attention. He called back in five seconds. I could hear muffled hubbub in the background.

"Jesus, Hannah, where did you get that photo?"

"That's your reaction? You want to know who sent me a photo of you cradling a baby in the delivery room of a hospital? I don't think you're the one who gets to ask any questions here."

He was so silent I thought the line had gone dead.

"I'll call you back in five minutes," he said, and hung up.

I stared at the phone and wept. Tears dripped down my face and my nose bubbled with each sob. I paced up and down the hallway. I felt a nauseous flutter in my tummy. The phone rang again.

"Hi," was all I could muster.

"Let me explain," he said. I could hear that he had moved into a closed space. His voice echoed. He sounded like he was in a closet or a bathroom.

"I love you," he whispered.

"Who's the woman in the hospital and whose baby is that?"

"You don't understand," he said.

"You got that right. Maybe you can enlighten me."

"I wanted to tell you, but I didn't want to ruin what we have together. I don't want to have this conversation on the phone. May I come visit you this weekend?"

"No. Tell me now."

I heard a weary sigh at his end. "Her name is Mariana. We met when we were teenagers. We've grown apart."

"Wait. You've skipped some time in there. What happened between teenagers and now?"

"Okay. We got married. We have two boys. But I love you. I grew apart from Mariana years ago."

I felt dizzy from the double bombshell. My mind flew back to the second we met on that plane. We were two people fated to come together. We were playing out the natural path of destiny. Weren't we?

"Why did you do this?" I sobbed. "You lied to me from the start."

"You made me feel excited and exciting again," he said softly. "I never meant to hurt you. I couldn't stop. I wasn't expecting to fall in love with you."

"How long did you think you could live this double life?"

His silence spoke far more than any words he could say. The reality was that he never thought ahead. He just thought of his immediate gratification. He was a guy who could compartmentalize and even rationalize his deceit.

I recalled our romantic trips to Menorca, Paris and Eskifoça. How hollow those adventures seemed now. I was nothing more than his escape from reality. I probably helped his marriage. He had the best of all worlds: the security of a wife and family with the thrill of having a secret lover.

"I have a feeling that your Mariana was on to your affair a while back," I told him.

"What do you mean?" he asked, a hint of panic in his voice.

"I've been getting hang-up calls for weeks. I didn't think much about them until recently when they became more frequent. Then she sent me the photo, and the penny dropped. I can't believe how stupid I've been for so long."

"She's been calling you? Why didn't you tell me you were getting hang-up calls?"

"Are you kidding me? How was I supposed to know the calls were from your pissed-off wife? That's what you're worried about? That your wife has suspected for quite some time that you had someone on the side?"

It was as if I was no longer on the phone. He was talking to himself, rattled. He sounded like a man who realized he had to conjure up a way out of a mess and was thinking of options out loud. Only, I wasn't included as one of his options.

"I can't leave Mariana. I can't ruin the boys' lives," he muttered.

"How noble of you."

"I need to protect what I have."

"Of course you do," I said sarcastically. My tone was lost on him. "I'm glad to hear that children mean so much to you."

"I need to get back on track with my family," he said. "I'm so sorry, Hannah."

"I'm pregnant," I said.

SOPHIE (Tall Girl)

I planned to call Hannah as soon as I got back to Turkey. I had spent my last day in Paris researching online to find out more about David Morales and his work. What I had to tell her wasn't good. Perhaps she'd be fine with the information, but I suspected she wouldn't.

I was also dying to tell her about my own news. I think she'd be as surprised as I was. But maybe for now, I'd focus my updates on what I had learned about David.

My cellphone rang the instant my flight touched down at Istanbul Airport. The plane hadn't even come to a stop on the tarmac when I fished out the phone from my backpack.

"Sophie, I've got some big news for you," Hannah blurted.

"Hello to you too," I laughed at her breathlessness. "I just arrived this second. Give me two hours, and I'll be at your apartment. I've got news for you as well."

"My news is bigger," she said.

"Okay. I can't wait to hear it. I'll see you soon."

She clearly wanted to share some news about David. My own intel on him did not paint a pretty picture. My news, coupled with the photo that I had found of David with the mystery woman at the beach, revealed some unscrupulousness that could make for a painful discussion.

On my taxi ride into Istanbul, I recalled all the times I had returned from assignments and Hannah had been my one-woman welcome committee. She was always there, ready to greet me, eager for a recap of what I had done, and raring to offer updates on Dove Street gossip. She was the constant in my life.

I fretted that her relationship with David and my discovery that he wasn't exactly an upstanding citizen might forever alter our friendship. I hoped that I could find a way to break the news to her, without breaking her, or us.

I understood why she had fallen for him. He was sexy and mysterious. He whisked her off to exotic places and was deeply romantic. No doubt he bought her something extravagant in Paris. I got all that. But I also saw a glimpse of his dark side. My gut was usually right about people, and, in this case, my instincts were bang on. I felt no joy in being right.

Hannah wanted a storybook fantasy. She always had difficulty finding a caring partner because she had a fairy-tale life in her head, one that didn't exist in any reality. The Welsh have the perfect word to describe Hannah's longing: hiraeth—a sense of yearning for a home, a place, or a person that is beyond any plane of existence.

Hannah's perfect life had been snatched from her at that perfume counter so many years ago. Her father had left her there and never came back. He couldn't. It certainly wasn't his fault. He wouldn't have known what was to happen.

David had suddenly appeared in her life and fit squarely into her idealistic imaginary vision. He offered her riches and magical hotels and gave her hope of having a family. She got sucked up in his world, like dust into a vacuum cleaner.

But what I unearthed about him made me angry, although not surprised. I felt sick about it. Scrolling through financial documents I received from contacts in Spain, I hit on that "aha moment" when I realized he really was the sleaze I had feared.

He wasn't a thief. He didn't break any laws. He just worked in gray areas and found the loopholes that would give him a large piece of the Russian oil pie and a comfortable, easy life. His financial deals were as suspect as his home life.

TED (Tall Guy)

There was a sense of permanence to the conflict. No more talk of quick victory. The war was grinding on. Zelensky urged G7 leaders to help stop Russia's invasion by the end of the year. That seemed a lifetime away. He pushed them to keep up the pressure and intensify sanctions against the Putin regime.

Ukraine was not just running low on ammunition. It was running out of men. Circumstances had become so dire that even Ukrainians with disabilities were joining the battlefields. If they could manage to fire weapons, they could be found on the front lines.

I even saw a group of ten-year-old boys manning their own checkpoint, armed with toy guns. They kept watch day and night, flagging down cars, on the lookout for Russians. They asked for IDs and a password for the vehicles to enter their neighborhood. This was their war effort. Everyone pitched in, no matter their age, gender, or physical capability.

The world was not turning its back on Ukraine, but the supply of weapons from the West was too little to end the war and just enough to prolong it. I had been on assignment for about six weeks, when the foreign desk told me to pull out and meet them in London. I certainly wasn't going to protest.

I missed Mila like crazy. What a luxury it was to have

someone waiting for me back in Istanbul, someone who cared enough to worry about my safety.

"I'm almost coming home!" I told Mila over the phone.

"What do you mean 'almost'? Come straight to Eskifoça. I can't wait to see you."

"I wish I could. Unfortunately, it'll be a little while before I can get down there. I have some meetings with the foreign editor. After that, I'll come straight to you."

"That's terrible! They should leave you alone so you can come to the beach and attack me."

"Now that's what I like to hear from a Russian," I laughed.

MILA (The DaNyet)

I missed Ted and was relieved he would be coming to see me soon. He seemed sad and weary about the war. Beach, sunshine, and afternoons of lovemaking would bring him back to life. Wow, he was a remarkable lover. When I thought about how we danced in bed, a warm rush filled me with lust.

I thanked Çiçek every day for literally pushing Ted and me together and for giving new meaning to my days. She had helped to turn my bleak world around. I thought back to only a few months ago when I despaired over escaping from under Putin's machinery. Now, I was in a stunning beach bungalow, making videos in protest of his depravity.

With Ted and Çiçek in my life, I felt secure and safe for the first time in years. They gave me a kind of superpower resilience to survive the loss of my life in Russia.

I noticed Çiçek's positive effect on Sandra Demirtaş too. Each day that Çiçek and I met her on the beach to film, she glowed with pleasure. When we first met her, there had been a subtle sadness to her, and she had readily admitted that something was missing in her life.

I wondered if her husband was a domineering sort or if they had a marriage of equality with mutual care and respect. She had mentioned very little about him, except that she wanted to keep our venture a secret from him for now. I didn't think that was such a good idea, but it wasn't up to me to change her mind.

I worried what might happen when our videos gained momentum and she became a viral sensation like Çiçek had. I wanted to caution her, but I also didn't want to scare her away. After a few days of filming, I felt obliged to warn her of the potential consequences.

"Don't worry," she told me. "I'm having so much fun with you and Çiçek. These mornings with you have given me new reason to spring out of bed and face the day. Besides, any online publicity can only help our restaurant. I know that Fatih will be thrilled."

I wasn't convinced, but at least I had alerted her. I hoped her husband was an understanding type.

SOPHIE (Tall Girl)

I had butterflies in my stomach when I buzzed Hannah's apartment. I had reported on the war in Syria, the resurgence of the Taliban in Afghanistan, and the conflict in Yemen, but I was terrified of how she'd react to my information about David.

We hugged each other tightly when I walked into her living room. She always welcomed me so warmly, no matter how long I had been gone or where I had been. Her embrace calmed me.

We usually picked up our conversation where it had left off. But this time I didn't know how or where to start. This chat would not be our typical Dove Street gossip session, Netflix recap, or update on the new shops in town. Hannah looked a bit drawn, thinner than she had been in Paris, with circles under her eyes and cheekbones more prominent. Her usual chirpiness seemed subdued, but her infectious smile never changed.

"Okay. You go first," she instructed. I had barely gotten comfortable on her sofa. "I want to hear your news, because whatever you have to say will never top mine."

She probably wanted to tell me about whatever extravagant gift David had given her, something he'd bought at Cartier or Tiffany's to string her along further.

"Okay. But please don't kill the messenger."

"I wouldn't do that no matter what you're going to tell me," she said.

Encouraged to proceed, I confessed. "I had a bad feeling about David when I met him in Paris. We didn't exactly hit it off. We weren't together for more than a few minutes while you were in that public bathroom, but it wasn't pleasant. I'm so sorry, but I decided to do some online investigation on him."

"What did you find?" she asked flatly.

Surprised she wasn't outraged at my audacity, I jumped right into it. "Well, in a nutshell, he's trading Russian oil, and he's making millions from it."

Hannah laughed. "That's your news? That's it?"

"I'm not done," I told her. "He's not exactly doing anything illegal, but he is definitely operating in the margins of morality. While most Western traders have scaled back their purchases of Russian oil because of sanctions, David has created a dodgy work-around."

I watched for a reaction to the news that her boyfriend was helping to fuel Putin's war, but her expression gave nothing away.

"Go on," Hannah said.

"Well, he has set up some kind of non-EU domiciled company so that its oil-trading activities would not be affected by the sanctions."

"And?"

"Well, that's it for his business dealings. He's making a bundle off the war. He's come up with a way to legally do it, but it's sleazy."

"I agree," Hannah said. "Did you dig up anything else?"

Gobsmacked by her calm, I showed her my phone. "Well. I did find something else, but I'm not quite sure what it means. This photo of him on the beach…it could be him with his sister, but I doubt it."

Hannah looked closely at the picture and simply responded, "Nope. That's not his sister, that's his wife."

I was stunned by her nonchalance. Then Hannah told me all of her news. And I understood. She was right. Her news topped mine. And I hadn't yet let her in on my own secret.

HANNAH (Happy Girl)

When I told David we were having a baby, I thought he had hung up on me. He hadn't. He was just stunned into silence.

"So, what happens now?" he eventually asked.

"I have no clue," I told him.

"Well, I'm not leaving my family," he said emphatically.

"So you said. Too bad you didn't tell me you already had a family."

"Too bad you didn't use birth control," he countered.

How quickly our relationship had shifted from what I thought was love to what was pure loathing. I must have been temporarily insane, trapped under the spell of a sweet madness that allowed me to overlook David's deceptions. How remarkable it was to feel the same physical reactions to him now that I did when I was falling for him: excited heartbeat, nervous sweating, and heavy breathing. Sophie had been correct all along. She had warned me to slow down.

"I made a mistake, being with you," David said. "I can see clearly now, and I'm to blame. I shouldn't have pursued you. It was a huge blunder. Mariana knows what I did. I have to make it right with her. I love my children. I cannot let anything destroy that."

"By anything, you must mean me, the woman carrying your third child. Or perhaps, there are more children you've had with other women you've lied to?"

He went quiet again, and then tentatively posed the question I knew was on his mind. "Have you considered not having the baby?"

"If you're asking me if I want to have an abortion, David, then you can at least say the word out loud. Abortion."

"Have you considered putting the baby up for adoption?"

"It's really not your concern. I'm having this baby. I won't ask you for money or support or involvement, okay? You can deal with it any way you want."

"I guess I could consider myself just a sperm donor," he said.

He was talking to himself again, rationalizing his way out of his association with our baby. It finally dawned on me that he was such a dreadful person that I didn't really want him to help me raise this child. Clearly, he was just trying to assuage his guilt and excuse himself from any responsibility.

"So, let me get this straight. You take me to romantic islands, beach resorts, and to Paris. You visit me in Istanbul. Yet, you're just a sperm donor? That's how you see this?"

"Exactly. That's all it was," he said.

I wanted to scream that he was a complete prick. But I remained silent. He could tell himself whatever he wanted. I knew then that I didn't need David at all.

I also didn't want this child—my child—to destroy his family. That was not my aim. I had no desire to hurt his boys or his wife. Revenge would serve no purpose. On top of that, my child would likely be better off without him. He wasn't exactly a pillar of decency.

But regardless, as I was about to hang up, I made a plea for the child that was growing inside me. "If you ever change your mind, if you want to see the baby, you can contact me. I hope that if he or she wants to meet you one day, you'd be open to the possibility."

"Not a chance in hell," he said.

His response stunned me.

"What?"

"Never," he said. "This is your choice alone. I oppose your decision. If you proceed with this pregnancy, you are the one who has to raise the child without a father. All alone. I don't want to live my life knowing that one day a kid could show up on my doorstep wanting to meet me."

"Lovely of you," was all I could manage to say.

"I have to take care of my family," David added. "I think we're finished here."

"Yep," I told him. "We're finished."

Then I vomited.

SOPHIE (Tall Girl)

Hannah's news stunned even me. "Are you absolutely certain you want to be a single mother?" I asked. I knew she had always wanted to have children, but I was sure this was not what she had in mind.

"This is how my life has worked out, and I'm going to seize and embrace it," she said.

"You've thought carefully about this?" I ventured quietly. "You made a mistake with David, but are you ready to handle the consequences for the rest of your life?"

Instead of anger, she smiled. "I want this baby more than anything else. I believe there is a bigger plan out there, and everything happens for a reason."

I thought she sounded like a bumper sticker, but I wasn't going to argue. She seemed at peace with her choice.

"I met David and thought that I fell in love with him," Hannah continued. "Obviously, he wasn't at all who he said he was. I slipped up with my birth control for a couple of days, and so I got pregnant. But maybe this happened because I'm supposed to have this child. That's how I've decided to look at it."

I had no words of wisdom or encouragement. Nothing she said made sense to me, but that didn't matter. I saw how perfectly content she was being pregnant. After that discussion, I would never question her decision again. I accompanied her to most of her doctor's appointments because I wasn't going away on assignments for a while. It was a treat for me to be in town long enough to help her.

I was there to watch the early days of summer and feel the excitement of the city vacating for the beach. By the time Hannah was about three months pregnant, her morning sickness subsided. She now reveled in her pregnancy and most days felt good. And she definitely ate for two.

She found a reliable assistant to help run her shop, which was flourishing. It seemed that many people seeking diversion from the sinking Turkish economy had taken up art as a hobby. New customers of all ages wandered in to pick up supplies for watercolors or stenciling, while a loyal group of art students and teachers continued to order materials.

Hannah now had free time to prepare for her new life. We read all the English language baby books we could find and decided that I would accompany her to birthing classes in a few months. Our Turkish was abysmal, but we would get the gist of it, how to breathe and when to push when the time came. Hannah decided no to a natural birth, no to a planned Cesarean birth, no to cloth diapers, and yes to an epidural.

We had fun planning for this new creature that was growing inside her.

"You give me confidence that all is going to be fine," she told me at the doctor's office, "I don't know what I'd do if you weren't with me through all of this."

Oddly, her pregnancy gave us both new purpose. Hannah had always been desperately looking for someone to make her life complete, with baby and house and garden to top off the dream. None of those things mattered to me. Until now.

I had my career. But Hannah's situation made me recognize that family can be found in unconventional forms, and in unlikely locales, with people who are not necessarily the family you're born with, but instead with the friends you find along the way.

"Let's go see Peter the Coffee Guy. I think we could use a cup of his good cheer," I told her. Maybe it was time for me to reveal my own news.

MILA (The DaNyet)

Our new PeaceDog videos with Sandra had an immediate impact. The number of followers crept up to four million, and the analytics showed we had increased our older demographic.

To avoid gawkers while we worked, I filmed Sandra and Çiçek in the tide water in remote areas of the beach. Sandra's blue and yellow one-piece swimsuit added just the right political splash of color to their videos. Çiçek loved the sand and salt that formed a mask of beach dirt on her face and added to her appeal. I decided we would stay through the whole summer.

In our initial TikTok beach series videos, I used John Mayer's fifteen-year-old hit, "Waiting on the World to Change". The lyrics hadn't lost their power over the years and were as relevant as ever for this particular war. To accompany images of Sandra and Çiçek playfully spiraling beneath the waves, I edited Mayer's bluesy voice singing about owning information.

Almost immediately, copy-cat videos sprung up. Young influencers made beachside #PeaceDog knock-offs. Some of the older followers, closer to Sandra's age, copied her yellow and blue swimsuit colors and posted videos and Instagram pictures with #PeaceDog in support of Ukrainian refugee groups.

I had been certain that my plan to increase online followers would work in this summer venue with our spectacular new co-star, and so far, no one in Eskifoça had realized who we were or what we were doing.

What I hadn't expected to find were so many like-minded Russians living in Eskifoça. I could hear Russian spoken on the boardwalk and in grocery stores. With their Russian credit cards disabled, these younger refugees lived frugally on any cash they could pull from ATMs or their meager earnings from odd jobs in restaurants and hotels.

I was one of the lucky ones who arrived with funds of my own.

Russians came by the thousands to Turkey because they didn't need visas and they were not all jetsetters with tons of cash. Many were simply disillusioned youth who had only known Russia under Putin and watched as his government deepened its crackdown on dissent. Even before the war, many of them had gone to opposition rallies and witnessed the government tightening the screws.

Now that any resistance to the war was deemed a criminal act in Russia, these young people no longer wanted to live in a country that attacked a neighbor or supported an autocrat. They were too young to know what it was like to live behind an Iron Curtain, but they had no interest in sticking around Russia to find out.

In a recent speech, Putin called these self-exiled Russians "national traitors" who wanted to damage their country. He labeled them the "fifth column", a term used to describe a faction of subversive agents who attempted to undermine the nation's solidarity.

I met a group of them at a coffee shop along the beach. Most were a few years younger than me and had fled Moscow in disgust, without a clue for how they'd manage in Turkey. They were hardly subversive. I was relieved none of them mentioned #PeaceDog or seemed to know who I was. I wanted to enjoy anonymity as long as possible. They supported various online campaigns to help Ukrainian refugees even though they themselves lived on scant finances.

The general response for #PeaceDog was gratifying. Comments posted beneath her videos were uplifting and heartwarming. I scrolled down through them.

"Putin, you need to learn from #PeaceDog."

"PeaceDog has my vote for Peace Prize."

"#PeaceDog is the CEO of peace."

Pleased with our results, I was about to upload our newest video and then head to the beach for a sunset swim when an anonymous comment caught my eye. I gasped. My hands shook, and my heart thundered as I read and reread the ominous remark.

"I know where you are, PeaceDog. *My bite is worse than your bark*. Stop now."

Whoever wrote the threat knew who I was. The italicized phrase, *My bite is worse than your bark*, was a direct quote from someone I had interviewed in my anti-Putin movie, *City of Dreamers*. Was this a threat I should take seriously? They clearly knew my work and had connected me to PeaceDog, but did they really know where Çiçek and I were hiding out?

I kept scrolling hoping that the menacing note was a one-off. No such luck. Beneath several positive comments another chilling warning appeared: "Watch your step #PeaceDog. It's not safe for fifth columnists with two or four legs."

NENA (Sad Girl)

Taking care of Hakan in those early summer weeks in Istanbul had made me more restless than ever. Most of the city seemed to have adjourned for sunny southern Turkish beach resorts in Bodrum, Kaş or Izmir. I was stuck at home in steamy Istanbul, spending too much time watching Netflix.

I wasted even more hours of mindless binge-watching than I had during the COVID lockdown, and the current roster of movies had become even more unsatisfying.

I was pleased that Hakan was making good progress after his heart attack, but I still didn't feel comfortable enough to leave him alone again, as much as I wanted to take Mila up on her offer to go to the beach.

I was getting increasingly anxious to find Fatih Demirtaş and put that painful mystery behind me. I also longed for a dip in the sea.

But I had to remain patient. Hakan wasn't quite strong enough to take care of himself. He encouraged me to go away and enjoy a break, but I still felt guilty about my last trip.

I was so bored in our apartment, I'd downloaded TikTok to follow Mila's PeaceDog productions. She was prolific, and new amusing videos popped up all the time. The beach series with an older woman and Çiçek was a brilliant move. Watching the dog cavort with this graceful woman in the water as a soulful singer urged the world to change was sheer joy.

I walked with my phone over to Hakan, who was lounging on the living room couch, to share the video with him. He was generally dismissive of videos on TikTok. He didn't get the point.

"They're expressions of nothingness by supreme idiots. I don't understand how people become famous doing this," he would usually say.

The exception was Çiçek's videos. Hakan was fascinated by the dog's online persona. He adored that animal. He was missing her while she was away at the beach and thoroughly delighted in watching her performances.

"Take a look at Çiçek in Eskifoça," I said. "You're going to love these seaside vignettes. She's got an onscreen co-star now."

He squinted to see the images on my iPhone and reached for his glasses to get a better look.

"Aren't the two of them mesmerizing?" I asked him.

He stared intently at the screen. I thought I saw a momentary hint of surprise in his eyes and a small intake of breath, like a restrained gasp. Then he said, "Nena, that looks like fun. You should go to the beach. Enjoy yourself with Mila and Çiçek, and maybe you'll find out once and for all if Fatih is there."

TED (Tall Guy)

My meeting with the foreign editor in London was mostly an annoying side trip tacked on to so many weeks in Ukraine, especially since I was eager to join Mila at the beach. The foreign desk wanted me to update some insurance documents, meet new staff, and take a quick safety course for overseas correspondents because their records showed I was long overdue for the refresher class.

In all honesty, I always found the first aid part of the course extremely helpful for those of us who covered wars. The instructors taught us important front-line skills, like how to stop bleeding, treat an open wound, and temporarily set a broken bone.

The course organizers included a twisted joke in the simulation of battlefield injuries using a man who really was missing part of his leg. The reporter who had to tend to supposedly fake injuries nearly passed out when he ripped off the man's trouser leg to discover half a limb. I was glad I didn't have to dress that wound—I had seen too much of that in real life.

I had just completed the last day of the safety course when I got a disturbing note from Mila with the intimidating comments on PeaceDog's TikTok account. She was obviously scared and, having lived under constant threat in Moscow, I guessed she wouldn't ring unnecessary alarm bells.

The threats needed to be taken seriously, but she had no interest in alerting the local police, owing to her ingrained mistrust of authorities. She didn't want to call attention to herself or risk a leak on their whereabouts.

"I'm coming to you as fast as I can," I wrote. "I don't want you going anywhere alone. Take Çiçek with you."

"She's hardly a guard dog, but I won't go out without her. Please come soon. I need you. I want you."

Her last comment made my heart ache.

Mila was right about that goofy dog. Çiçek wouldn't harm anyone. Even though her strong shoulders and beefy frame made her appear menacing, she was more Marmaduke than Rottweiler. The more I thought about that gentle giant of a dog, the more I grasped how urgently I needed to fly to Mila. She was not safe alone by herself.

ÇIÇEK

My life got weirder. The DaNyet fell asleep in the back bedroom and forgot to feed me. She must have been overly tired from our long day at the beach with that nice lady who gave me big hugs and let me jump all over her. But still, she should have put a few morsels into my rubber dish. I was starved.

I tried to sleep but needed to eat before I could curl up in a ball to snooze. My stomach growled so loudly, I thought for sure I'd wake up the DaNyet. I dug through a small carpet in the hallway and found nothing. I turned over the trash can in the bathroom only to discover tons of crumpled paper and a banana peel. I jumped on my hind legs to reach the dining room table and pawed at some bread. That loaf was better than nothing.

My ears perked up at a faint noise in the kitchen, and the fur along my spine rose. I trotted out of the dining room and peered through the doorway where I could see one sneakered foot and then another slide through a window over the kitchen sink. I whimpered and half growled as the feet kept pushing further into the room.

A pint-sized person hunched through the opening and whispered, "PeaceDog". That word again. The man did not look familiar, but the unmistakable odor of a fresh juicy steak oozed from him. To my delight, he tossed the meat across the room, where it landed squarely at my feet.

Oh, this was my lucky night. This food delivery was better than anything those pizza guys carried on their motorcycles on Dove Street. I pounced on the slab of meat and discovered a thick bone attached to it. What ecstasy! I forgot there was a strange man in the house and set about devouring the beef. What a tasty treat, sweeter than any meat I had ever scoffed.

After I gnawed the last bit of gristle, I began chomping on the hefty bone. This was the gift that kept on giving. I looked up only for a moment to catch a glimpse of the tiny guy lifting himself onto the kitchen counter and folding himself back through the window with something flat and shiny tucked under his arm.

I demolished the bone, licked my chops, and climbed onto the comfy cushioned couch in a back room. I wanted to crawl into bed with Mila, but she had her door closed. As I sank into the pillows, exhaustion swept over me. My limbs felt heavy and uncoordinated and started to tremble. My whole body whipped into convulsions from the top of my head to the tip of my tail.

I couldn't help myself, I peed all over the couch. Foam filled my mouth and spewed out between my teeth. Panting heavily, I took a shallow shuddering breath that rattled through my chest. I closed my eyes and was treated to a slideshow in my head of everyone I ever loved: my lost family, Tall Girl, the DaNyet, even the Old Guy. They were all waving to me as if it were the last time we'd see each...

MILA (The DaNyet)

Always fuzzyheaded before my first morning cup of coffee, I ambled into the kitchen to make a strong pot and pop a piece of bread into the toaster. My first thoughts each day usually focused on my plans for the day ahead. After a minute or so, memories from the previous day would wend their way through my brain. Oh, right. Those online threats. My stomach clenched thinking about the menacing words.

I hoped Ted would hurry his trip. It was already July, and the beaches were heaving with tourists. I longed for him, surprised how much I needed him. I felt vulnerable alone in the house, knowing that some crazy might be nearby. I tried to shake off my early morning fears and concentrate on our filming schedule.

It was only when I walked into the living room that I noticed my laptop was missing from the desk in the corner. Panic-stricken, my heart pounded as I quickly scanned the rest of the room. Where was it? I dropped my breakfast onto the table and scrambled in search of my computer.

Think clearly. Calm down. It had to be there, somewhere. I looked beneath every stool and table. I checked between the throw pillows on the couch. I grabbed my purse and dumped it upside down. Nothing was missing. My wallet hadn't been touched and, fortunately, my phone had spent the night on the bedroom nightstand.

There was no doubt that someone had come into the house while I slept. My laptop was nowhere to be found. The thought made me sick. More terrifying was the realization that it hadn't been a random break-in. The intruder knew what he was after.

But the thief hadn't thought things through. If he wanted to put a stop to my work, he had wasted his time. Running off with my computer would not shut down our operation. I had copied all the videos and our raw footage onto an external drive, which was locked away with my camera in a safe in the bedroom. A lifetime of paranoia in Moscow had taught me all about back-ups.

My hand flew to my mouth. Oh my God, Çiçek! I screamed for her but heard nothing other than the chirping of birds and an airplane flying in the distance.

"Çiçek! Where are you?" I yelled. I hurried back to the kitchen to see if she was hiding in the corner, her favorite spot to escape the summer heat. That's when I noticed the small half-opened window above the sink. The thief must have been small enough to cram himself through it. A light morning breeze wafted through the opening.

I darted down the hall, first to the bathroom, and then to

the second bedroom. The safe with my equipment inside was unopened. Çiçek wasn't there. My hands trembled, and my entire body shook in terror. No Çiçek anywhere.

I pushed open the door to the study, a place where she rarely went. It was small and hot, so she usually stayed clear of it. But, oh, what a relief! There she was curled up on the pull-out couch.

"You gave me a scare, Çiçek."

She was in a deep sleep. I shook her, but she didn't move. I jiggled her harder, but she still didn't budge.

"Come on, girl. We have work to do today."

No reaction.

An ear-piercing noise rose in steady waves. I couldn't turn it off or turn it down, even though the deafening pitch was a scream coming from me.

HANNAH (Happy Girl)

Sophie and I nestled on the pillows on my living room couch while I skimmed the latest book we had found on giving birth abroad. The tips were wise, all about checking out insurance, hospital costs, citizenship, maternity facilities, and childcare. Neither of us knew any foreigners who were about to have a baby, so we couldn't learn from anyone else's personal experience.

"I think you'll be great at this," Sophie insisted. "It doesn't matter what country you're in, you'll be a natural at giving birth. Maybe you need to stop studying so hard."

"I just want to get it right," I told her. "I'm so scared and excited at the same time."

"You're not alone in this," she said. "Anyway, I've wanted to tell you for a while some news I have. Let me show you something."

Before Sophie could scroll through the photos on her phone, a headline popped onto her screen. She gasped.

"No, no, no!" she cried, going to the Twitter thread. "This is not possible. This is horrible."

I peered over her shoulder and saw a headshot of Çiçek. Sophie read out loud: "Beloved peace activist and TikTok star #PeaceDog reportedly found dead in a Turkish beach town."

"Oh my God! No! What happened?"

Sophie anxiously scrolled through more Tweets and read each one with increased agitation:

"Anti-Putin TikTok phenom #PeaceDog died suddenly at the beach."

"PeaceDog may have sung her last song. RIP you lovely peacenik."

"Has TikTok star #PeaceDog crossed the Rainbow Bridge?"

"I've got to call Mila," I told Sophie. "She must be devastated."

I dialed Mila's number, but she didn't pick up. I texted: "Are you OK? Do you want to talk? I'm so sorry about our beautiful Çiçek."

No response.

TED (Tall Guy)

Mila wasn't answering her phone. I was frantic. I texted: "My God. Are you alright? What happened? I'm worried. Please send sign of life!"

NENA (Sad Girl)

I couldn't reach Mila by phone after Hakan and I heard a shocking news report on the radio about the death of PeaceDog. We were crushed.

"What happened?" I texted.

SANDRA DEMIRTAŞ

When I received Mila's frenzied call after she found Çiçek unresponsive, I jumped in the car and sped to the address she gave me of her beach rental.

Fatih yelled to me from the front door, his coffee cup in hand. "Where are you going? You're still in your pajamas!"

I drove so fast through the winding roads in the Eskifoça hills that I don't remember making the two-kilometre trip to Mila's place. When I pulled up to her driveway, she was understandably in shock but miraculously still in control. She knew exactly what to do. I had never seen anyone so strong and composed after such a trauma.

When we returned to her bungalow in the afternoon, I told her she must move immediately to our beach villa. Our hillside estate was secluded and had plenty of rooms and garden space for healing. It wasn't safe for her to be alone.

"That maniac could come back for you," I warned her.

"But what would your husband say?" she asked. "He doesn't even know about our #PeaceDog project."

"Don't worry," I assured her. "I'll handle him. You have to leave this house right now and move in with us. Stay for the rest of the summer, stay as long as you like."

I was pleased at the thought of company for the summer and that Mila seemed relieved with the idea. She stepped out of the living room to call her boyfriend. He must have been thankful to hear from her. She hadn't had a free moment to answer any of the calls that had flooded into her phone.

"Don't worry, Ted," I heard her say to him. "I'm really okay."

She shut the bedroom door, and they spoke for quite some time, her muffled voice steady but with bursts of distress. When she emerged, she told me that Ted would be coming down in a week or so. He couldn't fly sooner because he had picked up COVID. Bad news definitely came in waves. He'd have to sit in London until he tested negative.

"Mila, I have room for Ted and any of your friends who want to come down and be with you," I offered.

She hugged me and let loose with deep heart-wrenching sobs. I had wondered when she'd give in to her sorrow. We held each other for several minutes until she pulled away and wiped her tears with the palm of her hand.

The emotional outburst seemed to wash away her pain and left resolve in its wake. Surprisingly, Mila had no intention of working with the police to find out who had carried out such a twisted crime. Her years in Russia made her distrustful of all authority, she insisted.

"Besides, I think I know who it was," she said. "I met a group of young anti-Putin Russians at a coffee shop the other day. One of them stood out because he was so small and had a mangled, bashed-in nose that barely protruded from his face. He never spoke, he just watched. There was something odd about him. And whoever broke into the house had to have been very tiny to fit through the kitchen window. I have a feeling it was him."

Her theory was that he was a spy, keeping tabs on the young Kremlin critics. He must have recognized Mila from her notoriety in Russia. Perhaps he'd followed her home after seeing her film at the beach.

But revenge was not on Mila's mind. She didn't want to waste time building a criminal case for the police. Instead, she jumped into a plan of action to maintain the #PeaceDog momentum.

Mila had not sent out Tweets about PeaceDog's death. The man who poisoned the dog must have been the one to inform the world that the famous canine was gone. Mila wanted to capitalize on the news for a good cause. Her plan was to flood social media with photos, videos, YouTube content and Tweets from the recent #PeaceDog beach footage that hadn't been posted. The dog's reported demise had invigorated public interest in #PeaceDog. People who hadn't known of the TikTok celebrity were now hearing about her.

I still had to break it to Fatih that I had been working on this project with Mila. I didn't think he'd mind because it could possibly be good marketing for the restaurant. My only concern now was safety. Our villa had cameras and alarms everywhere, so we'd be secure at home. As for the restaurant, we'd need to be vigilant. At least Mila's speculation about the identity of the criminal gave us a description of who to watch out for.

SOPHIE (Tall Girl)

I was going to be in Istanbul for the immediate future. My foreign desk had taken me off overseas assignments for a while and put me on the Ukraine beat, but from Turkey. I had filed a few short pieces about Russian oil t rading, but never mentioned Hannah's baby daddy, David Morales. Hannah probably wouldn't have minded if I outed David as a dodgy business operator, but I didn't include him in my pieces.

Besides, there were plenty of other sleazebags cashing in on the war. Business was booming for arms makers, energy companies, and even camping equipment manufacturers. And every other news organization was covering these obvious stories.

I did a quick piece on the Ukraine, Russia, and Turkey grain deal. The agreement would allow safe passage by merchant ships of commercial grain and fertilizer from three Ukrainian ports in the Black Sea. The goal was to help to prevent a rising global food emergency.

Standing around in the hot July sun with a hundred other reporters waiting for updates at the new joint coordination center in Turkey, I fielded a call from my editor. The first grain shipments would likely be delayed for several days, I told him, but he'd lost interest in that. There was a lighter story that he wanted me to investigate immediately.

"The death of that Istanbul street mutt PeaceDog is gaining traction. Twitter is raging about her demise at a beach resort somewhere in Turkey. I want you to do a follow-up."

"Why is that news now?" I asked. "She's dead. RIP PeaceDog and all that."

"Well, she may be dead, but she's not gone. The mysterious Russian filmmaker who produces the dog's TikTok videos and her other social media content is still actively posting."

"So?"

"She must have archive footage from before the dog died. In any case, the online videos continue to contain peace songs, and PeaceDog performs her antics in the sea. But what's changed are the political hashtags the filmmaker is using. Have a look and find her. I'll ask Ted if he's free to be your cameraman. He's been in the UK for meetings and that safety course."

My editor hung up. Typical. Too busy to listen. He had given me no chance to explain that I had somewhat of a connection to the Russian filmmaker and knew the town where she was hiding. Also, it seemed that Ted had never bothered to tell our bosses how directly involved he had been in making the PeaceDog videos in his spare time. Our editor had no idea we were the perfect team to produce a piece on Çiçek. Never mind. He wouldn't care as long as we got the story.

Maybe I could convince Hannah to come with me. The sea air was healthy for pregnant women. While Ted and I worked on the story of the afterlife of #PeaceDog, Hannah could float in the calm waters of the Aegean.

I went online to find out what my editor had meant about the new, more political focus of #PeaceDog. In the past, the dog's followers had used pointed anti-Putin slogans, while #PeaceDog herself had been more of a general pacifist.

Posthumous #PeaceDog was now aggressively promoting specific anti-Putin causes instead of just lip-syncing to iconic peace tunes. The Ukraine war was not slowing, even though people's interest had waned. Mila clearly wanted to make the most from the momentum of #PeaceDog's death to drive money and support to some hardline fundraising campaigns.

One of those hashtags belonged to an organization known as the "world's biggest activist network", whose focus was fundraising to prosecute war crimes. Ukrainians had recorded atrocities and taken pictures of mass graves, children's bodies in their playgrounds, and gruesome victims of torture. But that collection of evidence needed verification to be admitted into court. There were heaps of footage and photos, but investigators and legal experts needed immediate funding to get the verification job done.

Mila also included the Twitter handle for the International Criminal Court, @IntnCrimCourt, that was making appeals for war crimes witnesses to come forward. Who knew that #PeaceDog could still play a part in possibly the biggest prosecution of war crimes in history? Maybe my editor was on to something.

I asked Hannah for Mila's phone number. No doubt she was in mourning and the call could be difficult. I was never completely comfortable making sensitive requests of people who had recently suffered a personal loss.

I never expected the reaction I got.

FATIH DEMIRTAŞ

When Sandra dashed out of the house in her pajamas, I had no idea what she was racing off to do. My wildest imagination couldn't have come up with what she revealed that afternoon.

During her breathless rapid-fire account, I had to keep

telling her to slow down so I could understand the fantastical tale that had all the elements of a bad spy movie and ended with an angry Russian poisoning a dog. Sandra had to backtrack and explain TikTok to me. I had wondered where she had disappeared to each day these past few weeks. Now it all made sense. Her story was so insane that I knew she couldn't possibly have invented it.

She showed me the delightful anti-war videos. And while the point was to make the dog the star, Sandra was so beautiful and graceful in the water that, to me, she was the celebrity. After nearly thirty years with Sandra, I still got a kick out of her. She had spunk. Her energy was infectious, and her optimism brought us through the difficult time when we were creating our restaurant, Fat Demi's. I wasn't the least bit surprised that she had gotten caught up in this Russian intrigue. Sandra loved a new challenge, and the filmmaker offered her an amusing outlet for her vivacity.

I had fallen hard for Sandra the second she checked into the villa resort that Hakan and I had foolishly invested in so many years ago. She had a dewy glow and a beguiling smile that instantly captivated me, and still did. Sandra was the only good thing that ever came from that hotel.

I saw the writing on the wall with that resort and my other overseas ventures with Hakan. They weren't sustainable. I had to get out, but he felt betrayed. I had found a new love and wanted a new slate. He claimed that I fell in love with Sandra's money and walked away, although I knew nothing about the extent of her wealth until later. Her affluence definitely gave me the boost to build my own restaurant without interference from investors or partners.

Sandra had been the best partner in love and life that I could ever have dreamed of.

I immediately agreed that her new friend Mila and her friends who would be coming to cheer her up could stay in our villa. As an extra precaution I would beef up security around the house. The restaurant was another matter. If people recognized Sandra from the videos, or if that zealot who poisoned the dog could connect the dots to her, we could be in danger. To be on the safe side, I would hire an undercover guard at the restaurant.

NENA (Sad Girl)

When I finally reached Mila by phone, she seemed remarkably calm but didn't want to dwell on what happened to Çiçek. She said that her boyfriend who had recently contracted COVID would be joining her as soon as he tested negative.

"Please come down and stay with me," Mila urged. "I've moved into a huge villa that belongs to my new friend Sandra who's in the videos. The place has plenty of room. You'll really like her and her husband."

This time, I accepted Mila's invitation. I needed a blast of sea and sun and a bit of distance from my caretaking of Hakan. He could now manage for a while on his own.

I also thought that if I did find Fatih Demirtaş in that town, I'd get to understand my past. The truth was long overdue.

Hakan was happy and relieved that I planned to go to Eskifoça to help Mila through this difficult time.

"You deserve to enjoy the spectacular weather, and you can't get much of that sunshine from inside our apartment," he said. "Where will you stay down there?"

"At the villa owned by the woman in the videos, Sandra, and her husband, who also owns a restaurant," I told him.

For a long moment Hakan was silent. I couldn't read his face.

"That's generous of them," he said.

MILA (The DaNyet)

I was happy that Nena agreed to visit. Her arrival would do us all good. She'd get some joy away from her aging partner. And Sandra and I would have a distraction from the Çiçek trauma.

I also got a call from the reporter who worked with Ted. Sophie sounded quite genuine, especially for a journalist. I thanked her for her sympathy after she told me, "We're all so devastated about Çiçek, but we're also worried about you. I hope you're doing okay."

Sophie gently segued to her real reason for calling, which was to tell me about her assignment that would focus on PeaceDog's new advocacy campaigns, and she seemed uncomfortable that she had to broach the subject of doing an interview with me. I think I liked Sophie.

I was relieved that she didn't ask about the specifics of what happened to Çiçek. She was more interested in the political angle of #PeaceDog's current online presence. That suited me fine.

I wanted the publicity for our causes, particularly if it meant that more people would come forward as war crimes witnesses, along with donations to fund the investigators.

When Sophie told me that Ted might be the cameraman for

the story, I was confused. "But won't that delay your piece?" I asked. "He's stuck in London with COVID."

She was surprised.

"I had no idea. In fact, I don't think the foreign desk is aware that he's sick," Sophie told me. "You've been in touch with him since the two of you filmed Çiçek on Dove Street?"

"Yes, you could say that," I smiled.

I tried not to allow my grin to come through the phone. She evidently had no clue that Ted and I had become lovers. I was gratified that Ted was so discreet about our relationship that he hadn't even told his own colleague. That made me cherish him even more.

"Well, maybe I'll come ahead of Ted and do some off-camera interviews. Is that okay?" Sophie asked. And pledged to keep my identity and location a secret.

I told her I appreciated that and looked forward to meeting her. She probably wouldn't be alone, she said. She was thinking of bringing our mutual friend Hannah.

"No problem," I said.

I liked Sophie's forthrightness. I could trust her. That was an alien feeling for me because I'd been programmed to be wary of all reporters who in Russia broadcast pure government propaganda. During this war, they doubled down on their lies. They had to. Otherwise, how would they ever explain the atrocities in Ukraine?

This was an unprecedented war provoked by a nuclear power with a permanent seat on the UN Security Council. Publicity for PeaceDog's new campaign wouldn't stop the war, but it was attracting enormous resources to help mete out justice.

Sophie's news story could help. She had been honest with me. She simply wanted to report on PeaceDog's online afterlife. But I'd need to tell her more. I'd have to tell her the whole truth.

SOPHIE (Tall Girl)

I called Ted after my conversation with Mila.

"You big sneak!" I laughed.

"What? What are you talking about?" asked the groggy voice at the other end. I could hear Ted fumble with the phone, drop it on the floor, and retrieve it.

"You've been holding out on me," I said.

"Hi, Sophie! Sorry. I haven't told anyone I've got COVID. I just took the test, saw the pink lines, and fell asleep. I haven't even told my editor. I was too tired."

"That's not what I'm talking about."

"What do you mean?"

"You and that Russian."

"You mean Elena, the model? She's history. Or rather, she was never anything. I mean. Nothing ever happened. I met with her only twice. I never saw her again."

"Not her! The other Russian. Mila the filmmaker."

"Oh, her?"

"Yes, her! I just talked to her. Mila. I could tell she was beaming through the phone when she talked about you."

"Why were you talking to Mila? Have you even met her?"

"You're not allowed to ask me questions," I teased. "The foreign desk wants you and me to do a story about #Peace-

Dog's posthumous advocacy campaign. I gave her a call."

Ted said nothing.

"Are you there?" I thought his phone had gone dead.

"Yeah. I'm here." He paused for several seconds. "That might be a conflict of interest."

"Because you're sleeping with her? I knew it!" I laughed. "You just can't help yourself, can you? Anyway, she sounded great on the phone. Maybe you've actually found someone wonderful this time."

"I'm serious. I may not be able to shoot this story with you."

"Oh, come on. You just have to tell our bosses about your affair. It's a fairly straightforward story about #PeaceDog's push for justice, even in death."

"It's not like that. I need to talk to Mila before I talk to the desk. Besides, they haven't called me directly to tell me about this assignment. I'm hearing it from you for the first time."

"Okay. Give your girlfriend a call. I just spoke at length with her. She seems up for the story."

"Really?"

"Yes. And since we're sharing big surprises, I've got another one for you. Wait for it. Hannah dumped her Spanish boyfriend, and she's pregnant with his child."

"Oh, man. That's big. That's real big." He was quiet again. "I hope she's ready to be a single mom. This is a lot of news." Silence again. "Let's talk about this later. I'm feeling kind of crappy, like I could sleep for a year. Maybe when I wake up, COVID will be history."

"Right. And the war in Ukraine will be over too. Sleep

well, Ted. I hope you feel better soon."

Well, that was strange. There was far more to the story than either Ted or Mila let on. She was willing to talk to me while Ted seemed skittish about the whole idea. Both of their reactions whetted my appetite to quickly get to the beach.

HANNAH (Happy Girl)

Sophie uncharacteristically invited me to go with her to the beach. She always kept her journalistic and personal lives separate.

"This story is different," she explained. "You loved that old mutt, Çiçek. Besides, it's an easy story. You can hang out on the beach while I do my interviews. Ted won't be coming for a while because he's got COVID. I'll do radio stories in the meantime."

It didn't take much to convince me to fly down with her. Floating around in cool turquoise water, doing nothing but reading beach novels and staring at the clouds sounded like the perfect remedy to ease my mixed-up head.

I still giggled when I woke up each morning and realized I had a baby growing inside me. But when I pulled myself out of bed, a heaviness stole my bliss. Momentary thoughts of David spoiled my contemplations. No matter how hard I tried, I couldn't stop blaming myself for my stupidity, for falling so hard and fast for him, and for being conned by him. The signs of his double life were always there. I just chose not to recognize them.

I craved stability so much I had overlooked David's deceptions. I realized that much of my life I had been searching for any man who could fill the hole that remained in my heart ever since my father left me at the perfume counter. If only my father hadn't dashed off. I had waited and waited until the crowds disappeared.

"Are you here by yourself?" the saleslady had asked me as the store emptied.

"My father is coming back," I insisted. "He just went somewhere."

Her narrowed eyes and furrowed brow frightened me. She ran off and returned with a policeman.

He knelt down to meet me at my level. His kind eyes looked directly into mine as he asked me to describe my father. When I told him he had been wearing a Yankees baseball hat, the policeman glanced up at the perfume counter lady and nodded.

I don't remember much after that, just my mother meeting me at the store, trying to wipe tears away with the back of her hand, but they dripped too fast. She held a large stuffed dog in her hand and put it in my arms.

"Your father is no longer with us," she said. "Let's go home."

I didn't understand what she meant until we reached our house and she talked to my brother and me. My father had dropped dead from an aneurysm at the toy counter while buying the fuzzy dog I now clutched to my chest.

I loved that stuffed animal. But I needed my father. If he hadn't gone to buy me a present, maybe he would still be with us at the dinner table. Maybe he would still go to the park with me on weekends, and walk me to school, and holler loudly from the sidelines of my soccer games.

"Will you be okay going back to the town where you and

David went together?" Sophie asked. Her question pulled me back to the present.

"Don't worry. I'm fine." I meant it.

Packing for the excursion proved to be a challenge. The process required a treasure hunt through my closet and drawers. Nothing fit anymore. I threw my biggest shirts and baggiest pants into my small suitcase. I still needed to find a new bathing suit because my standard black swimwear with the crisscross ties in front would no longer stretch over my expanded belly.

With less than five months to go, I still didn't look pregnant, just round. Fortunately, a speed-shopping expedition turned up a bright pink one-piece suit for plus-sized women. Perfect.

As I stood in front of my full-length bedroom mirror, assessing my choice of the fuchsia-colored swimming get-up, I thought of Çiçek. My flamboyant swimsuit brought to mind her pile of bright-colored toys that she hoarded in the back of the parking lot. I couldn't hold back the tears.

Çiçek had been my buddy and my confidante. I talked to her about everything. My fears of abandonment, of never finding love, of never having a family of my own. She listened. She'd always leaned her head against my leg to let me know that she was there for me. She'd gently touch my thigh with her paw if I stood too far from her. She wanted me near, and I wanted that too.

I was overly emotional these days. I guess pregnancy does that for you. But each time I walked past the parking lot, I was seized with the sadness that comes from great loss. My tears stung as I glanced at Çiçek's vacant wooden house and her dirty mound of squeaky toys. I would eventually get over David, but I didn't see how I'd come to grips with the loss of Çiçek.

TED (Tall Guy)

My Lord, I felt shitty. I thought I'd suffer only a sore throat and a dry cough. But my throat hurt so much, I couldn't even swallow water without gagging. The excruciating pounding at the front of my head felt like the Russian army was marching through it.

I pulled the hotel curtains closed and tried to sleep. Even blackout curtains wouldn't have helped. The slightest speck of light shot piercing agony through my brain. Fortunately, I was too weak to focus on work. I had dug myself into a hole with Sophie and Mila. But how was I supposed to know that I'd be assigned to do a story on my girlfriend? That never crossed my mind. But I couldn't tell Sophie everything or I'd betray Mila.

For the immediate future, my main concern was how to get out of bed and maneuver to the bathroom. I shuffled halfway to the toilet. Almost there. So wobbly. But just my bad luck, my phone rang. I reversed course and inched back towards the nightstand, reaching for the phone to stop its shrieking. I saw Mila's name on the glowing screen and knew that this was one call that I'd always take, even if it were my last breath, which maybe it was.

"How's my sick boy?" Mila's concerned voice, so soothing to my ears.

"How come no one told me how awful I'd feel? I thought this was supposed to be mild."

"COVID hits everyone differently. It's an equal opportunity

plague that doesn't discriminate. And it's full of surprises."

"That's for sure. Listen, speaking of surprises, I can't believe the desk is going to assign me to do a story on you and PeaceDog. Sophie filled me in."

"I know. What are you going to do?"

"Well. They haven't been able to reach me. I've not answered the phone or looked at messages for a while. But I can't hold them off too much longer. COVID has given me an excuse to hide from them, but I've got to call them back soon."

"I'm thinking we should just be truthful. Why hide?" Mila asked.

"I want to keep you safe."

"I understand," she said. "I've been thinking it over. I trust Sophie. I think we need to be totally honest."

"I agree. But you can hold off for now, as long as I'm still sick in this hotel room."

"I hope you're better soon. I miss you so much," Mila said. "I'll call tomorrow and check on you."

"I'm glad to know there's someone out there thinking about me...besides my bosses."

"Take care, Ted. Try to get some rest."

FATIH DEMIRTAŞ

Mila and Sandra were in safe hands. At the house I added cameras and updated the alarm system, and at the restaurant I installed cameras in the dining room and others that pointed in both directions on the boardwalk. I also hired the undercover guard at the restaurant. We could keep tabs on who was coming and going, and we'd have footage if anything happened. God forbid.

Mila gave our guard a description of the Russian guy she believed had poisoned the dog. A diminutive man with a messed-up nose would be easy enough to spot. Sandra told me that a friend of Mila's, someone she'd recently met on her street in Istanbul, would arrive in a day or so.

Mila was also expecting the imminent arrival of a female reporter and another woman, but the journalist felt it best if they had a place of their own. I suggested renting a comfortable villa near us that belonged to a friend who was out of town. It had a large pool and would be perfect if they wanted to avoid the beach crowds.

"I don't mean to be a controlling," I explained to Mila. "But you and the reporter are welcome to conduct your interviews at our house or at the restaurant. That way, you both will be safe."

"I've got this," Mila assured me, thanking me for my concern. "Don't worry. I've been in much worse danger. But I do plan to take the reporter to Fat Demi's when she first arrives. After all, you serve great seafood and mezzes. And having a bodyguard nearby is a definite bonus."

Planning for the arrival of all these women reminded me of the good times that Hakan and I once shared running our resort on the hill. I rarely thought about that era in my life. Hakan and I did have fun running that hotel. Until we didn't. At its peak, tourists came from all over Europe to be pampered in the spa, splash in their own secluded cove, and luxuriate in their private villas.

I wished that one day I could meet Hakan and fully explain

my actions. He wouldn't hear of it back then. He was so judgmental. So inflexible. So angry. They say that when one door closes another opens. Hakan slammed a door shut after I met Sandra, and my life took on new meaning and direction. I hoped that Hakan eventually had found someone to open new doors for him.

Speaking of doors, I needed to go outside and close all the windows and hatches in our backyard cabana. A black sky loomed ominous above Eskifoça. Weather reports predicted a big thunderstorm rolling in from the north. A real doozy, a heavy downpour accompanied with possible massive flooding. It wouldn't last long, but it could leave a mess in its wake.

HANNAH (Happy Girl)

I squeezed my eyes shut, but occasionally stole glances out the window, praying, that I'd see a glimmer of daylight. Suddenly, an updraft catapulted the airplane and its petrified passengers away from the earth and above the tumult. A collective sigh of relief spread seat to seat.

"That was interesting," Sophie said. A statement that reflected her typically calm and unflappable demeanor, although I sensed she had been as terrified as I was. She was still squeezing my hand.

"Why did they take off in the middle of such a storm?" Sophie asked.

She was furious but had no place to register her complaint. I was too petrified to feel anything. No sooner had the pilot steadied the plane when we hit another spate of rough air pockets, and the plane shook sideways and rattled like clicking stiletto heels on a marble floor.

"I'm not enjoying this, Sophie," I whimpered. Some people around us sobbed quietly, and a few vomited into their barf bags. Sophie stared ahead, bug eyed, silent. Her fear was now palpable, which did zero to calm my nerves.

I forced myself to visualize life a few weeks from now. By that time, I would be feeling a small tickle in my belly from the baby growing inside me. That thought calmed me. My baby! I would be feeling my baby. Maybe by then I would sense a gentle poke from inside. A silent recognition of something glorious. In that instant, with that notion, nothing else mattered but that tiny person. All would be fine. And it was. I could see from my window that the pilot had adroitly pointed the nose of the plane towards an opening in the clouds that separated the two storms we had traversed. For the remainder of the hour-long flight, the plane followed a smooth and steady path.

Sophie exhaled heavily in relief while I sat blissfully with my hand on my belly and my eyes closed. I don't remember much about the windy landing or the way we bounced and skidded roughly to a halt on the runway, too busy imagining random kicks from the depths of my body.

Outside the cool air-conditioned airport, we stood in a hot, crowded line of tourists waiting for a taxi to whisk us to the beach. The cabs were slow in coming to the airport to pick up passengers. When the next taxi that had been meant for us pulled up, an oversized couple pushed in front and lumbered into the back seat. As we shook our heads in disbelief, wondering when another taxi would arrive, a commercial van driver pulled up and offered us a lift. He had two vacant seats left. The remainder of the vehicle was filled with tourists who had booked ahead for a ride to Eskifoça. Perhaps our luck had turned after such a rocky start to the trip.

SOPHIE (Tall Girl)

Thank goodness a van driver had been hanging out at the airport and had two empty seats to offer us. My phone rang from the depths of my purse as soon as we settled into the vehicle, but by the time I fished it out, the ringing had stopped. It was a missed call from Mila, probably just making sure we had landed. I would call her back once we reached the rental accommodations that her host had kindly organized.

Two minutes later when my phone rang again, I answered it. Mila obviously wanted to reach me.

"I'm so glad you made it safely," she said by way of a greeting. "I hope that storm didn't give you too much trouble."

"It knocked us pretty hard, but we're on our way to the villa now," I said.

"Great! If you're not too tired. I'd like to meet you right away. I need to tell you some things. I can pick you up at your place and take you to the Fat Demi's restaurant. It's one of the best places to eat along the harbor. And Hannah is welcome to join."

"The restaurant sounds perfect. I'll bring a lunch back to Hannah. She's very tired, so I'll let her rest."

I didn't tell Mila that Hannah was pregnant. It wasn't my place to do so.

We decided that Mila would fetch me in two hours. I was

curious about the urgency. I'd had a feeling she had been holding something back when we last spoke.

Hannah was already asleep in the van when I closed my eyes to catch a quick nap. But I couldn't turn off my brain. I peered over the seat at the teenager in front of me, who had white ear buds in each ear and was bouncing to music on his phone, silently mouthing lyrics to a #PeaceDog video.

Out of curiosity, I tapped the kid on his shoulder and asked him why he liked to watch PeaceDog.

"She's always singing great music," he told me. "And actually, I'm studying her." His accent said he was American.

"What does that mean?"

"Well, my teacher in Boston gave us a summer project to write about a social media campaign. I started watching #PeaceDog a while back and decided to write my paper about her."

"Your teacher doesn't mind you writing about a dog you found on TikTok?"

"I don't think so. She's happy that #PeaceDog got me reading about the war. I didn't know anything about it before. I don't usually watch TV news or read the newspapers."

"Did you know that PeaceDog died down here?" I asked.

"I heard she was gone, but I didn't know she died here. She's still alive online."

He pointed to his phone as proof.

SANDRA DEMIRTAŞ

After Mila gave me a heads-up that the reporter had landed and would be coming with her to the restaurant for a late lunch, I alerted Fatih and our newly hired guard. We would need to be extra vigilant when Mila was away from the security of our house. Although there had been no more online threats, there was still a maniac on the loose who had it out for her.

I kept urging Mila to report the short Russian to the police, but she said there was no proof, and besides, she had no confidence in the police. She was probably right on both counts.

I set up her table on the outer edge of the restaurant, close to Fatih's perch. She'd be under his watch and would have a convenient vantage point to see down the boardwalk as well as into the restaurant.

The attacker had been clever. He'd discovered her habits and had followed her to the bungalow she'd rented. She was much more cautious now and rarely left our villa, spending most of her time editing footage and creating social media content. But for her own sanity, she needed to get out of the house for a while.

This meeting would be a test of our security systems. We were confident that we could keep her safe, at least while she was in our dining area.

"The guard is here for your protection too," Fatih reminded me. "You are in those videos and could also be in danger. I wouldn't be able to live with myself if something terrible happened to you, especially under my own watch in our restaurant."

"You're taking good care of all of us," I assured him.

I never felt that my life was at risk. I just had a bit part in the whole #PeaceDog campaign and was too far removed from the politics to be on anyone's radar. But then again, Çiçek wasn't exactly a political radical, and look what happened to her.

MILA (The DaNyet)

I picked up Sophie from their villa but didn't get a chance to see Hannah, who was already in a bedroom sound asleep. The rough flight and early morning departure must have knocked her out for a welcome afternoon nap.

I had only seen Sophie on television. In person she was slim, dark-haired, and unruffled, professional but warm.

"Thank you for being willing to talk to me and for arranging this beautiful home."

"That was Sandra and Fatih's doing," I explained. "You'll meet them in a few minutes at their restaurant."

Sophie and I made small talk during the winding drive down the hill to the harbor. There was so much to tell her, I didn't know where to begin, but I wasn't yet ready to get into details. Fortunately, she seemed fine exchanging pleasantries about the passing storm, the turbulent flight, and the beauty of Eskifoça. I was surprised how unhurried and unaggressive she was for a reporter.

Sophie knew nothing about that fateful night with Çiçek. No one did, except Fatih, Sandra, Ted, and the veterinarian. Whomever had sent out the Tweets about PeaceDog's reported demise never mentioned the poisoning.

Sophie was completely unaware that any crime had been committed. PeaceDog's followers, of course, were also in the dark. They only knew what they had read online that the dog had died at the beach.

I had to come clean with Sophie. I was prepared for the consequences, but I'd neglected to tell Fatih not to mention the attack. So Sophie was understandably confused when he greeted her at the restaurant saying, "I'm so pleased to meet you in person after seeing you so often on TV. Don't worry. I've arranged extra security so all of you will be in good hands while you dine."

She laughed and looked perplexed.

"I didn't realize my life was in danger. But thank you for looking after me."

I pulled her away so Fatih couldn't say anything else. Sandra shot him a glance to shut him up. The poor guy didn't know what he had done wrong. Sandra escorted us to our table and handed us two enormous encyclopedic menus, replete with detailed explanations and photos of seafood, mezzes, wine, and raki options. We kept it simple, we each ordered a salmon salad and some sparkling water.

I scanned the room to find the undercover security guard, a former Istanbul policeman who made more money doing private jobs for wealthy entrepreneurs like Fatih than he ever did on the city payroll.

Sophie noticed me giving the room a once over and asked if I was okay.

"I need to tell you something," I responded.

"So you've said. Please, go ahead."

She pulled out a reporter's notebook from her purse, poised for work. Her professional instinct must have told her it was better not to turn on her iPhone to record the conversation. I wasn't ready for that, and she wanted to encourage me and not scare me into silence.

"Look, Sophie, I wasn't completely…"

My sentence was interrupted by a commotion in the back of the restaurant. Diners were screaming, tables overturned, and plates crashing. We both jumped to our feet. I saw someone scrambling on the floor, trying to crawl away, but the guard went after him and kicked him in the head. More shrieks from diners and a loud groan from the crumpled man on the ground.

"My God, it's him!" I muttered.

Aside from his small size, his crushed-in nose was unmistakable.

"Who is it?" Sophie asked.

"It's the Russian I think poisoned Çiçek."

She gave me a look of horror. "Poisoned?"

The guard had pulled the hobbit-sized intruder to his feet and shoved him against the wall. He was no match for the beefy guard and didn't struggle. The guard's kick left him with a bloody gash above his ear. In the frenzy, something spilled out of his pocket.

"A syringe!" yelled a woman at a table near the mayhem, prompting a stampede of tourists out of the dining room. I lost Sophie in the pandemonium but found her with her iPhone held high, filming the chaos. She strode over to the guard and the Russian, whose face was pressed against the wall with his hands cuffed behind his back.

Nothing riled her. She stuck her phone in the Russian's face throwing questions at him. His response was some choice words that she'd never be able to broadcast. The proud guard in contrast was happy to give a full account of his heroism. He pointed to a side door, describing how he spotted the interloper, based on my description. No doubt Sophie would have a mile-long list of questions for me.

The blaring of police sirens heralded the arrival of a half-dozen officers running into the restaurant. One knelt on the floor, picked up the syringe with a gloved hand, and placed it in an evidence bag. Sophie filmed it all. I watched her get the name and number of one of the officers before he jumped into a squad car. She definitely would want to follow-up to find out what was in the syringe. I wanted that information even more than she did. After all, that needle was intended for me.

ÇIÇEK

Barf. Poop. Barf. Poop. Barf. Poop.

SOPHIE (Tall Girl)

I wanted answers, and fast. I confronted Mila about her mention of poison and Çiçek and a Russian who had just tried to storm the restaurant. How did she know he was Russian? And what really happened to Çiçek?

"I need to take you somewhere," was all she said.

I wasn't usually in the habit of hitching rides to unknown destinations with people I hardly knew. But I assumed that if Mila were sleeping with Ted, she wasn't likely to whisk me off for nefarious reasons.

"I'd rather show you than tell you," Mila said.

We drove for a few minutes in silence away from the harbor and towards the main drag leading to Izmir. I'd already sent the phone video of the frenzy in the restaurant to my editors and needed to fill them in.

On one level, it was just a bizarre local news item, but depending on what the syringe contained, and what Mila revealed, it could become an international story.

We passed some fruit stands and a simple roadside café with no one inside but the wizened owner who sat nursing his Turkish tea, staring blankly from the depths of the unlit shop, trying to ward off the heat.

We pulled into the dusty parking lot next door. A set of sliding glass panels served as the street-level entrance to a single-story building with the Turkish word "Veteriner" in red letters on the stucco wall. A young boy perched in a plastic chair outside chatted quietly to a cat mewing in a carrying case.

A stooped gray-haired man in a white medical coat approached us from a back room as we entered the veterinarian clinic. He shook Mila's hands with both of his and smiled broadly across his lined face.

"I have good news," he told her. "She's out of danger. She's in the last stages of recovery and getting her strength back."

"You're a miracle worker," said Mila. "I don't know how to thank you."

"We were lucky. She is such a large animal that there wasn't enough in her belly to do permanent damage. And you got her here just in time. Come. She'll be happy to see you."

I was beginning to understand. I pulled out my iPhone and began video recording without asking permission. Mila owed me that. We walked into a small side room with a thick blanket on the floor and a large water bowl next to a furry heap. Çiçek. Her ribs poked through her thinning coat that lost its thick mat. Her glassy eyes came alive at the sight of Mila, and her enormous tail thumped feebly on the floor. The ailing animal struggled to stand, but her spindly legs were too weak to hold the heft of her body, still prodigious despite her ghastly weight loss. Her whimpers squeaked like faulty brakes on a car.

The reunion was heartwarming. Even if you didn't like dogs, this one was a tearjerker. I wished that Hannah had been with me. She'd be overwhelmed with emotion, even more so than usual.

"Don't get up, girl," Mila whispered. She embraced the dog, and tears rolled down her cheeks. "I'm so sorry I let this happen to you. I promise I'll bring you home soon."

The dog blamed no one. She simply licked Mila from chin to forehead and let out a weak bark of joy.

I interviewed Mila and the veterinarian for more than an hour. This was a story that my editor would want, especially because it was still unfolding with the capture of the restaurant attacker whom Mila was certain was a Russian who had poisoned Çiçek.

The timing for my story was perfect. During the last few days, my office had been laser focused on the first shipment of grain to leave Ukraine since Russia invaded. The boat, the Razoni, was full of Ukrainian corn and had just been cleared to travel through Turkey's Bosphorus waters.

With the grain story over, my editor was eager to air the Eskifoça escapade, despite the shitty quality of my iPhone footage. They had already arranged for me to use studio facilities at a local television station in Izmir. Ted would be disappointed to have missed this breaking news piece.

While Mila drove me the hour to the TV station, I wrote my script and over the phone gave the foreign desk my input about what parts of the video and interviews to use. I was on a deadline, so our other conversation would have to wait, the one about why she didn't tell me that Çiçek was alive. Ted, too, had some explaining to do on that front. I suspected he had just wanted to protect Mila.

Clearly, my original plan to file a feature about the #PeaceDog TikTok campaign to encourage witnesses of war crimes to come forward had been overtaken by a shocking tale of attempted murder and PeaceDog's resurrection.

I settled into the unfamiliar studio and did a quick sound-check with the local technician, who was connected by earphone to my broadcast team in London. My story was slotted at the top of the hour. The foreign desk anchor introduced it as Part One of a two-part report called "War and PeaceDog". I looked straight into the camera and read my notes.

> "Remember that loveable TikTok canine that brought messages of love and peace to our iPhones? We mourned #PeaceDog after a slew of Tweets indicated that she had died at a beach resort.
>
> Her followers will be glad to know that PeaceDog is alive and well. She is recuperating after surviving a deliberate poisoning. As reported earlier, a self-exiled Russian film maker is the content creator for #PeaceDog.

> She and the dog had recently received online threats. Soon after, an intruder broke into her rented beach home in Turkey.
>
> The trespasser fed the dog a steak bone laced with a popular anti-tuberculosis drug, often used by dog hunters in Russia. Dog hunting is an underground sport in Russia and not practiced here in Turkey.
>
> The common drug that was used has a strong neurotoxin effect on canines. Fortunately, the antidote is simple: pyridoxine hydrochloride, better known as vitamin B6.
>
> 'I recognized the symptoms—the frothing mouth, the convulsions—as soon as the dog arrived at my clinic," said veterinarian Dr. Vedit Engin. "She was barely alive, and there were only minutes to spare. Fortunately, I had recently read an article about the dog-hunting sport and the medication that they administered to kill the animals. I had nothing to lose by trying large doses of vitamin B6 to counteract it. Thankfully, it worked.'"

My story ended with the anchor informing viewers that the "War and PeaceDog" report would continue over the coming days. She teased the next episode with a glimpse of my video clips from the mayhem at Fat Demi's restaurant.

And she closed by posing a question: "Did the same criminal who tried to kill #PeaceDog also attempt to murder her Russian producer? We are following this story closely and will share details in the next installment."

The reactions to the story were instant, including among our Dove Street friends.

TED (Tall Guy)

"*What the fuck*, Mila? Someone tried to kill you?" I texted when she wouldn't answer my calls.

HANNAH (Happy Girl)

I was not surprised when Sophie didn't answer my call. "Çiçek is alive! I can't stop crying with relief! Call me back, Sophie. Oh, and I ordered a pizza for delivery since you never came back with my lunch. I see that you got a bit busy."

NENA (Sad Girl)

Maybe it was a bad time for me to go to Eskifoça. "Mila, I can't believe that Çiçek is alive. What happened down there? I saw a video on the news. It looked like some craziness at a restaurant. Do you still want me to come?"

HAKAN (Old Guy)

I couldn't help myself. "Hey, Fatih," I texted. "It's me, your old friend. I just saw some strange shit on the news, and it looked like video from your precious restaurant. You better fasten your seatbelt because you're about to be hit with another shitstorm soon. And it couldn't happen to a nicer guy."

SANDRA DEMIRTAŞ

I was quite worried about Mila, but she was not picking up her phone calls. "Hi, Mila. Please call me back. You disappeared after the police came. I'm so glad our guard caught that awful man, but what a close call. I hope we're all safe now. Maybe no more surprises?"

FATIH DEMIRTAŞ

Just what I didn't need now—a threatening message from Hakan. I had no idea what his menacing words meant.

ÇIÇEK

I didn't die! Like I told you, "You can't always believe what you think."

MILA (The DaNyet)

Sophie understood the reasons for continued security, and I was grateful she did not mention my name or location. We'd soon learn more from the police about the man with the syringe. I hoped they could prove he was the same maniac who tried to kill Çiçek. That meant he'd be off the streets, and we'd be safe, provided he had acted alone.

I needed to explain to Sophie why I hadn't been honest about Çiçek. I should have told her from the beginning that the dog was alive. But I was not responsible for those false Tweets announcing PeaceDog's death. The Russian who poisoned her must have done that in the belief he had succeeded in killing her.

I never expected that the dog would get so many new followers after her reported death. Even financial donations for the war crimes investigations kept pouring in despite PeaceDog's demise.

I had no idea that the Tweets about her would actually increase her influence, and I didn't want to stop that momentum. I kept the falsehood going and rationalized it by convincing myself it was all for a good cause.

I was afraid that Sophie wouldn't understand that there was another front in the war in Ukraine, apart from the one she had witnessed firsthand in the physical war with ground troops and fighter planes. The other front was online. The digital world was essential as a means to bring the conflict to different parts of the globe.

By continuing to appear online, PeaceDog kept Ukraine's plight alive in the international conversation at a time when other headlines, like soaring inflation, the American elections, and climate change, were competing for attention. PeaceDog was a powerful weapon, even more so in death. Millions of people followed her. Many of them had learned about the war because of her.

I knew I could face backlash for continuing to post #PeaceDog videos. But I hadn't been the one to alert the world of her demise. I believed it was more important to do something and face criticism for it than to do nothing.

Whatever Sophie thought of my deception, she could not dispute the fact that #PeaceDog once again had put the war in Ukraine in the headlines. The social media content was not just silly videos and absurd memes. #PeaceDog was an important element in the battle for the hearts and minds in support of Ukraine.

On the drive back to Eskifoça from the Izmir television station, I started to explain all of that to Sophie. She stopped me cold. "I understand why you did it, but please, don't keep anything from me or lie to me again while I'm covering this story."

I nodded and she continued. "I understand now why Ted was conflicted about working on this. He knew all along that Çiçek was still alive. I'm only going to let him off the hook because he cares for you."

We both smiled. I definitely liked Sophie.

"And can you do me a favor while I'm following up this story at the police station?" Sophie asked. "Please take Hannah with you when you get Çiçek from the vet. She saw the news and is ecstatic that she's alive."

FATIH DEMIRTAŞ

Fortunately, our guard was professionally trained and had thwarted a potentially lethal attack in the restaurant. He had spotted the small Russian sneaking through the side door near the kitchen and immediately pounced. At first, I thought the kick to his head was a bit over the top. But when the syringe fell out of the man's pocket, I knew how lucky we were.

I wasn't too worried that the incident would hurt the reputation of our restaurant or scare people away. After all, it happened quickly, and no one was hurt—except the Russian who deserved everything he got.

I waited several hours and then drove to the police station to get some answers. Most of the cops were friends of mine from way back, so they'd tell me whatever they knew. The local police and I had an understanding. Over the years, I had bribed them to look the other way when we extended our dining tables too far into the boardwalk or had accidentally allowed one of our operating permits to lapse.

As it turned out, it wasn't difficult for them to determine the man's identity and intent. He admitted everything, unprompted. He considered himself some kind of Russian hero whose actions would be rewarded by Putin. He was completely deranged. His rantings in the police car and at the station were translated by a Russian interpreter who worked with the cops.

"I killed that stupid dog," he bragged. "No more songs of peace from that idiot mutt. And next time, I'll get her treasonous bitch owner."

From what the police told me, the attacker seemed like a caricature of a right-wing Putin fanatic. He called himself Z-man. His chest and upper arms were fully tattooed with variations of the letter Z, a pro-war Russian symbol that began when the country's armed forces painted a zigzag Z onto their vehicles to avoid friendly fire. The Z markings went viral, and pro-war Russians began painting a Z on their cars, doors, and windows, as well as T-shirts, hoodies, stickers, and posters.

I was certain that the national police would pull out all the stops to make sure that the Z-man never saw the light of day again. Perhaps whatever they discovered in the syringe would warrant his lock-up for a very long time.

I'll let Sophie know what I learned, but she would need to get it firsthand from the police, which I could facilitate. I don't want my face in the news or my restaurant's name sullied. Hopefully, she will keep us out of her coverage.

I normally love publicity, but this is different. I want paying customers, not gawkers. I don't need any more unwelcome excitement at Fat Demi's.

All was well, except for that sinister message from Hakan.

TED (Tall Guy)

The world now knew that #PeaceDog was alive. But I wanted to know what the news anchor had meant about an attempt on Mila's life. And what was that frenzied video footage from the restaurant all about?

When I got through to Mila, she explained that the madman had gotten dangerously close. Thank God that the security guard was a seasoned patrolman. He likely saved her life.

"We don't know yet what was in the syringe," Mila told me.

"Syringe? What are you talking about?" I yelled.

"Oh, sorry. I forgot to mention that he had a needle with him. Don't worry! The cops came and took it. Sophie is heading to the police station tomorrow to find out anything she can about the attacker and his intentions."

"I'll tell you about his intentions. He wanted to kill you!"

"Calm down, tough guy. He's behind bars now. We're all fine."

I admitted to her how helpless I felt stuck in a hotel room while she was in danger. I hadn't been with her to protect her. I could have lost her.

"I'm safe! I don't need protection. But please come soon."

"No problem. I'll be there by late afternoon tomorrow. I finally tested negative for COVID."

"No way! That's the best news I've heard all week, second only to Çiçek's recovery," Mila laughed.

"You really do care about that dog more than me."

"Don't make me choose between you two," she teased.

I called my foreign desk and apologized for my radio silence. COVID had been good for one thing—it gave me plausible cover to have evaded my bosses. Now that the story of PeaceDog's resurrection was public, I felt obliged to disclose my relationship with Mila.

"I saw that lanky blonde in Sophie's footage," my editor said. "I'd be surprised if you *weren't* having a relationship with her. Anyway, I don't see a conflict of interest. Get your ass down there as fast as you can and get the "War and PeaceDog" story finished. Your girlfriend is probably missing you. You've been gone a long time."

That was an understatement. Between the unending war, the security training, and COVID, I felt as if I'd been gone a year. This assignment at the beach was just what I needed. Finally, some peace.

ÇIÇEK

Oh freedom at last! The DaNyet returned, and with Happy Girl! The two of them sprang me from that dark room. I would miss the man in the white coat who had talked gently to me, even though he jabbed my butt too many times with something that stung like an angry bee.

Happy Girl looked bigger than the last time I saw her. She also couldn't stop crying. I figured it was that cheerful kind of sob because she laughed in between gulps. She had a bulge where I used to nudge her tummy to let her know that I wanted mine rubbed. At closer sniff, I knew exactly what that bump was. Happy Girl was going to be a mom. That was big news. I think I missed a few things.

I'm sorry that I disappeared for a while and dropped the story I was telling you. I can't fill you in on everything that happened because I don't remember much. I have visions of a man's foot coming through a window. Then, eating a delicious steak bone, and the next thing, I woke up in a dim room.

At first, I thought I must have been hit by a car, but nothing was broken, not my legs or my rear. But, wow, my stomach hurt. That's when I met the man in the white coat. He was my new friend, and I was pleased to make his acquaintance. Don't ask me how long I've been at his place. I've been napping a lot.

Anyway, I felt better when my old buddies from Dove Street came to take me home. They struggled to carry me to the car. That was embarrassing. My legs barely held me up with their support, and my voice was kind of funny too, like one of my squeak toys. Nobody seemed to mind. I didn't mind either. I was going home at last.

The smells outside the car were vaguely familiar. Salt. Sand. Coconut oil. The beach! We were at the seashore. But the DaNyet didn't drive the car to the water. We bounced and bumped and turned up a winding road. I wanted to swim in the water. I was hot and slobbery. My saliva made a slippery mess of the car seat.

The Happy Girl wouldn't stop touching me. She sat in the back of the car, right next to me, and scratched behind my ears in just the right spot. I couldn't quite flip over for her to rub my belly, but I knew she knew that I wanted a tummy rub. I barked with joy, but only a croak came out.

"Easy, Çiçek. We're happy you're here too," the DaNyet said from the front seat.

SOPHIE (Tall Girl)

The foreign desk called to let me know that Ted was on a plane and would arrive soon. Finally, I'd have a cameraman for this PeaceDog story. It wouldn't be possible for Ted to arrive in time for a full day of work, so I headed to the police station to do some background interviews on my own. In any event, the cops would be more likely to chat with me if I arrived without Ted and his camera gear.

Fatih had filled me in on what his police friends had told him. The crazy Russian attacker called himself Z-man and had freely admitted that he had poisoned Çiçek and had his sights on Mila. I had to find out what was in that syringe. That was an important missing piece of the puzzle.

I politely declined Fatih's offer to introduce me to his police contacts. They could have been helpful, but I wanted to work solo. I had made a quick connection with one of the officers during the fracas at the restaurant, and he seemed amenable when I followed-up with a call.

While Fatih had been gracious and certainly generous in finding the dazzling house for Hannah and me, I found him a bit slimy. He seemed to throw money around and buy his way in and out of problems. He bragged about the bribes he had paid to the police over the years and how they "owed him". I didn't want to owe him anything. I liked his wife, Sandra, just fine. But I wanted to keep my distance from him.

I wondered why so many women I knew seemed to find men who weren't quite honorable. First Hannah and now Sandra, although she seemed to have had a successful marriage, family, and business with Fatih. Maybe she looked the other way or was simply oblivious to his crass behavior.

Hannah's new friend Nena was coming down to visit and would stay at the Demirtaş house. From what Hannah told me, Nena was another woman who had an unusual arrangement with her man. Apparently, Nena lived at the far end of Dove Street with a husband old enough to be her father. Whatever worked was their business.

I hadn't been involved with anyone for so many years, I had forgotten how relationships were supposed to operate. I'd missed that euphoric feeling, that flutter in the heart that accompanied attraction to someone. Until now.

SANDRA DEMIRTAŞ

Fatih should have been thrilled that the guard he hired did his job well and probably saved Mila's life. But something was troubling him. He was on edge. What was wrong, I asked.

"Sophie snubbed me. After all I did for her, she turned down my offer to help her at the police station."

"I wouldn't take it personally," I said.

His agitation was disproportionate to his concern about Sophie's treatment of him. He was using her as a smokescreen. She wasn't the reason for his anxiety. Something else was unsettling him.

I had never seen him this tense since the days we first met, when I vacationed at the luxurious establishment he ran with a partner, Hakan.

My heart had throbbed furiously when I first spotted Fatih at the front desk of their resort. I had never felt such a visceral rush of attraction for anyone. The sight of him left me breathless. He had the looks of a classic male lead in an old Hollywood movie, with ice-blue eyes and a commanding presence that exuded confidence. Tall and fit, with prematurely gray hair, he was hard not to notice.

Before long, we were taking lengthy rambles along the shore and spending romantic evenings on the beach, watching the moonlight over the Aegean.

On the surface, he appeared to be living a dream life. In reality, he was terribly despondent. He told me he felt suffocated, like his whole life was overextended. The resort was barely breaking even, and other ventures overseas with Hakan weren't doing well.

"I'm on a high-speed train heading into a wall," he admitted. "I want a new life."

Fortunately, he decided that he wanted a new life with me.

My father was enraged. "Don't give all the money that your mother left you to that dreamer. I don't trust that Fatih. What do you even know about him? You've only known him for five minutes."

I didn't listen to my father. I listened to my heart. My inheritance helped Fatih follow his dream. He was able to get out from under the resort and start Fat Demi's restaurant without any partners except me. Neither of us has ever looked back. I believe his happiness was the best investment I ever made.

But the reason for his recent distress was a mystery. The

restaurant was flourishing. The attack in the dining room had been traumatic, but Fatih's guard had managed to keep it under control. He had no financial worries. He and I had never fought about much of anything. Our boys were doing well with the business.

But Fatih wasn't sleeping at night and roamed the hallways of our villa in the dark. I was thankful that our place was big enough that Mila hadn't heard him or seen him during his middle-of-the-night wanderings.

One night, around midnight, I found him staring blankly out of our front window. When he came back to bed and eventually fell asleep, he muttered jumbled, incomprehensible conversations. I couldn't make sense out of any of the words. He even called out a name and whimpered in desperation as he said it. But the name also was garbled.

NENA (Sad Girl)

I was grateful that Mila had invited me to the beach, which gave me the chance to get to know her better. But I was also apprehensive about the trip.

I didn't tell her that I had an ulterior motive, that I needed to tie up some loose ends in my life. Mila only knew that I needed a break from caretaking Hakan. She had no idea that I was also on another mission.

What if I didn't find Fatih? Would I be relieved? And what if I did find him? Then, the only reality I had ever known will have been nothing but a grand deception. I was afraid of how I would react.

"Please travel with me, Hakan," I begged. "I need you to be with me and give me strength."

His kind eyes looked back at me with such deep sorrow.

"I can't do it. I'm feeling better, but I don't want to push it. Besides, I really think this is something you need to face on your own to get closure."

I'd have Mila down there to give me courage and support me, no matter what happened, he pointed out. However, she wasn't aware that I was on a hunt. Apart from Hakan, I had shared the details of my past life with only one other person. And Çiçek, she knew all about me.

I did look forward to a reunion with my dear furry friend. I had missed Çiçek more than I realized. She was part of my everyday existence. I had depended on her to lift my spirits when I walked by her parking lot each morning. Her absence had been disturbing.

Hakan was as relieved as I was to learn that Çiçek was still among the living. Mila would no doubt fill me in on what had actually happened to the dog. The news reports indicated that someone had poisoned her, but there were no follow-up stories. It made no sense that someone would want to kill that lovely creature.

Hakan watched me pack. He reminded me of a child, watching his mother getting ready to take a long trip alone. I thought I saw tears welling in his eyes, but he turned away. You'd think I was leaving him for good.

"If this is upsetting you, then do something about it. Come with me," I implored.

He merely shook his head.

My previous trip to the beach hadn't upset him nearly as much as this. I suspected that his heart attack had left him more vulnerable. To make his life as easy as possible while

I was away, I left him plenty of healthy meals that he would only need to heat up. I laid out the various medicines for his heart, diabetes, and cholesterol, and wrote instructions about the frequency and dosage of each.

"Last chance," I told him as I headed to the door.

The taxi was downstairs. My arms stretched towards him to give him a hug. He buried his head in my arms and squeezed me as if the world was about to end.

As we pulled into the airport, my phone buzzed with a citywide weather alert that more high winds and severe thunderstorms were moving in. My flight would be delayed for hours. I wouldn't get to Eskifoça until the middle of the night.

TED (Tall Guy)

I was desperate to feel my arms around Mila and to plant some kisses on that long, smooth neck of hers, as just a prelude to what I wanted to do with her. I hadn't seen her for months, and I eagerly anticipated some leisure time in the sack.

But my horny impulses had to be put on hold. Soon after I landed in Izmir, while waiting at the luggage conveyer for my bags to make the rounds, Sophie called.

"Hey, stranger," she said. "I know you're heading for Mila's place, but I need you to come directly to the police station in Eskifoça."

"Hi, Sophie, I missed you too."

"I'm sorry to ruin your romantic reunion, but the desk wants a rough cut of our story tonight. I thought we'd have more time to put together the final installment of "War and PeaceDog", but we don't."

"That's a quick turnaround. I'll grab a cab as fast as I can."

"Oh. And before you go, I wanted to let you know that I'm down here with Hannah," Sophie told me. "I thought it would be good for her to get out of her head for a bit and let the sea distract her."

My quiet reunion with Mila was turning into a circus. Sophie sensed my concern.

"Don't worry," she told me. "Hannah and I are not staying in the same house with you and Mila. Our place is five minutes away from yours. And we can keep Çiçek at our place if you want."

"Thanks a heap," I muttered.

I hung up and called Mila.

"Hey!" Mila answered, "Are you here?"

"Yes and no. I've landed but I can't see you until later. I'm so sorry. Sophie and I have been given a tight deadline for her latest story. We'll be filming and editing until late tonight."

"So close and yet so far. I'll just have to be patient. I'll text you the address of Sandra and Fatih's villa. Come over when you're finished, even if it's the middle of the night."

"I hope they've given you a private wing so we can make lots of noise."

"We'll have plenty of seclusion to do anything we want. Their villa is enormous."

"I can do anything I want with you?"

"Yes," she laughed. "And as many times as you want."

"I'm going to have a tough time concentrating on editing tonight's story. But at least I'll have you all to myself tomorrow."

"Not exactly," Mila informed me. "I hate to tell you, but when you were sick with COVID, I didn't know you'd make it here so quickly, so I invited a new friend of mine from Dove Street to come down."

I didn't respond. I had hoped we could be together, with no one around to bother us.

Mila picked up on my disappointment.

"Don't worry. You'll like Nena. She won't need entertaining. She wanted some time at the beach. Besides, it could take her a while to get here. She just texted that her flight will be delayed due to bad weather."

"Good. I don't want to share you with anyone. I'll come and attack you in bed once Sophie and I finish this story."

"You better," Mila laughed.

It seemed like the whole neighborhood was intruding on my overdue reunion with Mila. At least we weren't all staying in the same place. Small consolation.

SOPHIE (Tall Girl)

I worked on my script while I waited for Ted to arrive at the Eskifoça police station. My new friend the police officer confirmed that the guy who planned to kill Mila was the same one who had made a hash of Çiçek's attempted assassination. Both Mila and the dog were alive because the would-be murderer twice bungled it.

I outlined the text of my story.

"Beloved TikTok anti-war phenom, PeaceDog, survived an attempted poisoning in Turkey by a pro-Putin Russian zealot who calls himself Z-man. The letter Z has become a symbol for support of Russia's invasion of Ukraine.

The so-called Z-man broke into the beach home of the Russian filmmaker, who is the creator of PeaceDog. The filmmaker, a political refugee from Moscow, now lives in Turkey. She had recently begun to use PeaceDog's influencer status to advocate support for war crimes investigations in Ukraine.

As we noted earlier, Z-man reportedly confessed to using an easily obtained anti-tuberculosis drug to attempt to kill PeaceDog and silence her anti-war messages. A simple vitamin B6 antidote saved the canine.

We have just learned the assailant then reportedly tried to stab the Russian filmmaker with a syringe full of potassium chloride as she dined at a beachside restaurant in Turkey. The dosage was enough to cause a cardiac arrest within minutes.

An undercover guard at the restaurant easily foiled the assault.

The Russian reportedly admitted to the police that he had attacked the dog and

> was planning an attack on the filmmaker, for political reasons. He called them both traitors to Russia.
>
> While PeaceDog recovers from the poisoning, her Russian producer behind the videos says she is more motivated than ever to expand the dog's online presence and bring her messages of peace to an even wider audience. It seems that PeaceDog has no intention of resting in peace anytime soon."

The script still needed some work, but at least Ted and I would have a jumpstart on the story, and we'd make the ridiculously tight deadline.

I called Mila to let her know that her theory had been correct. Çiçek's attacker was also Mila's would-be assassin. The Z-man had worked alone and was safely behind bars.

HANNAH (Happy Girl)

Mila had dropped me and Çiçek off at our villa. I floated around the luxurious infinity pool like a giant water balloon as Çiçek splayed her shrunken body on the hand-painted Turkish tiles circling the swim-Correctionming area.

Mila soon returned with a woman who looked familiar as they approached the pool, but I couldn't quite place her. Then I remembered that I had seen her working at Fat Demi's several months ago when I had visited with David.

Mila introduced me to Sandra Demirtaş.

"I once ate at your restaurant and met your husband there,"

I told Sandra. "In fact, I think that was the same night I got pregnant."

Sandra looked bewildered. I immediately realized how awkward my comment sounded.

"That's not what I meant," I laughed. "Your husband is not the father of this child," as I pointed to my belly. "I had a dreamy meal at Fat Demi's with my boyfriend. We fell into bed soon after, and well, here I am months later, pregnant."

"I'm glad to hear our food and raki inspired such a happy result," Sandra said, her grace covering my awkwardness.

I smiled and rubbed my small baby bump.

"You and your husband have created a beautiful restaurant that made for a memorable evening for me."

I didn't have the heart to tell her that my boyfriend was a married shit who had lied to me from the start of our relationship. My trip to Eskifoça had been a romantic adventure for me but nothing more than a dirty weekend for him.

I wasn't even sure if Mila knew about my predicament. I hadn't told her about my pregnancy or talked to her about David. Even when we drove together to pick up Çiçek, I hadn't filled her in on my situation. I was certain that Sophie was far too discreet to have told Mila my story. Besides, Sophie was so focused on her assignment that my personal life would not have been a topic she'd bring up with Mila.

Sophie had invited me to come with her to Eskifoça so I could get my mind off David and enjoy some sea breezes. Her plan was working. The trip was also intended to boost my morale after the devastating news that Çiçek had died. But Çiçek was alive and well, and I was feeling the joy. Best of all, David was slowly slipping from my heart and mind.

"Let's catch the sunset at the beach," I suggested. "Çiçek should come with us."

Mila and Sandra agreed. The timing for our sundown seaside plan was perfect because Ted and Sophie were busy with work at the police station. Mila explained to me that she had also invited Nena down from Istanbul, but that her flight was delayed because of heavy storms outside of the city. It seemed that all of Dove Street was descending onto Eskifoça. We'd have a mini reunion, and Çiçek would be part of the gathering.

Mila and Sandra hoisted the dog into the back of the car while I eased into the front passenger seat. Off we went. The car bumped and skidded over the loose rocks on the winding road down the hill to the beach.

We parked as close to the surf as possible. Mila and Sandra strained to maneuver Çiçek out of the car and onto our enormous beach blanket that could accommodate all of us. We sat in a row, the dog in the middle, staring at the horizon while the hypnotic whisper of the gentle waves lulled us into a peaceful stupor.

MILA (The DaNyet)

While Hannah and I sat with Sandra and Çiçek on our beach blanket watching the sun sink below the skyline, Sandra disrupted our serenity. "Something is bothering Fatih."

We said nothing and waited for her to explain.

"He's not himself. It's not just the attacks on Çiçek and our restaurant that are disturbing him. He's agitated about something. He doesn't sleep. He roams the house at night."

She shook her head and asked, "Have you heard him?"

"I haven't noticed a thing," I assured her. But the Demirtaş' house was so big I could easily have failed to hear Fatih's nighttime ramblings.

"What do you think is keeping him up?"

Instead of allowing time for Sandra to answer, Hannah chimed in. "When a man goes quiet and seems anxious, it means he's feeling guilty, or he's worried about money, or he's hiding something."

I laughed. "That's a bit harsh." Clearly Hannah had gone through something tough that neither Sandra nor I knew about.

"Yes, it's harsh," Hannah admitted and proceeded to tell us about her ill-fated love affair with David and how she ended up pregnant with his child. Sandra and I were too stunned to comment.

"The longer our affair continued, the more restless David became," Hannah explained. "At first, I thought he was worrying about his big business deal. That was part of it, but when his double life came to light, I realized he had been afraid that his wife would catch him."

We sat in silence, digesting her tale. It was a chunk of trauma to digest.

"God, I was so stupid," Hannah continued. "Anyway, all of this is to say that if you think something is bothering Fatih, then something is bothering him. My biased guess—he's feeling guilty about something that he's done, and he's afraid he's going to get caught."

"I'm so sad to hear how David treated you," Sandra said softly. "You have such inner strength. As for Fatih, I don't think he has a girlfriend on the side. He's too busy with the restaurant."

More silence as the three of us stared off into the distance.

"Speaking of lovers," I blurted. "I've not ever told you about mine."

"What? I thought you just worked all the time, and your only love interest was Çiçek," Hannah teased.

"No. I actually started seeing Ted before his latest trip to Ukraine," I confessed.

"That's incredible," Hannah said. "That makes perfect sense. He's a great guy. Good for you! You certainly kept that on the down low."

"I know," I admitted. "It was all so new and then he went on assignment. But we've been in close touch."

We continued to watch the sea, each of us mulling over our revelations. None of us had any more theories about Fatih's behavior. We certainly had nothing to add to Hannah's horrendous story about her ex-boyfriend. I was lost in thought about how wonderful my reunion with Ted would be.

Çiçek broke the silence with a loud fart. We laughed uproariously, and it gave me the perfect opening to move the subject away from men.

"I forgot to tell you that Sophie knows who poisoned Çiçek. It was the same guy who tried to jab me with potassium chloride."

"How horrible!" Sandra exclaimed. "But what a relief. Maybe we're out of danger now. Who is he?"

I told them about the pro-Putin zealot, Z-man, who thought that offing Çiçek and me would end our online anti-war campaign. "Sophie's story about him will air as soon as she and Ted have the video from the station and can put it together."

"That's amazing news," Hannah said. "I'm so glad that this Z-man is locked away. That means you're safe to continue your videos."

"We've been making them, anyway," I said. "In fact, so much has changed in Ukraine in the last few weeks that we need to revise our messaging."

Çiçek barked to remind us that she was feeling better and required some attention. As we took turns hugging Çiçek and cooing over her, our conversation shifted to Ukraine. We talked about how the country had recently launched a game-changing counteroffensive against the Russians occupying their eastern territories. Ukraine forces had destroyed Russian arms, command centers, and supplies behind Russian lines with American-supplied precision rockets.

Draft-age Russians were fleeing conscription, many of them pouring into Turkey to avoid fighting in a war they didn't want. One Turkish governor said that as many as nineteen thousand Russians were coming to his province every day. For now it seemed that Putin was losing the war in Ukraine and support for it at home.

"What if he uses nuclear weapons to make up for the failings of his troops?" Hannah asked.

"That's a question no one can answer," I told her. "Maybe he'll just use his stockpile as a way to extort concessions that he hasn't been able to gain on the battlefield."

"It's like waiting for a big shoe to drop," Sandra said as

she stared far away at the horizon. She seemed to be talking to herself. Hannah and I looked questioningly at each other. Was Sandra referring to Putin's next move or Fatih's mysterious anxiety?

ÇIÇEK

I still couldn't fully stand up without help. My legs wobbled, and my head felt fuzzy. Lucky for me, the ladies were strong and could lift me from the sand back into the car.

I was so happy to be with those girls again as I listened to their chatter. They did their best to calm me and return me to my old self. But whatever had happened to me wasn't good. I still didn't feel whole. Sometimes I trembled uncontrollably, and sometimes I howled for no good reason. I don't know who I was howling at, but it felt so darned good to release that noise. My tail used to thump constantly with joy, but now, it mostly stayed tucked under me.

The worst thing of all was my fear pee. I couldn't control it. If I got spooked, I peed. And I got spooked really easily. So, I peed often.

I was scared of most things. Windows that went up and down. Anything thrown at me. Fast movements. I wondered who or what had taken over my body and made me such a scaredy cat. Ha! Scaredy Cat. That's a name I didn't really understand because most cats I knew were fearless.

We drove up that bumpy hill again. I got a big hug from Happy Girl as she got out of the car and opened the gate to her house with the big pool. This time, I didn't go with her.

The DaNyet and the other nice lady drove me further up the hill to another house. I think because I peed so much, they let me stay outside in the closed garden. Good decision. I preferred to be out in the open. I felt safer there. The evening grew cool and dark, and I couldn't keep my eyes open even if they came out to feed me. I was so very tired.

NENA (Sad Girl)

The airline should have delayed my flight to Eskifoça much longer because the storm hadn't completely passed when we boarded. What a petrifying journey that was. The plane bumped and twisted through the clouds for an hour outside of Istanbul, and the smell of vomit wafted through the cabin. I've never been so glad to see the landing lights on a runway.

I texted Mila to not to worry about me. After my long taxi ride, I'd reach her place around sunrise. I was looking forward to seeing Mila again and meeting the lovely woman I had seen online as Çiçek's PeaceDog co-star. All I knew about her was that her name was Sandra and that she was very generous to allow me to stay at her home.

I planned to get to know Mila better and to allow her fully into my life. I was finally ready to share more with her. That article and old photo had dredged up so much sadness I believed I had long buried. Hakan was right. I needed to confront my past. I hoped I could solicit Mila's help in tracking down Fatih Demirtaş if he still existed. Maybe her friend Sandra could be of assistance too, especially because she was a local.

TED (Tall Guy)

At last! Sophie and I wrapped up the final "War and PeaceDog" story. God, how I despised that fanatic Z-man. He had come way too close to murdering Mila, not to mention Çiçek. No doubt we'd eventually have to report on his trial, but for now, all I could think about was reuniting in bed with Mila.

The taxi moved too slowly up the hill from Sophie and Hannah's villa where we had edited the final story. I needed to feel myself inside Mila now. Just the thought of her drove me wild as the taxi pulled into the gravel driveway at the expansive estate where she was staying.

She had given me the gate entry code so I wouldn't wake up anyone. I tiptoed across the front lawn to the north wing where Mila had instructed me to enter, but before I reached the door, I tripped on a soft lump that let out a high-pitched whimper. I knew that sound. Çiçek! She immediately recognized me and struggled to stand to lick my face. I plunked down on the cool grass to get a good look at her bony body and matted fur as she climbed on top and slobbered all over my face.

"I'm happy to see you too, girl. But it's too early to play. We'll wake up the house."

I rolled Çiçek off me and sat with her until she fell back asleep. The anticipation of touching Mila's soft skin was overpowering. I couldn't wait another second. I padded across the lawn and entered the front door that Mila had left unlocked for me. I slinked into a hallway bathroom to quickly wash off the dog smell.

Across the vast living room, I found the door I had been

waiting for these past months. I pushed it open with such anticipation that I feared I had taken it off its hinges. The moonlight streamed through the window. Mila's luscious blond hair splayed across the pillow. At last.

"Mila," was all I whispered.

She sighed and rolled into my arms. As the moonbeams shined on her sleepy face, she stripped off her silky nightgown and I yanked off my own clothes. Our naked bodies slid against each other. Our lips met and desperate urgency rose between us. I slipped into her, and Mila embraced me tightly, arching into me. I swelled within her until we both released with waves of pleasure.

When Mila came back to herself, she smiled, closed her eyes, whispered, "More of that later, please" and promptly fell back to sleep with a satisfied grin on her face.

I was far too jazzed to snooze as we spooned in the afterglow of our lovemaking. I gently pulled back the covers and returned to the living room, leaving Mila to her dreams.

Through the floor-to-ceiling windows I watched as the sun began to peek above the horizon, and said out loud, "What the fuck is *she* doing here?"

MILA (The DaNyet)

I thought I was dreaming but definitely remembered some gentle lovemaking with Ted. Jolted from my sweet slumber, I heard him swearing in the living room. I tore out of bed to check that he was okay. My recent trauma with Çiçek had made me more skittish than I realized. I had an illogical fear that something terrible had happened to Ted.

Relieved to find him standing half naked, glaring out the

window, I followed his eyes, staring intensely at someone in the middle of the lawn.

"That's my friend, Nena," I exclaimed.

We watched her squatting next to Çiçek. The dog squirmed with excitement, frantically licking and pawing affectionately at the woman.

"You know her?" Ted asked, his question weirdly aggressive.

"Of course. I told you I had invited Nena down here. She's a neighbor."

"Her name is Elena, not Nena," Ted snapped.

"What is wrong with you?" I demanded. "She's Nena. I asked her to come down here because she's going through a rough time. Her partner is quite a few years older than she is. Taking care of him has taken the joy out of her life lately."

"Oh, really? That's what she told you?"

"Of course. I have no reason to doubt her. I even met her partner."

"She never mentioned any partner to me," he said.

"What? How do you know her?" I asked. "When did you meet her?"

"It was before you arrived in Turkey," Ted explained. "She charmed me in a neighborhood restaurant. We shared two intimate conversations together and she told me about her traumatic childhood. I only saw her once after that, standing on a street corner. By then, I had met you and my life changed…for the better."

I reached out for Ted's hand. He and Çiçek had forever changed my life too. So much of any person's existence is altered by the people they meet, the lovers that come and go, the friends who drift in and out through the years. I had no reason to doubt Ted's love for me.

"She's a model," Ted continued. "A photographer friend tracked her down for me through her modeling agency. Her name is Elena Petrovich."

"You certainly researched her," I commented. It came out harsher than I'd intended.

"Like I said, I met her before I met you." Ted was miffed that I sounded accusatory. "She told me quite a story. She was born in Russia and is the love child of a Turkish businessman and a Russian woman, both of whom died when she was not quite a teenager. She said that she survived on a suitcase of cash that her father had had delivered to her Moscow apartment."

"That all makes sense," I said. "She told me that she had a difficult childhood. And maybe 'Elena' is just her professional name."

"You're probably right. But she never mentioned a husband."

"Well. Maybe she felt that would have put a damper on your evenings with her. Maybe she enjoyed your company and didn't want to ruin it."

"That's a big omission," Ted said.

"Yes. But not a lie."

"I can't believe you're defending her!" Ted pulled me into an embrace.

"I wouldn't be so charitable if I thought she was pursuing you. But she isn't."

Together, we watched Nena, or Elena, or whatever her name was, as she hugged the dog and nuzzled her fur. Both of us questioned who this woman really was. I thought

I knew her. Ted thought he knew her. Çiçek knew her and clearly loved her. But what was her real story?

FATIH DEMIRTAŞ

Another night without sleep. I was too anxious about Hakan's threatening message. What did he mean that a shitstorm was coming my way? What was he planning? And why now?

I wandered into the kitchen to make an early morning cup of coffee and get a grip before Sandra woke up and Mila and her friends joined us. The sun had started to peek through the trees, and it looked like the beginning of a beautiful clear day. I grabbed my coffee to park myself on the front lawn and greet the morning.

Çiçek was there licking the face of a woman whose long chestnut-colored hair cascaded over both of their heads. She must be one of Mila's friends, I thought. When she heard my footsteps, she pulled away from the dog and looked up at me.

Her eyes, large and inquiring, recognized me instantly. She inhaled a loud shaky breath and covered her mouth with her hands. The answer to Hakan's ominous message was right in front of me.

"It's you," I whispered, dropping my cup.

"Otets?" she asked. She called me father.

We stood just a few yards apart, our eyes locked, our bodies frozen in shock. Silence hung between us as Çiçek parked herself at our feet. The dog whined loudly, sensing the intense emotions.

Suddenly, our moment was interrupted.

"You must be Nena," Sandra called from the front door. "Welcome to our home. Mila told me you'd be arriving early in the morning. I'm Sandra Demirtaş."

She reached out for a welcome embrace. Nena collapsed in her arms.

A confused Sandra pulled Nena more tightly into her embrace and slowly guided her towards the house.

"What's wrong with her?" Sandra turned to ask me. She noticed a single tear streaming down my face. "What's going on, Fatih? Do you know her? Is this Mila's friend, Nena?"

"Yes, she's Nena," I told her. "My daughter."

If Sandra were stunned, she didn't let on.

"Let's help her inside," she said flatly.

Her emotionless tone terrified me. I would have been less panicked if she had gotten angry or demanded to know what I was talking about.

Instead, she calmly turned to me. "You two clearly have some catching up to do."

Her questioning eyes met mine. She turned away before I could say anything. I felt like a shit.

SANDRA DEMIRTAŞ

I didn't realize how much my insides were trembling until I reached the far wing of the house. Questions tumbled through my mind. My husband of so many decades had a daughter. How could Fatih never have mentioned her? Where did she come from? Did Mila know that her friend Nena was Fatih's daughter?

I found Mila and Ted gripping cups of coffee and looking baffled as they stared out their living room window. They were obviously as surprised as I was by Nena's emotional arrival.

"Mila, I think you've unleashed an apocalypse," I told her.

"What just happened out there?" she asked. "Why did Nena collapse like that? We couldn't hear anything, but we witnessed the drama."

"Well, it seems that your friend is Fatih's daughter," I explained.

"What?" Mila and Ted asked in unison.

"I know nothing more than that," I told them. I looked to Mila to tell me everything she knew about Nena.

"She's a neighbor. She struck me as lonely, kind of sad, married to a much older man who has been ill. I invited her here to cheer her up," Mila explained. "I don't know much else about her. She didn't want to talk about her early years in Russia. However, Ted met her separately and knows a bit more."

I hoped he did. Maybe Fatih hadn't known that he had a daughter. Perhaps Nena's mother never told Fatih that she was pregnant. But that was wishful thinking. Fatih's reaction at seeing Nena indicated that he knew his daughter. That meant only one thing. My husband had harbored a shattering secret that he had kept from me and our sons for decades. He had known all along that he had a daughter somewhere out there. What kind of man had I married?

"Please, Ted, tell me what you know," I pleaded.

"I met her by accident in a neighborhood restaurant. She told me her name was Elena and her father was a Turkish businessman who frequented Moscow for work in the 1980s. He fell in love with her Russian mother, who worked the front desk at a hotel where he stayed."

"That makes sense," I told Ted. "I knew that Fatih had construction business in Russia back then, before we met."

Ted continued. "When she was only ten years old, a man showed up at their apartment with a suitcase full of cash and informed her mother that her Turkish lover had died. Two years later, the mother also passed away."

That poor child, I thought. Left an orphan before she was even a teen. It dawned on me that the money Fatih had someone deliver to the mother and child was part of my inheritance. I had given much of what my own mother had left me so that Fatih could buy out his partner in their floundering Eskifoça resort and open the restaurant. He had used some of my cash to assuage his guilt and walk away from his own daughter and lover.

I hoped there was more to the story. I didn't want to believe that Fatih had left his own flesh and blood out there, alone, to fend for herself at such a young age. Had I married such a selfish monster? It didn't fit with the loving husband and father who I knew. I didn't think that Fatih and I had any secrets between us. How wrong I was.

FATIH DEMIRTAŞ

You're alive? All these years? Nena asked. Her voice low and quivering. She shook her head in disbelief. "Why? How?"

I wasn't ready to answer her questions. My excuses were too horrible to utter.

"You look exactly like your mother," I deflected. "I thought I caught a fleeting glimpse of you at my restaurant a while back. But I wasn't sure. You're an exact likeness of the beautiful Elena, the way she looked so many years ago."

I didn't know what I was saying or what words to choose. "How is Elena?" I asked.

Nena's response hit me like a sledgehammer. "How is my *mother*? Are you kidding?" she shouted. "My mother died two years after *you* did. Only you're here, and she's not. I tried to keep her alive in my heart by using her name in my modeling life."

I had no idea. If Elena had died so many decades ago, it meant that this woman in front of me, my daughter, had grown up an orphan. That dreadful realization swept through me like a chilly wind announcing a winter storm.

I was overwhelmed with shame. "Oh, Nena. I didn't know."

"Of course you didn't. You thought a trunk full of money could make us go away."

"You're right. I did. But I had no clue that you lost Elena as well."

Her eyes grew large, her expression incredulous. She swallowed and blinked. Her face tightened in a controlled rage that quickly shifted to anguish.

"How is that possible?" she asked. "You never checked up on us."

"My excuses are weak. At the time they made sense. I was young. My work in Russia was winding down. I couldn't return so often anymore. I met Sandra. You and your mother were far away, and my life shifted completely back to Turkey."

"So you abandoned us, just like that?"

"Yes."

"How could you?" she demanded. "You didn't love me anymore?"

"Of course I did. I loved everything about you. I loved your joy. I loved your sense of humor, the way you always called me by my first and last name. You thought that was so funny. I did too. You rarely called me 'Otets,' but that was fine. You called me by my full name and that became our inside joke. I always looked forward to my trips to Russia. I counted down the days to see you."

"But what happened?" Nena pleaded.

"I was afraid if I told Sandra I had a lover and a daughter in Russia, she wouldn't understand. She wouldn't want me. I fell in love with Sandra and didn't want to jeopardize our relationship."

Suddenly, Sandra's voice bellowed from behind us. She had heard everything from the doorway. "You were wrong, Fatih! If you had told me about Nena, it would not have affected my love for you. But what you've done is reprehensible."

Both of us jumped. Nena and I turned towards my wife. Sandra approached Nena and enveloped her in her arms.

"You poor dear," she said softly.

I watched the two women rocking back and forth, one convulsing in restrained sobs, the other glaring at me, her expression shifting from contempt to pity to sadness before she closed her eyes.

"I suppose you want me to leave," I mumbled.

"You stupid fool," Sandra sighed. "Sit. You're not done here."

SOPHIE (Tall Girl)

I woke up Hannah by gently placing a hot cup of coffee on her bedside table. The rich aroma and the sunlight streaming through the beach house window roused her.

"I'm not supposed to have coffee," she muttered. "I'm pregnant. Remember?"

"You can have one cup to get revved for the day," I said. "Get up. Let's go to the beach. I'm done with work for a while, and I crave the sea right now."

"Don't you want to go up the hill and see Ted and Mila, and everyone else up there?" Hannah asked.

"You know about Ted and Mila?" I probed.

Hannah rubbed her eyes and sat up in bed, still groggy from sleep. She slurped some coffee.

"Yes. Mila just told me they had been seeing each other before he left for Ukraine. Ted was gone so long, and I was so preoccupied with my own David saga that I never put them together as a couple. But they make so much sense. I'm happy for them."

"I think we should let them sleep," I advised. "Ted and I edited late into the night. We shouldn't interrupt their reunion. Put on your Big Mama bathing suit and let's go for a swim."

We called a taxi to take us down to the shore, which gave Hannah enough time to finish waking up and struggle into her maternity beachwear. At the beach I sprinted as fast as I could and dove into the soothing water while Hannah spread out our blanket and watched me frolic.

The water held its summer warmth. I paddled through the

balmy surf for only a few minutes before heading back to shore. I noted that many of those around me were young men who had turned the town into a refuge for Russians who didn't want to fight in Ukraine. The draft dodgers were easy to spot on the beach, with their meagre belongings and out-of-place winter coats tied to their packs.

In the midst of the throng of males sitting on the sand with their knapsacks, my eye caught one outlier who stood out from the crowds. He sported bold-colored Paul Smith swim trunks, as expensive as they were conspicuous. I kept out of his line of sight but walked close enough to get a better look as he cuddled with a young blonde woman who seemed to hang adoringly onto his every word. Yep. It was him, alright.

Hannah could handle this. She was ready. I walked back to her.

"You're not going to believe this," I said. "Take a look down the beach. Do you see the guy with the bright orange and yellow swim trunks?"

Hannah stood up and squinted with her hand above her brow to shield the sun as she followed my directions.

"Oh my God! You've got to be kidding. What's he doing here? Who's that with him? What a shit!"

Hannah stood up and ordered me to follow her.

"Pull out your phone and record," she commanded. "This is going to be fun."

We strode down the beach so quickly that I could barely keep up with her. She was on a mission.

"Hey! Morales! David Morales!" she shouted.

I pressed "record" and watched the scene unfold. This was going to be interesting.

David pulled his face away from an intimate moment with his blonde companion and searched the crowd for whomever was calling his name. It took a moment for him to register the situation. He squirmed on the blanket as if trying to flee from the raging woman coming at him. His jaw dropped and his eyes widened as he scooted away from her, but there was no escaping Hannah's wrath.

"Did you return to Eskifoça to spawn?" Hannah yelled. "You could have gone anywhere with your new girlfriend. I guess this place has special meaning for you."

David sputtered, but no words came out.

"Meet your child," Hannah continued, as she pointed to her belly. "This is the baby you said you didn't want in your life."

She turned to the blonde and warned, "Be careful with this creep. He has trust issues. That means you can't trust anything he tells you. Have you met his wife, or his two sons? I bet not."

Hannah turned around and hollered, "Did you get that on video, Sophie?"

I gave her a thumbs up.

"Great. We're done here."

As she began walking away, she half turned to face them again. "Bye, David. And good luck to you," she smiled to the young woman.

I had no words. Hannah had found a voice of her own. At last. I was proud of her. She was clearly done with that idiot.

"Okay. Let's send that masterpiece video to the wife," she instructed. "I've still got her number in my phone. I hadn't intended to destroy their marriage. I didn't want any kind of revenge, but she really needs to know that he's at it again."

She pressed SEND. There was no joy in her expression, merely closure for a task completed.

"So much for a relaxing swim at the beach," she laughed. "Let's go see our friends and have a more peaceful morning with them."

We rolled up our blanket and searched for a taxi to take us back up the hill.

"And thank you for having my back."

"Always! But you didn't need me."

I was in awe of her newfound strength. I had watched her evolve from being willfully gullible and childlike to an independent woman with kickass determination.

TED (Tall Guy)

Mila and I didn't want to wander down the hall to join the father-daughter reunion. We couldn't imagine the emotional explosion that was bound to be happening, especially with Sandra now part of the unexpected family get-together.

There was another reason for us to stay away for the moment. Nena, or Elena as I knew her, had no idea that I was in Eskifoça. The last time we saw each other was months ago. She also didn't know that Mila and I were a couple. She didn't need that kind of shock on top of everything else.

Mila helped me understand Nena in a different light. Perhaps our random meeting in Istanbul had indeed offered her a momentary escape valve. She probably used her professional name, Elena, because I was merely a stranger whom she had met unintentionally and could use as an uninvolved outlet for whatever was bothering her. It's sometimes easier to do that with a stranger than it is to tell those closest to us.

I couldn't fault her. I was the one who had read way too much into our brief encounters. Thank goodness that Mila had stumbled into my life back then and saved me from wasting more time living a fantasy.

To stay clear of the mayhem in the Demirtaş home, we walked down the hill to wake up Sophie and Hannah. Their house and pool would be the perfect refuge. Just as we arrived at their front gate, a taxi pulled up with the two of them. Sophie and Hannah jumped out and greeted us excitedly, exclaiming that they had a crazy story to share. Their tale, I thought, couldn't be anywhere nearly as wild as ours. I was wrong. It turned out to be a toss-up.

We went first. I filled them in on Nena's childhood abandonment, and how I came to know her as Elena. Their questions flew.

"You mean, Nena's father has been living here all along?" Hannah gasped.

"Sandra didn't know her husband had a love child?" Sophie asked.

Next, it was their turn to recount their animated morning. They described David's reckless return to Eskifoça and their video recording escapade. I was appalled at how stupid and arrogant the guy had been. He could have shown a bit more creativity in his choice of locales for his dirty weekend.

Mila seemed to delight in their story.

"You actually sent the video to his wife?" she chuckled. "Wow. That's rough."

ÇIÇEK

Oh, the commotion that morning—way too early in the morning. And all those people from Dove Street were now here in a new house near the beach. But they all didn't seem so happy together. And who was that man making them cry?

It was too much. I was feeling stronger and I could stand up on my own. But I slept so frequently I can't really recall everything about this part of my story. I think I saw Tall Guy and the DaNyet take a walk. They left the gate open, but I was too tired to stroll outside. I got bored so I dug up a bunch of flowers, created a cool hole for myself, and nestled in for another nap.

A truck pulled up outside the gate. I normally would have barked at the uniformed guy as he walked across the lawn, but I couldn't be bothered. He wasn't a normal mailman. I hated those guys. I nipped at them anytime I could just for the fun of it. This delivery man was different. I didn't have the energy to torture him when he deposited some kind of stiff flat package at the front door. I watched him drive off.

I could have gone to investigate, maybe even chew up the packet. But what was the point? I wasn't terribly hungry, and my body ached, so I took another snooze. I would investigate the package later. Maybe I'd wake up starving, and I'd find a treat inside.

NENA (Sad Girl)

Sandra's kindness was calming. I sat in the kitchen with her while Fatih positioned himself at the far end of the room, as if the distance could shield him from his transgressions. We sipped tea and I munched on some morning biscuits.

Sandra asked me to tell her about my life in Russia after my parents were gone. I explained about the money I had and how it lasted most of my teen years because I lived such a basic existence. I had a roof over my head, enough food to keep me healthy, and cash to buy clothes and household supplies. An old lady down the hall fended off the authorities so they didn't take me away. The money proved useful there too.

I told Sandra that what I lacked was love and guidance and encouragement and hugs when life was mean. It hurt that I had my parents in my heart, but I couldn't be in their arms. I played back a hundred memories of the few years I had with them, but even those had faded over time.

I turned to Fatih and said, "Nothing hurts more than realizing you meant everything to me, but I meant nothing to you."

"You were always in my heart," Fatih protested.

His words sounded hollow. But then I flashed on a sweet recollection of him. He had bought my mother and me a TV, and we'd watch the Russian news together in the evenings when he was in town. We didn't pay much attention to what was on the screen because he would put me on his feet and swing me as I giggled. We'd pretend I was on a plane, flying around the world to exciting cities.

"You were fun. You could have been a great father," I conceded. "But then you abandoned me."

Sandra squeezed my hand. Her warm touch again soothed my anger. She urged me to tell them more about my journey and how I made my way to Turkey. I told her about the odd jobs I found over the years, in Russian bars and restaurants and hotels. I described how I traveled to Germany, my first foray outside the country. I was twenty.

"I met a wonderful man in Berlin. Hakan. He changed my world."

"Hakan?" They both boomed.

The vehemence of their question made me jump. Hakan is a common name in Turkey. Their reaction seemed odd.

"Yes, Hakan. He's quite a bit older, but we fell hard for each other. He was kind and generous and believed in me. I suppose he was the father figure I longed for, but I also was attracted to him. We married about twenty years ago."

Their silence prompted me to continue. "I wanted to bring him with me on this trip, but he's quite ill now."

"You told him about me?" Fatih asked.

"Of course. I told him that you were my father, and you died when I was young. He knows my whole life story. He encouraged me to come and try to find you down here."

"Try to find me?"

"Yes, I thought I saw your photo in *Why Not Spend It?* magazine. But the date on the photo was long after you were supposedly dead."

"That's how you came to my restaurant months ago," Fatih muttered. "I knew I saw you there."

"I thought I saw you too," I told him. "You were walking with two men, but I wasn't certain it was really you. I needed to return to find out."

Sandra reached for my hands again. "Those men you saw are your brothers."

"I have brothers?" I smiled. "I want to meet them."

"You will," said Sandra. "But they'll be shocked to learn of your existence."

Funny how life and our circumstances can change so quickly and unexpectedly. I woke up this morning an orphan and now I have a father, a stepmother, and two brothers. I could feel my cheeks burning from the excitement. I wasn't alone in the world with just Hakan.

"I'm someone's sister," I whispered.

"And you're also *our* daughter," Sandra said quietly.

Fatih said very little. He listened to my tale, his face etched in regret and shame. He put his head in his hands when I shared details of my mother's death.

"I didn't know," he kept repeating. "I would not have left you alone, if I had known your mother was gone."

I glared. "You certainly did nothing to find out."

"I don't expect forgiveness," he said softly.

He stared at the floor. I assumed he was talking to both Sandra and me.

After all, the revelations had hit Sandra hard also. The man she thought she knew, the father and husband who had doted on her for decades, had hidden an important truth from her.

Neither Sandra nor I spoke.

Fatih looked directly into my eyes, his face pained, his brow deeply lined.

"So many lost years," he admitted. "I can't ever make

up for them. But I hope, one day, you'll allow me to be the father I once was to you."

I had no energy to answer him. I needed time to think. To be alone. To understand the full importance of discovering him, meeting Sandra, and learning I had siblings. My entire life had been turned upside down in a matter of minutes.

Sandra kept her feelings private and gave nothing away to Fatih. She too had a great deal to process, and to decide how, when, or even if to forgive her husband.

She wasn't yet finished filling in the blanks of my life story. She was curious and caring. Her sons were fortunate to have such a compassionate woman as their mother.

"Tell us more about your husband, Hakan."

As I gathered my thoughts to best describe him, we were interrupted by the pawing of Çiçek at the front door.

"Çiçek! We've all forgotten about her," Sandra said. "She must be starving."

Sandra pulled open the front door and the dog came loping into the house. Sandra bent down to pick up something on the front step.

"Yuck. Çiçek has peed on the cardboard packaging. It looks like a letter that came special delivery." Sandra's brow furrowed. "It's addressed to you, Nena. Who even knows you're here, besides Mila?"

"Hakan," I replied. "He asked where I'd be staying in case he changed his mind and decided to come down. How strange that he's sent me a letter. If it's alright with you, I'd like to go somewhere and read it."

"Of course! Let me clean it off first," she laughed. "I'll take you to the guestroom."

ÇIÇEK

I followed Sad Girl to her room down a long hallway. She still smelled like peppermint. I loved that about her.

She climbed onto the bed with the package I had tinkled on. I was still too wobbly to jump up with her, so I curled down on the floor beside her. I watched her rip open the cardboard and study the paper inside.

Something was very wrong. She shook and cried and yelled, but there was no one else in the room to hear her despair. I licked her hand as she dropped the paper on the floor. Nothing I did seemed to calm her. She just kept wailing. I felt hopeless.

I can do many things, but I can't read. So, I'll just hold the letter in my mouth for you to see it. I think it's an important part of my story. I hope I haven't slobbered too much on it, and you can still make out the words.

> *My dearest Nena,*
> *If you're reading this, you know by now that your father, Fatih, has been alive and well in Eskifoça. I wonder if they've told you yet that I knew Fatih. I was even part of his dreadful duplicity.*
>
> *Why did we lie to you? We were selfish and cowardly. Our joint businesses in Turkey and Russia were spiraling. Fatih fell in love with Sandra and no longer had interest in his Russian chapter. He wanted to simplify his life, open his own restaurant at the beach, and settle down with his wealthy British wife who backed his new venture.*
>
> *The resort we ran was my dream. But without Fatih, it floundered. He was the charismatic front man who brought in all the wealthy tourists. I was the back office*

who couldn't run it alone. We were a partnership, but he wanted out.

I can't put all the blame on your father. He was ready to move on from our business, and I was not. As part of his deal to pay me handsomely to close down the resort, I had to do some of his dirty work. That included bringing the cash to your house and delivering the Big Lie to your mother. However, I couldn't get you out of my mind. The little Russian girl who watched me from her bedroom window.

I had a friend in Moscow who sent me periodic updates about your life. Between us, we made sure you always had some kind of job and were safe, even as your cash dwindled. He had friends with restaurants, cafés, and hotels, and could easily persuade them to offer you positions.

I never made an appeal to Fatih to reach out to you. I should have urged him. He was your father, after all, and owed it to you. I just couldn't bring myself to speak with him. Fatih had no idea that I followed your life over the years. He could compartmentalize. I couldn't forget or forgive what I had done.

My Russian contact informed me one day that you relocated to Berlin. Your moving so far away inspired me to find you and finally tell you the truth. No matter how much I had traveled the world, I could never completely forget the abandoned child in Russia.

I had every intention of telling you the whole story, but that plan changed the moment I found you in Germany. I fell in love at first sight. I knew you'd despise me if I revealed the secret that I had withheld for so many years. So, I said nothing. I didn't want to lose you. But in the end, I fear I've lost you anyway. I hope it's not too late for you to find the happiness you deserve.

I've loved you with all my heart,
Hakan

I think you'd be mad at me if I ended my story here. Don't worry. I don't want to leave you hanging with too many loose ends. But I can't wrap up everything in a tidy package like the ones I often discover in the trash.

Sometimes I chew those bundles and uncover tasty left-overs of chicken and beef. Other times I find bitter chard. And sometimes, I find that the most promising packages turn out to have nothing inside.

But you have to keep on believing and searching and sniffing. Life is full of many treats just waiting to be discovered. But back to my story. I'll let my friends update you from here.

EPILOGUE

NENA (Sad Girl)

I haven't returned to Dove Street to talk to Hakan about the hurt he caused. I can't quite come to grips with that, at least for now.

Despite all the anguish, some remarkable changes happened. I gained a mother in Sandra. She is kind and generous. She treats me like a daughter. I'm getting acquainted with my brothers too. As soon as we met, they accepted me as their sister.

For the short term, I've rented a house in Eskifoça to be near all of them. And unexpectedly, my modeling career picked up. I'm now the face of a new resort down here. You'll find me on billboards all over Izmir. They're in Russian, Turkish and English.

As for my reconciliation with Fatih Demirtaş, that will take time. I may always be conflicted about my father. But maybe not.

FATIH DEMIRTAŞ

I wait and hope.

SANDRA DEMIRTAŞ

I have the daughter I always wanted. At first, just the idea of her hurt. But soon, I realized what a good person she is. I wanted her in our lives. Yes, my husband disappointed me. What man or woman hasn't caused disappointments? But it's amazing what good can come if you stick around long enough and work through the bad patches.

MILA (The DaNyet)

I still make #PeaceDog videos with Çiçek. The war has dragged on. Right now, there seems to be no end in sight to the conflict. Çiçek and I remain dedicated to shining a light on the war so that the West doesn't forget, and the world doesn't give up on Ukraine.

#PeaceDog now has ten million TikTok followers.

Also, Ted and I moved in together on Dove Street. I worry every time he gets on a plane to cover the war or other crises. He just left to film the aftermath of a devastating earthquake in Turkey and Syria. It's another unimaginable catastrophe.

TED (Tall Guy)

I'm crazy about Mila. She had been right in her assessment of her friend. I was a stranger to Nena and therefore a perfect sounding board for her to share everything that hurt. Nena didn't want me to find her, but she did want me to be around to listen. Her mother's name, Elena, was her safe persona.

Elena/Nena never knew it, but she pulled me through that first difficult assignment in Ukraine. She was a beautiful and mysterious distraction that I could concoct any way I wanted.

I'm glad I'll have Mila as a safe haven after covering this devastating earthquake. This is a tough one. It's as if an army moved in and leveled ten provinces in sixty seconds.

HANNAH (Happy Girl)

I named my baby Pax, the Latin word for peace. I believe that it suits these less-than-peaceful times. I never heard from David after our last encounter in Eskifoça, but his wife contacted me. She wants me to be a witness in her divorce proceedings. I'll bring Pax with me. That should be entertaining.

Also, I haven't told Nena yet, but I think I'm crushing on one of her brothers. I think he kind of likes me too.

SOPHIE (Tall Girl)

Hello from Denmark! I'm here with Peter the Coffee Guy. I never found the right time to tell anyone—he's from Copenhagen. I found my Dane.

ÇIÇEK

So, there you have it. That's my story of love on Dove Street. What you see here is not so different from what you'll likely find elsewhere in other neighborhoods.

My street is humanity's pageant.

My friends are folks who come together in search of companionship. They are all just trying to do the best with what they have, to make a mark, to matter, to care, to be cared about.

I told you I'm not a writer, but I had a story to share with you. I hope my friend Boji can help me find an agent. He has important friends. But I didn't tell this tale to become famous.

I wanted you to know that life is stormy. One minute it bathes you in sunlight, and the next it forces you to run for shelter. What makes it worthwhile is when we find friends along the way and watch out for each other. Gentleness and kindness and a few juicy bones make for a better world.

You can move half-way around the world to find your perfect life, but it always comes down to who you meet. And it's important that we all join together in the power of love. Because if we don't, we'll keep moving towards a world run by people who love power.

Peace out.

Acknowledgments

I am indebted to many who contributed to this book, including my four-legged friend and loveable muse, Çiçek.

The first person I want to thank is Marta Vallejo, who despite claiming she doesn't like dogs, remained my relentless cheerleader from the start.

Derek Williams offered his insights into what wartime cameramen really think about while filming. Our lengthy Zoom call was followed by urgent emails from him advising me to make sure that "Ted got enough".

Brice Laine, another fearless and talented cameraman, sent me detailed corrections during his limited vacation between assignments in Ukraine.

Without Servet Harunoğlu, I would never have known about the Soviet-era business ties between Turkey and the USSR. He helped me understand how construction deals and long-distance love affairs during that period could run their course.

Edmée Van Rijn was my dog whisperer who kept Çiçek as real as a talking dog can be.

To Orla Guerin, Wietske Burema, Tim Facey, and countless other foreign correspondents in our neighborhood, I am in awe of your courage in covering the world's crises, and thankful for your willingness to answer my endless questions about your demanding work.

To Gwen Yount Carden, Bill Gossage, Sarah Price, and Noémie Terzian-Balsamo, thank you for your extreme patience and generosity in reading early versions of the manuscript. I am grateful to Karen Emmons who painstakingly fixed inconsistencies, for which there were many.

To Pat Rowe, your compassionate approach to life allowed me to explore my characters' better angels, especially at the end of the book.

A huge thank you to Zahia Hafs for designing this book and urging me to keep going with it. The brilliant cover art is another work of creative genius by Damien Chavanat.

To Kaela Bleho, our youngest daughter who grew from a child with nits in her hair to an editor who meticulously picked nits in my plot holes, thank you for saving me from myself.

To Casey Bleho, who would never let me abandon the book, thank you for always loving a love story.

I especially want to thank John Bleho for keeping me laughing, inspired, fed, caffeinated, and feeling loved. You make every adventure more fun and every verb less passive.

About the Author

Cherie Hart is a writer and award-winning documentary producer from Virginia. She wrote for the *National Enquirer*, was a TV reporter, and a magazine writer. She worked as an overseas press officer for the United Nations Development Programme and traveled to more than 60 countries. She has two daughters and lives with her husband in Turkey and the US. This is her third book.

By the same author:
The Chat in the Flat (2020)
From Hollywood to Holy Wars (2018)

Cover design by Damien Chavanat
Interior design by Zahia Hafs
Jalan Publications – Paris (France)
contact@jalan.fr

First published in 2023

Made in United States
North Haven, CT
04 October 2023

42362979R00154